CRIMSON BLADES!

First upon him was a guard, swarthy and mustached, fitted out like a mercenary in bronze cap and boiled leather vest. His sword had a longer reach than Conan's heavy scimitar. Therefore it was necessary to whittle away at him while dodging his thrusts—first at his shoulder, with an ill-directed slash that barely wetted his leather sleeve with blood. Then his ear; Conan grazed it with a resounding cut that rang against the man's helm, goading him to a dizzy rage.

Swearing fiercely, the defender slashed his blade at Conan's face. It was a reckless stroke, one that was easily turned aside by the pirate's scimitar . . . an instant before the curved blade lashed up under the hauberk into the man's vitals, doing terrible damage. The guard went down with an agonized shriek, dropping his sword to clutch at his red-streaming belly. . . .

CONAN
OF THE RED BROTHERHOOD

——BY——
LEONARD
CARPENTER

A TOM DOHERTY ASSOCIATES BOOK
NEW YORK

CONAN OF THE RED BROTHERHOOD

Cover art by Ken Kelly

A Tor Book
Published by Tom Doherty Associates, Inc.
175 Fifth Avenue
New York, N.Y. 10010

Tor ® is a registered trademark of Tom Doherty Associates, Inc.

ISBN: 0-812-51413-0

First edition: February 1993

Printed in the United States of America

0 9 8 7 6 5 4 3 2

To Ron Andrini

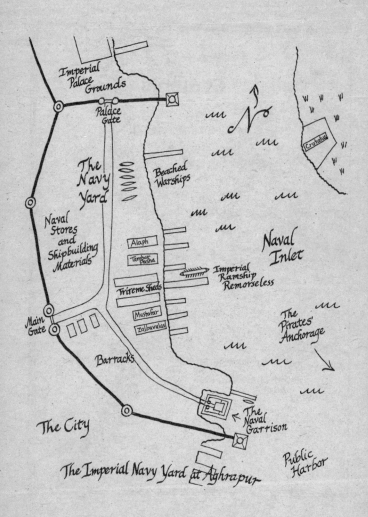

Imperial Palace Grounds

Palace Gate

The Navy Yard

Beached Warships

Naval Stores and Shipbuilding Materials

Alaph

Tambur Pasha

Trireme Sheds

Mustafar

Zalbuvulus

Imperial Ramship Remorseless

Main Gate

Barracks

The City

Naval Inlet

The Pirates' Anchorage

The Naval Garrison

Crotalus

Public Harbor

The Imperial Navy Yard at Aghrapur

Contents

ONE

Blades of the Red Brotherhood

The sail was a white speck on the horizon, scarcely visible in dayglare off the Southern Vilayet. From the coastal hillside, looking out beyond the pale ribbon of beach, the sea spread glassy-bright, stirred in places to glinting shards by fickle westerly breezes. Overhead, a scattered fleet of clouds sailed cottony-white . . . whiter even than the fair limbs of Olivia, who languished in the meadow grass near at hand.

"Conan, what are you gazing at? Look back to me, my love!"

Lithe arms twined about the Cimmerian's neck and drew him down to the crumpled greensward.

"I swear to you, my darling, my eyes never tire of you! I wish we could remain here forever, lying together like this." The supple arms enfolded him, drawing his face down into the soft curvature of neck and dark, fragrant hair. "As a lover, you are beyond price to me . . . more

1

than ever I could have wanted . . . my husband, my master, my Captain!'' The woman's murmured rhapsodies and twining caresses smothered his senses as she drew him down into the grass.

In time Olivia's breaths grew less rapid and insistent, slower even than the soft, rhythmic thudding of waves on the shoreline below. ''We had best get back,'' Conan told her then, adjusting his crimson kirtle and hitching his sword-belt about his middle.

''Must we, really?'' The woman reluctantly sat up, gathering her silken blouse and skirt around her. ''Back to those coarse and brutish men, to hear their gibes and obscene mutterings?''

''Aye. We shall be putting out to sea soon.''

''They watch me all the time, you know.'' Olivia bent to fasten gilt-trimmed sandals about her shapely ankles. '' 'Tis a rare relief for me to get out of their sight.'' She rose to her feet, drawing her gown about her shoulders to protect her from the sun.

''I cannot blame them, the poor wretches! Can you? Tempted by such beauty?'' Grinning in good spirit, Conan administered a firm slap to the woman's thinly draped rump. ''Anyway, they'll be getting thirsty by now.'' Stepping into a double brace of damp, heavy earthenware bottles lashed to either end of a boat-pole, he eased the makeshift yoke across his shoulders and bore up the weight on powerful legs.

Waiting briefly for Olivia to gather up a pair of bulging waterskins, he let her lead the way down the faint, ancient footpath through the grass. They skirted the brook where it spattered down a rocky cliff on its way to the rank salt slough, then continued past it downhill. They went in silence, with Conan quietly content to observe the jiggle of the water bottles against Olivia's shapely, dampened hips.

Before they left the meadow he stopped her and pointed out the distant sail, which had scarcely progressed northward along the coast. "Say nothing of it to the crew," he instructed her.

Just below, the path crossed a fringe of piny wilderness; beyond it, sheltered from the sea by brushy dunes, a narrow inlet sparkled. On the slope of this inner beach lay a slender galliot, drawn up out of the water and lying askew on its keel. Around the scant shade of its hull, some two-score ragged and semi-clothed men loitered, some of them ill-humoredly raking the boat's weedy planks with sharp stones and crescent hunks of clamshell.

Here were swarthy, turbulent knaves, both bearded and shaven-headed, tattooed and earringed, men of motley races in ragged, garish undress. Some were maimed or half-blinded, but all moved with a fighter's wariness and glittered with sharp steel weapons—hard-eyed corsairs, pirates of the Vilayet coast.

"Curse this voyage for a liverless farce!"

"Aye, 'tis a Cimmerian hill-humper's pleasure cruise!"

The sharp-voiced complaints could have come from any of a dozen rogues muttering together in a pidgin mockery of Hyrkanian. Whether they were meant to be heard by the oarship's captain was anyone's guess. But when the Cimmerian and his woman arrived on the beach, all eyes turned their way.

"Look alive, ye scabby scuts! Here comes our captain now . . . and his fair shipmate!"

There was a general stir in the shadow of the hull, combined with a grudging half-willingness to appear busy at maintenance duties. The galliot was little more than an open launch, its narrow shell stretching a mere dozen man-lengths between the tall, curving keel-posts that rose from its bow and stern. Except for solid timber framing to hold

3

up the mast, whose sail was furled around a single long spar, the ship's side-wales were braced together chiefly by the rowers' benches. A brief quarterdeck built up over a low, cramped cabin astern was the sole stretch of level planking.

"Here is our water at last," one fork-bearded crewman proclaimed loudly from the shade of the hull. "And see, 'tis borne to us by a fairy-maid. A goddess, no less! Captain, may I take your place on the next water-hauling expedition? I can haul that set of jugs as well as any man," he proclaimed, to raucous laughs.

"Quiet, Punicos!" a gruff voice called from the other end of the hull. "Such a junket would cost you your life, I'll wager! Sure as my name is Ivanos, the trip would draw more blood than water." The jest brought further snarls of laughter from the crew.

"Enough now, you skulking pirate curs!" Conan thumped down his jars of water on the sand and accepted the sheepskin flasks from haughty Olivia. Carrying the bags over to his crew, he hove them firmly into the paunches of two of the most brazen idlers. "Here, Jephat, Ogdus—suckle on those, and pass them down! Then back to work careening. I want the *Vixen* fit for swift travel by noon." He glanced up at the steep-angling sun.

"Why should we scrape and polish this old barge," a gap-toothed, pigtailed pirate carped, "when there has been nothing for us to chase in days, and rations are short? Why not let the currents float us back to Djafur?"

The Cimmerian, whose bare, muscle-knotted shoulders bulked as tall as most of the other buccaneers' heads, loomed near enough the grumbler to make him skulk back toward the hull and set his holystone to the weedy planks. "You, Diccolo, should be keenest of all to keep the hull clean—" Conan growled at the offender "—so it will feel

4

smooth and pleasant against your skin when I keelhaul you under it!''

None of the others seemed inclined to take up the argument. After wetting their craws from the common water-flasks, they resumed work, with Conan diligently criticizing their labor to keep them at it. Olivia, meanwhile, found a shady spot well away from the crew's scrutiny. She combed out her long black hair and busied herself mending ship's tackle and the goods and garments obtained in the pirating trade.

When the time came to turn the vessel on its other side, Conan helped his crew manhandle the keel over. He then hoisted the wizened pirate-priest, Yorkin, bodily on his shoulder. The toothless elder cutthroat, thus borne up, ritually touched up the all-seeing eyes painted on the ship's bows above the waterline.

When the scraping was near complete, Conan dispatched a keen-eyed lookout up over the sandy headland. The man was Juwala, a mahogany-colored Keshan with pale, ornamental scars patterned across his face and chest. In moments he returned, his voice thick and deep with urgency. ''There is a ship offshore, Conan. A wide-bellied merchantman, a Turanian cog by the look of her. She has rounded the southern reef and stands well out from the coast.''

At his words, an exultant murmur spread among the pirates.

''A ship, by Dagon's teeth! A fat trader!''

'' 'Tis blades, then—the oar blade and the cutlass!''

''Alas,'' Diccolo bellyached, ''our so-called captain keeps kept us here doing slaves' work when we should be out farming the waves!''

''Aye, plowing them up with our sharp keel,'' old Yorkin's rough voice chanted, "and fertilizing them with merchant's blood!"

"Just what I did not want," Conan growled at them "—you pack of starveling curs racing out to frighten off our prey before she worked far enough downwind! I saw the ship at midmorn, but I said nothing of it. Better to keep you toiling, and save us a stern chase!" He strode among the men, shoving and buffeting them about the shoulders. "Come, dogs, now is the time! Launch this little fox-bitch of ours, and we'll hook into that merchant or run ashore trying us both! Shove hearty, lads," he cried, laying his shoulder against the keel. "Give us a heave, now, and again, a heave!"

In moments the *Vixen* was afloat, her keel scuffing the sand of the estuary, her red-painted eyes sloping sinister as she floated free. Olivia came along at a run, bringing with her a bundle of cordage and silken finery. Conan caught her up and boosted her over the prow, pulling himself close after. While others scrambled aboard, the captain and his mistress picked their way aft across the twenty-odd rowers' benches, amid crewmen cursing and jostling to fit their oars between the thole-pins.

"Look alive, now!" At last Conan sprang onto the quarterdeck, the swaying planks resilient under his sandal-soles. "Oarsmen ready!" Seizing hold of one of the long steering-sweeps whose pivots flanked the narrow cabin, he dipped its blade and agilely began plying it, turning the hull sidewise underfoot. "Olivia, fetch your flute, girl, and pipe us a tune! Ivanos, tell off the biggest rogues to man the boat-poles."

The burly lieutenant and several of the larger pirates had already anticipated Conan's order. The *Vixen*, propelled by the snub ends of poles against the sandy bottom, already gained way in the shallow lagoon. At the bow, a

6

pair of polesmen stood ready to fend the ship off sandbars; Conan, meanwhile, plied his sweep strongly enough to steer the craft and drive it forward as well.

"Steady, now," the Cimmerian ordered. "Keep under way, but no more speed till we cross the outer bar."

Along the seaward beach, dense, shrubby trees gave place to sculptured dunes; these presently dwindled to a windblown, brushy sandspit ending in a stretch of weed-draped, tilting rock spires. The *Vixen* slid forward easily before the thrusting poles, with forty dry oars poised over the lapping brine on either hand. Conan felt the first sea-swell lift the craft, scraping its keel against rough coral sand. He leaned against his steering-sweep, bending its long shank with his weight; then wave-tops began splashing in over the bow, and he bellowed commands.

"Oarsmen ready—stroke! Bravely, you sea-skites, stroke! Keep together and carve this surf. Stroke! Poles inboard, and man oars! Ivanos, take the port helm." Conan plied his long oarloom overhead, his muscle-corded body flexing like an elm in a gale as his lieutenant hurriedly unlimbered the second steering-oar. "Keep the bows steady against this chop and we'll soon be seaborne."

The captain ceased calling the rowers' stroke; in his stead, a shrill, rhythmic piping took up the tempo. Olivia, at Conan's order, had fetched her silver syrinx out of the cabin. With ankles tucked beneath her, and the hood of her gown puffing in the fitful breeze, she knelt at the break of the deck, blowing across the gleaming wedge of pipes with pursed, expert lips. The tune throbbed sweetly and steadily, with only the faintest overtone of the orgiastic gaiety associated with such music in the western hills.

Olivia's service as aeoliolite for the chase was a rare pleasure, and Conan appreciated it even as he labored. Her music and her womanly good looks kept the attention of the oarsmen far better than the charms of old Yorkin, who usually performed the office with his Brythunian bone flute.

Steering became surer as the last of the cresting waves surged along the starboard side, dousing the rowers in turn. The pirates toiled over low sea-swells, straining unevenly and cursing as their oar blades were dragged under or spewed aloft by coiling waters. But they pulled with fierce energy; those few who could tear their eyes from Olivia gazed over their shoulders at the sight, even more tempting, that was in Conan's view: a sleek, round merchant vessel, red-painted, with touches of gilt at bow and stern, idling northward toward them under slack-bellied square sails.

The cog, though well offshore, was already putting about to gain sea-room. Before the pirates' yearning eyes, the angle of her three masts changed; ivory sails shivered uncertainly before drinking in the new, tauter breeze. The vessel's lookouts and officers could have little doubt of the intent of a small, heavily manned craft putting out to intercept them along this wild coast. On a sea as broad and treacherous as the Vilayet, shipping almost universally hugged the shore or kept within sight of well-known islands; as a result, this whole southeastern coastline had become a noted hunting ground, both of pirates and for them. Yet here was no low, well-armed Imperial pirate-chaser, but a fat and tempting prize.

Luckily for their chances, the midday breeze remained slack even here on open water. And the sailing ship, having come so far downwind, did not dare run any closer inshore; she could only tack obliquely out to sea. Her sailing speed on that course was limited, and Conan judged her power under oars to be scant or nonexistent.

"Ivanos, work your sweep thus! Starboard rowers,

feather oars . . . hold them in, aye, four . . . five strokes!
Enough idling now, back to work, you miserable dogs!
Olivia, pipe us slow courage for the long haul!''

The effect of Conan's order, rowing with port oars only
and side-paddling vigorously with the stern sweeps, was
to shift the galliot's course to intercept the merchant some
way out along her new tack. The sea-waves now ran low
and even alongside, offering no resistance to the *Vixen*'s
high-stemmed hull, and seldom even casting spray in over
her bows. The pirates, encouraged by the steady, resolute
tempo of Olivia's fluting, toiled ably. They only occasionally burst out in yelping, hooting eagerness, like a wolf-
pack baying after the haunches of a weary stag.

The wind held, unfortunately, and the chase stretched
out to seaward. The hazy sky deepened about them, the
high sun showing off the Vilayet's blue-green sparkling
depths. The Hyrkanian coast dwindled behind to a line of
white breakers, a scatter of pale crystal sand, and a crumpled green tarpaulin of brushy hills. The men began to
scowl and curse, swearing vengeance on the cog's crew if
ever they caught them. Ivanos, securing his steering-oar
with a line, took the seat of old Yorkin, who then went
among the rowers with a bucket to splash seawater over
their toiling backs—and, later, to spray fresh water out of
the leathern flasks into eager, gaping, yellow-toothed
mouths.

"Save yourselves, rogues! Olivia, pace them slower, lest
they waste their strength!'' Conan steered the long, true
course, plying his sweep watchfully. To raise sail would
be useless, since the cog strained seaward with the wind
abeam and the little galliot lacked enough keel to work
any distance upwind. Watching the sails of the merchant
draw slowly nearer, Conan yet wondered if the discipline
of his crew would hold . . . or worse, if the breeze might

suddenly freshen, speeding their quarry hopelessly out of reach.

But the pirates, seeing the merchant draw gradually taller and more splendid alongside, gained in strength rather than losing it. Olivia's piping gradually, imperceptibly, quickened, lashing them on with carnival abandon; again Conan reminded her to slow down. But at last he joined in, roaring out a traditional pirate chanty to entertain them:

> *Row, you misbegotten dogs,*
> *Row till your backs break!*
> *Row till your oars crack,*
> *Row till your gizzards splinter!*
>
> *Row till your skin splits off*
> *And tendons peel like rotten leather.*
> *Row till your ribs snap*
> *For your shipmates and the hope of treasure—*

The song had more verses, many more, but Conan was not far into them before a twang and a thud sounded across the narrowing expanse of waves. The merchant evidently mounted a missile thrower on its high sterncastle; a faint whirring sounded high overhead, and a small gout of water kicked up some way off the starboard bow. None of the pirates noticed, or seemed to, since they were facing sternward and craning necks to port, toward the fleeing cog.

> *Row across the stinking brine*
> *Where your dead brothers palely float,*
> *The foul broth where they stew and bloat,*
> *Their mouths agape to call you hellward!*

The second projectile struck just aft of the galliot's bows with a vibrating blow. The missile was a heavy wooden ballista-bolt: a man-tall, wrist-thick shaft tipped with a square bronze head that pierced, luckily, through one of the oar-benches rather than the hull. By a miracle, none of the densely packed pirates was slain, though Atrox the Kothian howled a wrathful curse as he clutched a gashed shoulder with one massive hand. Oar-stroking was disrupted though the whole for'ard section—by the heavy shaft pinned down to the deck, blocking the swing of nearby oars, and by Atrox's loose oar dragging in the water. Conan left off chanting and barked orders to clear up the mess, even as he bore heavily onto his steering-sweep to hold the vessel on course.

The *Vixen* soon made way with more speed than before as the pirates, offended by what seemed to them a cowardly attack, strove mightily to close the distance between the vessels. At their insistence, the skull-jack—the flag of the Red Brotherhood, a white skull on a black field above crossed red sabers—was run up the mast. They sweated harder at their oars thereafter, their curses and blood oaths drowning out the thin tempo of Olivia's flute.

All hands made a show of ignoring the catapult, though bolts still twanged from the cog's quarterdeck and occasionally hit home. As they drew near, in any case, the projectiles flew in at flatter angles and with less accuracy, merely glancing off the bows or snapping an oar blade in the water. One lucky shot pinned a Corinthian rowdy's chest to a Gunderman's belly amidships, while another carried Zagar the Shemite's head clean away; but these events only served to speed up the oar-stroke, once the bodies were cast overside.

''Rein in, you mad devils, before you work yourselves to gasping, puking wrecks! Save some strength for the

fight ahead!'' Conan could see victory slipping away due
to his pirates' indiscipline, or, in truth, their frenzied fear
under the wrath of the catapult. He readied himself to
wade among his rowers and slow them down with fist-
blows.

But then, without warning, their cause found aid from
an unseen quarter. The wind, as if in annoyance at the
catapult's whine and the pirates' curses, abruptly fled . . .
or rather, fell still. The merchant cog's triangular sails
were left slack and pendulous; its masts stood near-
vertical, rocking in a fitful way that could hardly have
helped the aim of the catapult crew.

Conan's men, on sensing the change, set up a howl of
exultation, one that did not diminish as their craft turned
and bore in toward the drifting prize, and safely inside the
reach of the center-mounted missile thrower. At the last
moment, a handful of archers appeared at the cog's high
rail, unleashing arrows on the pirates with some passing
effect. But the rowers gaily disregarded the shafts falling
among them; some even thrust a wounded benchmate
down into the bilges out of the way and pulled two oars,
one in either hand.

''Ship the port oars, you hellhounds! Olivia cease piping! Jephat, Juwala, look alive with your grappling hooks!
Stand ready to board!''

Dragging his rudder-oar abeam, Conan braced its thick
loom overhead long enough to bring the galliot gliding
close in under the merchant's hull; then he abandoned it
and sprang to the rail. Snatching up a heavy bronze grapple and whirling it on its chain-lead, he flung it over the
stern rail of the cog and hauled it taut.

''Olivia, tend to the wounded as you can,'' he told his
mistress, meanwhile winding the braided rope tight around

a cleat. "Keep a sharp blade with you to cut away grapples and defend yourself, if need be!"

Then Conan, after seizing the woman in his arms and administering a wild, rough kiss to her lips, sprang away. Smoothly he mounted the grapple line, his loose-topped boots scuffing for purchase on the hull, his heavy scimitar swaying in its belt at his side.

All along the *Vixen*'s length, the marauders did likewise, swarming up ropes and chains and even hook-ended boat-poles amidships, where the cog's waist wallowed lowest. It was a stiff climb, like storming a fort wall, but the defense was thin and sporadic. Already wrathful cries and the clashing of weapons rang out from the cog's deck overhead.

Even as Conan hauled himself up to the foeman's rail, a spike-tipped pole was thrust at his face. Dodging aside, he seized its head just behind the barb and wrenched it back one-handed, causing the stout-bellied wielder to stagger after, clinging to its haft. Then, shoving forward just as swiftly, he smote the defender in the middle with its butt end, dropping the man breathless to his knees.

This bought the Cimmerian time to vault the rail and draw his scimitar—just barely—before others were upon him.

Two
Reavers of the Coast

First upon the Cimmerian was a guard or marine trooper, swarthy and mustached, fitted out like a mercenary in bronze cap and boiled-leather vest. His sword, a stick-straight estocade, had a longer reach than Conan's heavy scimitar. Therefore it was necessary for Conan to whittle away at him while dodging his thrusts—first at his shoulder, with an ill-directed slash that barely wetted his leather sleeve with blood. Then his ear; Conan grazed it with a cut that resounded against the man's helm, goading him to dizzy rage.

Swearing fiercely, the defender slashed his blade at Conan's face. It was a reckless stroke, one that was easily turned aside by the pirate's scimitar . . . an instant before the curved blade lashed up under the hauberk into the man's vitals, doing terrible damage. The guardsman went down with an agonized shriek, dropping his sword to clutch at his red-streaming belly.

There was no time for a mercy stroke before Conan faced the next man: a dusky-faced Ilbarsi or Iranistani, outfitted the same as the first. This one thrust mightily at Conan's chest, but stumbled over the slippery limbs of his still-writhing comrade. His staggering recovery brought his neck within range of the scimitar, which struck deep and sent him spinning away across the deck in a pinwheel of blood.

Turning, with a deliberate stroke of his blade, Conan struck the head from the gutted man, cutting off his monotonous screams. But an insistent squealing still sounded; looking up from his butchery, the Cimmerian saw the heavy, square-framed snout of the catapult pivoting noisily toward him, its cord-wrapped arms straining backward and a broad shaft nested in the arrow-trough.

At the same instant that he shrank aside, the arrow whanged free. Furrowing air with its force, it whipped the hairs of his loose black mane in passing. Less lucky was the man behind him, the pirate Ogdus, who had just stepped up onto the ship's rail. The heavy shaft struck him in the middle and carried his whole tattooed body away in a whirl of limbs, arching out of sight into the sea.

Conan, recovering his balance, darted forward after the lone crewman who had unleashed the catapult. He beat him down with the flat of his heavy blade, taking care not to slaughter the man; after all, he might need an able hand to work the catapult later.

Turning to survey the deck of the cog, he saw that it had all but fallen to his hellhounds' onslaught. The armed troopers, seldom seen on a merchant vessel, had made the fight all the fiercer, scattering the ship's pale planks with fallen bodies and besmearing them with blood. Now their presence pricked the Cimmerian's curiosity. What cargo, he wondered, might be precious enough to warrant such special protection?

All of the helmeted warriors, true to their mission, had fallen to the boarders' ravaging blades or been pushed overboard to drown. The last defenders huddled close by the poop rail, near the stepladders and the sealed doorway set into the break of the deck. These holdouts were a diverse lot: several sailors armed with boarding pikes and boat hooks; the paunchy, silk-clad officer who had tried so clumsily to spear Conan when first he hove aboard; a tousled, barefoot ship's-boy of scarce a dozen summers; and a couple of finely groomed, silk-turbaned men. These latter were Turanian nobles, undoubtedly. They held their slender sabers delicately poised, as if accustomed to plying them in duels rather than in battles.

Those few waited in a temporary standoff against the foes all around them. The pirates now thronged in the ship's waist and menaced their victims from before the side and stern rails, most of them strutting and jeering in their certainty of victory. Left to themselves, Conan saw, his men would soon overwhelm the survivors and put them to the sword. Striding toward the ship's waist, he bellowed his commands fiercely enough to claim everyone's attention.

"Throw down your weapons, prisoners! Yield to the law and might of the Red Brotherhood!"

"Aye, surrender and die!" a gruff pirate voice, Diccolo's, chimed in helpfully.

"Law, indeed!" one of the aristocratic-looking men answered in loud, highbred Hyrkanian. "Law is what you miscreants are skulking from," he accused, waving his expensive saber at the boarders "—the true, righteous law of the Turanian Empire and of His Divine Majesty in Aghrapur, Emperor Yildiz, scourge of the sea-brigands!"

"Now, now, Khalid Abdal." The plump officer, hearing the rancorous murmurs and menacing shouts his companion's words drew from the encircling pirates, expostulated with him. "These seafarers have their own laws and traditions, 'tis will known. Perhaps their captain will consent to deal openly with us." He glanced warily up to Conan, who had shouldered his way to the afterdeck rail.

"Nonsense, Tibalck! Where are these famed piratical laws written or graven down, I ask you? These ignorant brutes cannot write, and they know but one stylus—the slinking dagger for cutting purses and throats! If I have my way," the noble declared, his saber flicking brightly overhead, "I will take a few more of them with me, and die cleanly in combat—"

"Aye, truly! Fight!" blood-lusty pirates bayed. "Let it be blades, then!"

"But nay, Khalid Abdal." The portly merchant Tibalck showed calm determination in restraining the nobleman. "You do not have your way here! As the *Hyacinth*'s owner and commander, I instruct you to listen to our adversaries. Hear them out, do not provoke them further. Be silent, for the good of all concerned."

So saying, the ship's master threw his sword down onto the deck. Most of the other survivors followed suit. Khalid only half-complied, lowering his weapon to waist level; his fellow aristocrat did likewise.

"Aye, merchant, a wise course," Conan affirmed. From his place along the poop-deck rail, he gazed down on the captives and on the bulk of his own men. "As you say, we are ready to dispose of you fairly by our laws. Yield up to us what treasure you have, and your fate will be honestly decided."

"Just kill them, take the loot, and burn this rotty hulk!"

a pirate's rough voice—brash Punicos's, it sounded like— echoed Conan's.

"Aye. The sack, the blade, and then the brand!" cried another, heralded by widespread cheers. "Why invoke the law? They unleashed their catapult on us first, remember! 'Twas their fight!"

"Yes, and they skewered Arkos and Scorpho, and struck off poor Zagar's head!" The troublemaker Diccolo managed to sound primly self-righteous. "They ought to be butchered in kind!"

Swords glinting, the mob stirred restlessly. Conan, sensing an insurrection near at hand, roared out fiercely, "Back off, you yapping dogs!" He threw a leg over the quarterdeck rail, bestriding it threateningly. "Who first breaks my oath will answer to me—known to you as Amra, the Scourge of the Western Ocean!" He turned to the topic closest to every captain's heart. "What of enlistments? Are they not called for, to replace the oar-hands we have lost?"

"Aye, yes, enlistments! Let us have some sport!" The pirate mob, fickle enough to follow their commander's urgings as much as anyone else's, eased back from their victims. "Who among you wants to join the Brotherhood?" lusty voices demanded.

"The law in this matter is well established." Juwala, the black Zembabwan, respected by his fellow pirates as a scholar and arbiter of fights, was brought to the fore. "If any member of the captured crew wants to sail with us as a free pirate and gain untold wealth, he may choose to." He flashed his dazzling grin around the small group of survivors. "To enlist, he must do only one thing—spill the blood of one of his former lords and oppressors."

"What?" Tibalck exclaimed. "Captain, is this part of your fair dealing?"

"Aye, merchant," Conan avowed. "It is our way."

At these words, the look that passed among the captives was a queasy one, compounded of mistrust, uncertainty, outrage, and desperation. The righteous Khalid opened his mouth to protest, but the fork-bearded pirate Punicos spoke first.

"What about you, Hyrkanian?" Edging close to one of the barefoot seamen—a rough-shirted, pantalooned youth with the squat build and yellow-gold complexion of an eastern steppe rider—the corsair coaxed him in resonant tones. "What are you? A war captive, a pressed man?" With a swift motion of his blade he flipped up the man's shirt-back, exposing whip scars, to the laughter of the pirates. "A slave? Or an apprentice, little better! What is your name, fellow?"

The sailor regarded him proudly but uncertainly. "Tamur, boss. Tamur-Laga of the Hradyu tribe."

Punicos laughed. "As I thought, an impressed landsman! Well, Tamur, would you not wish to buy life and freedom—say, with the blood of one of these arrogant Turanian fops? Here, I'll make it easy for you."

So saying, with a cunning sidelong move that misdirected attention, he seized hold of the younger, slighter nobleman's sword-hand and sent his weapon clattering to the deck. Simultaneously, two other pirates grabbed Khalid. Disarming him, they held him pinioned some distance from his brother noble, who was also weaponless.

Punicos, picking up one of the fallen Turanian sabers, handed it hilt-first to the young sailor. "There, fellow, have at him! A swordstroke or two will buy you a place in our brave company . . . with all the loot and easy living you could want!" He stepped aside and waited. "Well, man, what say you? Use it and the sword is yours! Fair enough, my fair-minded Captain?"

Conan, from his place at the rail, gave solemn assent. "So be it. If you have been good masters to your crew, there is nothing to fear."

The young Hyrkanian, holding up the finely curved blade uncertainly, looked from Punicos to the tall figure of Khalid Abdal. The elder Turanian returned his look sternly, drawing himself up in a proud, imposing stance. The sailor hefted the sword above his shoulder, yet checked himself, restrained by loyalty or fear.

"What troubles you, Tamur? Cannot bring yourself to slay a noble, is that it?" Grinning, Punicos reached to the cutlass hilt at his own waist. "It is not hard; here, I will teach you—"

On the instant, with a pained, inarticulate cry, the young Tamur raised his sword and lashed out—not at the captive, but at the taunting fork-beard, hacking at him with frenzied strokes. Punicos's blade rose swiftly to meet the other's, clashing against it twice, thrice. With an expert lunge, the fork-bearded pirate flicked the narrow saber aside; he ran its owner through, smoothly between the ribs.

The Hyrkanian, sliding down off the red-smeared cutlass, sank to the deck amid a thunder of shouts and jeers from the pirates.

"The whelp was a-scairt," one observer cried. "Cowed to death by a strutting turban!"

"He never would have made a good rogue of the Brotherhood!"

"Come then," Punicos said to the remaining captives. "Who among you will have this fine sword for the stabbing of a scented lordling?"

"*Uu-aahg!*"

The merchant Tibalck, instead of voicing further protests, emitted a dull groan and fell forward to his knees, then onto his face. Behind him, the half-grown, sandy-haired cabin boy extracted a dagger blade from his back and waved its bloody length on high. "I did it!" he yelled, dancing and skipping about the deck. "I am a pirate now, hurray! But I'll have no sword, this dirk is enough for me!" From his grimacing and mad cavorting, it seemed the lad must be addled or feebleminded. "Death to old Tibalck!" he howled. "Hail the Red Brotherhood!"

"Huzzah!" the pirates cheered him. "Excellent, lad. You set a fine example for your elders. A pirate in the finest sense of the word!"

"No more will I toil for him," the boy rejoiced, "bend to his whims, nor warm his mattress at night! I am a pirate, huzzah!" he crowed, brandishing his knife.

"Death to Tibalck. I say it, too." Another of the ragged crewmen, a thick-mustached Turanian, accepted the costly saber hilt-first from Juwala. Turning with its gleaming length, he hacked into the merchants' lifeless body, reddening the blade with a swift blow. "My name is Iliak . . . of the Red Brotherhood!" he added to exuberant cheers.

"So, Tibalck," the noble Khalid Abdal bitterly remarked, "now you know the reward of bargaining with thieves!" His words were all but lost in the hubbub as several more of the sailors stepped forward, taking the keen saber in hand to hack at the corpse.

"Point of law!" the pirate Punicos protested during the proceeding. "Is it fair that so many enlist in the Brotherhood by drawing cold blood out of a dead merchant? I say, have them hack at some of the others for good measure!"

Juwala drew breath to render a judgment, but was prevented from doing so by Conan. "Enough! I have heard all I want of sea-lawyers this day!" He vaulted down from the poop rail amid pirates and captives. "An end to this

21

idle sport," he growled, swaggering among them with his scimitar in hand. "Let us see to the spoils." He waved his heavy blade at the sealed hatch set in the break of the deck.

"Aye, the spoils!" the pirates agreed. "Slay the captives and steal the treasure!" Eager corsairs moved forward with raised cutlasses.

"Nay," Conan barked at them. "No more killing for now, unless I do it!" He strode through their midst on the balls of his feet, in aggressive readiness. Seeing his broad, muscle-cabled form clad only in kilt and soft boots, and the blade he gripped at his waist, none doubted that he could sell his own life for a dozen or more of theirs. He fixed his gaze on Juwala. "Hold these prisoners under guard while we see to the loot."

"But, Captain," the black Keshan pointed out with an air of wearied patience, "is that not putting the mizzen before the main?" He gave Conan a tolerant smile. "I know you do not always follow the ways of the Brotherhood, but our tradition is to slay them first and avoid trouble. At least drown them, if we do not wish the bodies to bear marks—"

"I do not intend to kill the nobles," Conan declared. "They can bring us a ransom more valuable than this tub's cargo. I'd have kept the owner hostage, too," he said, regarding Tibalck's butchered body. "Had he lived. Of these others—" he waved his blade at the pale-looking survivors who now watched him, daring once again to hope "—they will be set loose, adrift."

"Set adrift!" Fork-bearded Punicos led in the general chorus of astonishment. "By Bel-Dagoth, such a thing is unheard of! They can tell of our whereabouts, and recount our crimes to the Turanian and Hyrkanian Admiralties!"

"Fool," Conan said curtly. "There is no way to collect

a ransom without risking that! Anyway, we are Red Brothers, proud of our reputation and fame. I am not bound to slaughter every witness just to enable us to skulk away from the authorities! Let some of them live and spread the word of our exploits far and wide.''

''Captain Amra,'' Juwala joined in angrily, ''do you know the rudiments of the pirating trade? As it stands, this merchant and her crew could have been lost in a squall with no survivors, or gone aground on an offshore reef; none will know any different. But fame, such conceit as you talk of—'' he shook his head soberly ''—that kind of notoriety is the enemy of a pirate! It causes the waters he sails in to be shunned by merchants, and to swarm instead with the toothed beaks of Imperial warships. It turns every hand against him, including those of his false brothers—''

''Nay, Juwala,'' Conan interrupted firmly. ''Such fame works to my benefit. Henceforth when I chase a ship, they'll lack the stomach for a fight if they know it is Amra the Corsair hauling up alongside. And no merchant will be able to shun or outrace us when we have both oarships and sailships to hound them out with.''

''What? You mean to keep this prize rather than scuttle it, and to sail in two ships?''

''Two ships or twenty . . . all I need are crews to man them and staunch officers who can follow my commands! That is how it was done in the Western Sea.'' Conan knew that the latter statement was more wish than fact, but guessed that few of these Vilayet hands would know it. ''It is the path lowly pirates like ourselves can tread to become sea-kings!''

''Captain Amra! Look here, sir—''

Some pirates had not been following the debate with shouts of encouragement or murmurs of controversy; those few were engaged in prying open the stout door that slanted between poop and main deck. Firmly fastened both inside and out, the oak panel had so far resisted the leverage of boarding pikes and oar blades. Now, as jamb and coaming were on the verge of tearing loose before incessant attacks, the pirates sought Conan's attention. "I cannot tell it for sure, Captain, but just now I heard voices inside."

"Oh, did you?" With a stride, Conan was before the straining panel. "Come, lads, stretch your thews this time! Ready, heave!"

The door groaned free of its fastenings and fell outward, and Conan strode forward onto it. Brushing aside a splintered, sagging chunk of the jamb, he peered into the dimness between decks.

Within was dank, spice-scented gloom, with a glittering array at one side—no gleaming heap of treasure, but a silk-draped table spread with mirrors, bottles, and trinkets. At the back of the cabin, outlined against the slatted paleness of sterncastle windows, stood two figures, both female.

"Oh, aye," Conan heard the addled cabin boy prating behind him, "our brave pirate captain seeks the *Hyacinth*'s treasure. A rare, dangerous cargo it is, you will see!"

"Get him away," Conan rapped out. "Dogs, keep back from the door. Some of you try yonder hatchways and see what lies in the lower hold," he added, so as to furnish them a temporary distraction. "Now then, out with you! Come forth into the light! Who might you wenches be?"

"Innocent sea-travelers." One of the women, silk-gowned, high-sandaled and black-haired, stepped through the ravaged doorway, raising a dainty hand to shield her eyes against the afternoon brightness. "I am Philiope, daughter of Count Aristarkos of Shahpur. Yonder is my handmaid Sulula.'' She presented the second female, less sleekly beautiful but just as finely costumed, who hung back in the shadowed doorway. ''You, then, are the one called Amra the Lion?''

''Aye, and what if it is so?'' Conan found it strange to hear his pirate name murmured in such delicate, gracious accents.

''If you are he, then I throw myself upon your protection!'' Sinking forward on one knee, the girl Philiope seized Conan's blood-crusted hand and pressed it to her face, speaking in fervent tones as she did so. ''I know this ship has fallen prey to fierce invaders, to the evil Brotherhood. So I look to you, the strongest and most feared of all, to protect me and mine from the ill fate that overtakes their victims! Please, I beg you, see that no great harm befalls me or Sulula, my faithful servant—nor either descends on those who tried to save us, under my father's instruction. If you would undertake this, I swear to you—'' here she turned her face aside to plant a kiss on the hard knuckles of his hand ''—I would be most grateful.''

As she spoke, gazing up at him, Conan felt desire stir through his chest, belly, loins. The maid was winsome indeed, a lithe, dusky Turanian beauty, full-chested and firm-thighed in her seagreen gown, a puff-sleeved affair that dragged behind her in a ruffled train, yet retreated sharply enough in front to expose one dark-tipped breast and one bent knee. Furthermore, the wench had brass to her, in spite of her claimed noble origin; Conan liked her way of taking the initiative.

''It was you—'' against his will, he found the back of his hand caressing the velvety cheek pressed against it ''—that the troop of soldiers and the catapult were placed on board to protect?''

''Yes, by arrangement of my father, to guard me and

25

my cousins." Relinquishing his hand, she waved to indicate the pair of noblemen backed up along the rail with the rest of the prisoners. "And, of course, my dowry in the hold below. It was being sent to Hyrkania to guarantee my marriage . . . my prearranged marriage," she added in unasked explanation, "to a rich and senior official of the most dignified repute."

"So you ask me to keep you safe—for a ransom, I would hope."

"Yes." The girl Philiope rose to her feet before him. "Both for myself and my beloved servant," she added with a nod to her timid companion. "Unless you see fit to release her."

"Should I apply for ransom to your lordly father, then, or to this rich fiancé of yours?"

"Why, ah . . . my father, Count Aristarkos, would be more responsive to your demands, I should think." She nodded to the prisoners. "These others could be set free— with adequate food and transportation, of course—on any Turanian land or sea. They would carry your message to my home, I am sure. My cousins have always been most devoted to me."

The arrogant Khalid Abdal, from his place at the rail, nodded to her with a wry, supercilious smile. "Very well spoken, my dearest Philiope!"

"I see." Conan turned to Ivanos at his elbow. "What is your report from below decks?"

The tall, lean Corinthian, wearing a purple damask cloth draped about his unshaved neck and a silver soup tureen inverted atop his close-cropped head, beamed triumphantly at his captain. "It is a rich cargo, Captain—mixed, with fineware, fabric, spices, made-goods, and potted daintyfoods and relishes." His announcement was greeted with cheers and sea-jigging from the nearby pirates.

"Oh, is it?" Conan grunted suspiciously. He could smell good Kothian wine on his lieutenant's breath, and decided to conclude any necessary business before the whole pirate rabble was unmanageably drunk. "I warn you, do not relish your potted goods overmuch, not until I give leave! Set guards over the hold, three men at each hatchway. If any slinking thief tries to get in, bring him before me."

"Yes . . . aye, Captain!" Ivanos stammered.

"I will remain aboard this ship with the cargo and a picked crew. The rest of you can row with us back to Djafur—or tow us if the wind does not rise. The loot, aside from provisions, will be divided fairly at Djafur."

The pirates sent up a groan of disappointment at this news, yet did not protest strenuously, since most of them knew it was best to avoid fights and carousals in open sea.

"The prisoners will be set adrift—" he gestured to a small launch upturned in the ship's waist "—with food and water, along the coast. I can do no better than that," he assured Philiope, scowling into her wide-eyed face. "Fear not, they will easily find a ship bound south and west to carry them to Turan. Your ransom will be twenty talents of gold—" at this figure, the pirates murmured in amazement, though Philiope did not look surprised "—or an equivalent value in tradeware, provisions, and weapons. Have your father contact the sea-tribes near Djafur, they will set up an exchange. Until then, you remain with me, under my protection. Mark me well, you skulking sea-dogs," he proclaimed with a baleful look at his crew. "Amra of the Black Coast does not trade in damaged goods!"

"And my faithful handmistress?" Philiope was quick to remind him. "She can go with the rest, I presume?"

"Aye, well . . ." Conan hesitated. He felt awkward in

dealing with these female complications; furthermore, he had just caught sight of Olivia skirting past dead bodies on the *Hyacinth*'s deck, doubtless coming to learn the outcome of the battle. The look on her face as she saw the gowned woman was grim. He had all but forgotten Olivia; suddenly, an inspiration struck him.

"I will not set a woman adrift. But on the other hand, it would not do for a prisoner of the Red Brotherhood to keep a slave. Therefore, I give your servant Sulula to my mistress Olivia for the term of your captivity, to tend to her wants and, as time permits, to your own." He spoke in round tones so that Olivia, who came frowning, might hear. "You remain under my protection, of course, all three."

"Point of law, Captain!" It was Punicos who spoke, striding to the fore of the pirate assembly. "By the tradition of our Brotherhood, women captives taken with a ship are to be shared out equally among the brothers for use by all, for as long as they last. It has struck many of us as unfair that you should keep one woman to yourself . . . now you want three! And even assuming, Captain, that some noble landsman would be fool enough to pay you in gold for this little hussy—"

Punicos's speech went no further; Conan's steel scimitar, swung in a swift, pantherish lunge, flashed through the air and clove the man cleanly from collarbone to hip. The gory carcass tumbled to the deck, falling in two loosely attached pieces before his shipmates' hushed, appalled gaze.

"Any more business, any fine legal points?" Conan demanded hoarsely. "Enough, then. Cast these bodies overboard, and bring me a count of the living. Loosen up the grapples and ready the sails! I scent a wind rising!"

THREE
The Center of the World

Under the bright blue shell of Turanian sky, before the city's many-masted harbor, the Imperial Palace at Aghrapur spread vast and ornate. Its frescoed halls and inlaid galleries enclosed an area greater than the whole capital cities of some less powerful lands, all beneath one roof—or rather, an ever-growing assemblage of roofs, domes, towers, minarets, and arcades knit cunningly together. Through its expanses a visitor could walk for many days without retracing the same path or setting foot in inhospitable sunlight.

Nephet Ali gave little more than passing notice to these wondrous rooms and byways. The small, brisk vizier knew them better, perhaps, than anyone; in his years of service to the resplendent Emperor Yildiz, Grand Monarch of All Turan, he had decreed a good many of them himself and taken a hand in their design and furnishing. Now, even as he strode across silk-carpeted foyers and echoing mezzanines inlaid with costly gemstones, his mind roved other, more elaborate corridors and byways: the tortuous funnels, viaducts, and hidden passages of Imperial enterprise and Turan's military purchase system.

The procurement routes, not unlike these palace corridors, were strewn with dangerous spy-holes and ambushes. This current summons from the emperor, for instance—it might mean that some past or present theft of the vizier had been discovered—that he had been too greedy, and now as a consequence was to be stripped of office, possibly of life. If such was the case, he had best be ready to plead innocence or to deflect the guilt elsewhere. On the other hand, this meeting might merely be to unveil some splendid new opportunity for siphoning and profiteering; with that hope in his heart, Nephet Ali reminded himself to maximize his profit by making his demands sufficiently exorbitant from the start.

Arriving at the gold-bossed ebony doors of the emperor's apartment, he halted expectantly before the guards there: two hard-muscled, slim-waisted Hyperborean females. The women were well-matched in their towering height, their thick ropes of braided blond hair, and their identical costumes consisting of bundled fur waist-clouts, bearhide buskins, horned helmets, and round gold brassiere cups harnessed firmly in place by gilded chain mail. His Resplendency's idiosyncracy of maintaining a female bodyguard was well established, of course; yet Nephet Ali had to admit that this show of barbarous splendor in the midst of arabesque opulence caught his attention and made his pulse murmur in his temples.

Tamely he submitted while the Northern maidens searched him for weapons—a thorough search indeed, he noted as they riffled through his purse and groped up under his caftan of gold-embroidered silk. Satisfied at last, his captors opened the ebon portal; one of them led him through it, across a still-considerable distance of pillared corridors and vaulted chambers, to the broad, open archway of His Resplendency's bedchamber.'

Another pair of guards was stationed there, statuesque Kushite females. These two were armored in light turbans, vests, and harem pantaloons, all knit of diaphanous silver mesh that shimmered against their black skin. They did not repeat their predecessors' search, but parted their crossed pikes briefly to admit Nephet Ali into the lavish sanctum.

Emperor Yildiz was not on his bed, which was a velvet mattress afloat in a stone-curbed pool of shimmering quicksilver. Instead, the floating bolster was occupied by two of his fat concubines, either asleep or drugged. They lay semiclad across its rumpled coverlets like seals dozing on an offshore rock. Nephet Ali, gazing around at the cavernous elegance of the bedchamber, located the Resplendent One disporting himself with others of his harem along a farther wall of the room.

The emperor's well-known propensities dictated that his concubines be considerably softer and fleshier than his female bodyguards. Yildiz, a compact, olive-skinned monarch of thinning hair and ripening years, lounged slackly on a divan of yellow upholstery, watching two of his favorites at play. The women, largely unclothed, capered and squealed in a wine tub of aromatic purple grapes, tramping out the overripe juice with bare feet. As the vizier ventured closer, one of the maidens leaned copiously out of the tub and turned a golden tap set in its side. Filling a jeweled goblet, she handed it to Yildiz. He in turn offered the ruby vintage to one of the two male visitors seated upright and attentive in padded chairs at his side. The thin, bald guest, whom Nephet Ali recognized as Ninshub, the minister of finance, politely accepted, though he did not raise the cup to his lips.

Moving close to the cloying stink of the wine trough, trying to avoid the dark-violet splotches and footprints on the lapis-lazuli floor, Nephet Ali sank to his knees in greeting. "Your Resplendency, I humbly obey your summons."

"Nephet, is it?" Yildiz sloshed his wine cup high in salute. "Dear fellow, welcome to our revel! Aspasia, Isdra, another flagon for our guest!" As the two houris vied to work the tap, threatening in their girlish eagerness to overturn the entire winepressing onto the palace floor, Emperor Yildiz motioned his chief engineer to a seat beside him. "Of course you know Ninshub . . . and here, my young son Yezidgerd. He is the one who proposed this meeting. Now, fellow, drink up!"

Dutifully Nephet Ali accepted a beaker from the dripping concubine and raised it to his lips, sipping as much of the perfumy sweetness as he could stand. Meanwhile, watching through half-closed eyes, he calculated. He had never in fact previously seen Yildiz's son Yezdigerd, who heretofore was said to lead a quiet, studious existence in a secluded wing of the palace under the tutelage of his grandame, the Queen Mother Khushia. The prince was a taller, leaner, more sallow and thin-featured version of his father. In his grooming he obviously looked westward to the Hyborian lands, dressing in relatively loose, practical cotton pantaloons, a shirt with Kothian-style buttons in front, plain leather bootlets and a simple gray turban. He affected mild disinterest in the cavortings of his father's two floozies. Indeed, even amid this riot, he seemed entirely composed and purposeful . . . a man to be careful of.

"So, Nephet Ali!" the emperor beamed. "How pleasant it is to sample the the first pressings of the new harvest in such a convivial way, with boon friends! Help yourself to more wine if you wish. Or to the girls, for that matter, if such be your taste. There is no business so urgent that it cannot wait on the promptings of the flesh!''

"Thank you, Resplendency." Nephet Ali was well used to Yildiz's flaunting of outrageous distractions during high state gatherings. At first he had understood the practice as a clever means of sounding out his subordinates' true character and feelings, and of throwing them off guard against his initiatives. But in recent years, the habit seemed to have taken on a purpose of its own—that of merely appeasing the ever more debauched cravings of a jaded ruler. On this occasion, Yildiz himself seemed half-woozy, either with spirits or hashish fumes, and the orgy did not appear to be an act. Accordingly, the vizier elevated his hopes of a ministerial and fiscal triumph.

"I cannot say," bald Ninshub began, "that I could endorse a significant new military outlay at this time." The scrawny, skull-bald finance minister, generally uneasy at these licentious meetings, obviously hoped to dispose of the matter and escape with as little plundering of his coffers as possible. "Especially, I must say, on the heels of all the recent troop and sailor levys, galley-builds, and the cost of fortified outposts in the western marches. I should think the amount provided in the regular decree would be more than enough for our offensive plans—"

"Precisely, honored Ninshub." The young Prince's voice was firm and dry, unsurprised by the treasurer's opening gambit. "I share your rightful concern over undue expenditures. That is why I have proposed this idea . . . as an economy that will save us shiploads of gold in the future."

"Yes, but even so—" Ninshub was quick to dismiss the argument, almost laughing in the younger man's face "—you may not know, Prince, that nearly every expensive scheme is first brought forth as a cost-saving, or even a money-making, proposition. Alas, how few of them turn out to be anything

33

but a steady, escalating drain on the Imperial treasury . . . especially once the original costs have doubled or trebled, and middlemen have claimed further entitlements—"

"Aye, the middlemen," Emperor cried plaintively. "Eunuchs are the worst, forever parceling out my interests, demanding favors from above and baksheesh from below! The deal is done better, I say, if they can be cut out of it." He waved a hand, expostulating in air. "Why, the price of a nice Shemitish wench on the market-block, what is it? Five dinars? I often end up paying ten times as much after the eunuchs are through brokering and dickering!" He turned his head. "Nephet Ali, are you a eunuch?"

In spite of himself, the vizier felt his face begin to flush. "Nay, Resplendency. I have seven wives and twenty-three children."

"Oh, really? I can never seem to remember. Good then, no offense was meant, none taken. Would you care for another?"

"I beg your pardon, Resplendent One?" Nephet Ali was sufficiently off balance to proceed with caution, glancing down at his half-empty cup.

"Do you want another wife?" Yildiz gestured vaguely to the hussies in the wine vat. "Either one of these is yours for the asking."

"Nay, sire, a million thanks!" Shaking his head profusely to gain time, the vizier mumbled a polite excuse. "I try to make sure each new wife is younger than the last, to keep some semblance of rank and order in my home."

"I see." Yildiz nodded. "You are a wise man. Very politic." He looked away, finally letting the matter pass.

"I agree with you, Ninshub." Prince Yezdigerd resumed speaking as if there had been no digression from business. "The cost of maintaining our Imperial sway, and especially our naval dominance, is a heavy one. Of late, new conquests and infusions of plunder have been less frequent."

"Indeed, Prince," Ninshub said, nodding, "but the costs of our foreign adventures continue."

"But see here, my dear Minister," Yildiz protested from his divan, "what conceivable ground is there for complaint? Turan's borders are being enlarged, are they not? Our tributary states continue to pay as much tax as our satraps and foreign legions can wring out of them, is that not so?"

"Yes, Resplendent One, 'tis so." Ninshub nodded unctuously from his seat. "Your Resplendency's empire continues to flourish. Yet even so," he persisted with an apologetic air, "there are rising costs . . . not merely those of manning and maintaining our ships and legions abroad, but unforeseen expenses like bandit raids, revolts, and piracy on the high seas."

"Aye, 'tis most true." Nephet Ali, having recovered from his conjugal inquisition, felt the time was ripe to enter the discussion. Appearing to come charitably to the finance minister's aid seemed as good an excuse as any. "This pirate Amra, for instance," he expounded, "the one who recently abducted Count Aristarkos's daughter—there, now, is a case in point! The cost of suppressing such a menace before it erodes Turan's naval supremacy further or stirs up some kind of mutiny among the islanders and sea-tribes—why, that could be a ruinous matter if deferred too long."

"Come, now, Vizier," Emperor Yildiz protested. "The best-regulated empire will always be troubled by petty highwaymen and seawaymen! This Amra fellow is a nuisance, to be sure . . . in part because he challenges the noble class and plays to the rabble's fascination with bloody-handed corsairs. But can you really call such a trifling matter a threat to my rule, requiring some new naval outlay?" As the emperor argued, Nephet Ali observed that his air of drunken amiability continued, so that there seemed no real edge to his words.

"Nay, esteemed Father," Prince Yezdigerd reassured his parent. "I hardly think our vizier means to imply so much." He gazed at the two watchful subordinates. "The only way this brigand could ever become a significant problem, as I see it, were if our rivals the Hyrkanians manage to stamp him out before we do and then use the small triumph as grounds to claim naval prominence in the Vilayet."

"Hmm, true, that could be an issue," Yildiz observed. "Well-considered, Yezdigerd! Your royal grandmother has done rightly to recommend your counsels to me. What, then, is your proposal to deal with this nuisance and others like him?"

"In the naval realm, Father," the dour-faced young prince began, "daily costs are the vexing problem. A naval build is a major outlay, true; but then, well-founded ships can last for dozens of years in service and even longer in the sheds. Furthermore, past naval victories have netted us scores of sound vessels and reparable hulks. Fully half our fleet is made up of war prizes and commandeered pirates, smugglers, and such.

"As Ninshub says, it is the expense of manning and operating a navy that drags heaviest on the budget: recruitment, repairs, provisioning, and the cost of maintaining harbors and garrisons in distant ports. Sailors and navigators are skilled workers who cannot be had easily or cheaply. They have families, too, who must be kept alive here at home if their laboring-caste is to continue. Even oarsmen have to be taught, and will not perform satisfactorily without some pay or inducement. Their training is not cheap, requiring skilled officers to break them in, and many trial cruises in preparation for a single battle—all of which have to be fitted out and provisioned: a continual, draining expense."

"There are ships rowed by convicts and slaves," Yildiz

put in helpfully. "Some navies use nothing else. And, of course, in the event of a popular and well-publicized war, there is the chance of lively recruitment and a naval draft."

Yezdigerd shrugged minimally, as if too polite to flatly dismiss his father's words. "Forced labor has proven far from satisfactory. Slaves require even harsher drill; their life span is short and their battle performance sluggish at best. As for volunteers, or a civil draft . . ." The princeling shook his head with a frown. "Such measures are to be avoided, in my view. They raise dangerous feelings of kinship and self-reliance in the class they are drawn from, creating a restless, arrogant middle-caste or petty nobility—such as the one our Hyrkanian rivals, who often resort to such measures, are saddled with. Arming tenants and small-holders and training them in close cooperation is always a dangerous business. It leads to notions of self-determination, even to mob rule. A career-officer caste, with strict authority over line soldiers and seafarers, is much safer."

"Obviously, Yezdigerd, you have given the matter some thought." Yildiz nodded dryly. "But say, good Treasurer, your flagon is empty! And yours, dear Nephet. Isdra, Aspasia, you have neglected our guests! More drink all around!" Waving his goblet overhead, the monarch sloshed red droplets over the already-spattered nymphs floundering in the wine tub. "Ladies," proclaimed the emperor as they decanted more wine, "your fragrant distillations are as heady and sweet as divine nectar to my lips!"

When the resulting bustle had subsided, Prince Yezdigerd—who, obedient to the law of the holy prophet Tarim, imbibed neither the juice of grape or grain—coolly resumed speaking. His words had the sound of a prepared speech.

"We live in a time of powerful new learning and a growing commerce in ideas. Our Turanian Empire, most particularly this splendid capital of ours, straddles the center of caravan and sea traffic, dominating the crossroads of trade between east and west, north and south. Here in Aghrapur we stand, you and I, at the very center of the world. Thus far it has benefited us vastly, both in tariffs and profits, the enlargement of our empire, and the spread of our influence in foreign lands.

"Yet I wonder . . . have we really availed ourselves of the greatest benefit of all?" The prince paused rhetorically, earnest-faced. "In this city, in case you did not know it, dwell some of the keenest minds of our time. They are prodigies raised up amid the wealth of our libraries and scholarly gymnasia, or drawn here by their thirst for knowledge, abandoning remote, backward regions where their gifts were unappreciated. Some linger here only briefly on their world travels, beguiled by our city's opportunities for scientific investigation and the life of the mind.

"Aghrapur, for all these reasons, boasts the world's greatest healers, the keenest astronomers, the shrewdest alchemists, and the most accomplished mages the world has known. I have studied these men, and some of their ancient counterparts as well. I find that in most cases, their intellectual strivings are not narrowly specialized. These seers can usually bend their efforts to any problem posed to them, cutting through the heavy cobwebs of folklore and tradition to arrive at a fresh, inventive solution."

"You propose," Emperor Yildiz asked, "to direct some street-corner philosopher's discourses to the problems of empire?" The aim of the questions was obviously to speed the young prince along.

"Hmm. Yes, that could be," Yezdigerd replied, accepting the prod rather intensely, and fixing on his father a gaze that made Nephet Ali vaguely uncomfortable. "It may be that someday keen thinkers will take up the problem of controlling the unruly masses, or even, at our urging—yours and mine. Father—devise a self-consistent science of Imperial rule. Doubtless their methods, if put rigidly into practice, will be ruthless and efficient enough to secure our kingship for all time.'' He smiled vaguely at the thought, at last relieving the watchers of his stare. ''But for now, my aim is much more limited: specifically, this problem we have touched on, of how to man or drive ships without the awkward, costly vicissitudes of commanding oar-crews as we presently do.''

It was Ninshub's turn to ask for clarification. ''You mean, finding some way of propelling ships without rowers? Such a method has already been devised, O Prince—the power of wind upon sails!'' He smirked condescendingly. ''Is further investigation really needed?''

''Yes, Financier . . . if you consider that the winds of our desert sea, the Vilayet, are prone to blow sluggishly and fitfully, or else with tempestuous violence. For our safety and certainty, they force us back on the old expedient that has proven so cumbersome—that of oared galleys burdened down with crew and provisions, having little room left for cargo and armaments.''

''You mean to command these scholars to find some better way?'' Emperor Yildiz's attention was not, apparently, permanently focused in his wine cup. ''Which ones would your choose, then, and what would be the penalty for failure? Lifetime servitude on the oar-benches, perhaps?''

''Nay, Father.'' Yezdigerd shook his head, showing little patience with old-fashioned ideas. ''What I propose is a contest, a competition open to all recognized thinkers who care to offer a solution. The prize would be an award of gold. Five hundred talents should suffice, and possibly an Imperial warrant or appointment to oversee and develop the new plan for use throughout the navy.''

''Allow them a share of profit on the project, you

mean?'' The finance minister knit his hairless brow. ''Hmm, yes, that might prove interesting.''

''But my dear boy,'' Emperor Yildiz protested, ''what imaginable improvements could these experts concoct? Winds that blow at our will? There is a highly successful captain in our Northern service who claims to command that power already, you know. He merely wets his sails with the blood of war captives. Or perhaps these wizards could make the surface of the sea curve downhill, so that the rush of the flood would carry our ships to their destination . . . ? More wine here, fair Isdra! Such musing makes me dizzy.''

Prince Yezdigerd shrugged his lank shoulders. ''There is no guessing what might come to pass. Could anyone have envisioned a bronze war chariot, years before mortals had ever caught and harnessed a wild desert-horse? Or this contrivance . . .'' He fingered one of the ivory buttons on his shirtfront. ''It is a Kothian invention—very simple, but I think it has promise.''

''Speaking as vizier—'' Nephet Ali, having come to a decision, felt that he must speak up so as to guide the affair toward a profitable result ''—I think the young prince's approach could be most . . . fruitful. There are, of course, the vital questions of how to advertise such a contest, how to choose fit nominees, and ultimately, how to judge the worth of their schemes—''

''It would seem to me,'' Yezdigerd interrupted, ''that we three—or four, counting you of course, my dear Father—are the ones best suited to rendering a final judgment. That is why I suggested that we meet here. There must also, of course, be a member of the naval command involved. I have already broached this matter to High Admiral Quub, first in authority under Jamil, our minister of conquest. His ministry, I am happy to say, has expressed strong interest in participating.''

"Hmm, Jamil . . ." Ninshub shook his head unhappily. "A fine warrior, of course, but in the past, his demands on the treasury have been steep and incessant. If he were to seize authority over a project like this, and run away with it—"

"Do not fear," the young prince assured him. "Admiral Quub has promised me that control can be tightly limited to the Admiralty."

"Good, then," Nephet Ali said. "Of course, even though my own duties are financial, I, too, am in contact with nimble young thinkers. If I were to bring in a contestant or two—"

"They would be most welcome," Yezdigerd assured him. "The same is true for you, Ninshub," he said to the finance minister, who nodded thoughtfully. "Whatever the source, the best ideas must be allowed to rise according to their own merit. All that should be required is a proclamation and some interviews over the course of, say, a fortnight or so. I would be pleased to take charge of them. Then, for a period of several months, the contestants can be allowed access to the Imperial Navy Yard, with various nonessential ships and wares set aside for their experiments. And, of course, adequate slaves and recruits levied for their use—"

"Wait, now," Yildiz said, looking up from his goblet. "What is all this about experimentation? You mean for us to offer goods as well as gold to these conjurers?"

"Why, yes, Father. To be sure, the proposals will have to be tested." Yezdigerd, for the first time in the meeting, turned a strong-toothed, glinting smile on his parent. "An idea is nothing more than airy speculation until it can be put into some tangible form, or carried out as a process, with real men and solid objects. We can scarcely judge the value and practicality of a plan without first seeing it proven. And we cannot expect these lofty thinkers, most of whom are men of slender material means, to fund such experimentation out of their own purses."

Nephet Ali hesitated along with the others. He had felt fairly confident, moments before, of being able to sponsor a candidate of his own with a small cash stake, a candidate who might then, with his influence, walk away with the prize of five hundred talents. This new aspect of the plan, in effect an Imperial subsidy, threatened to stiffen the competition; but it also opened up wider possibilities in the form of the Imperial Navy Yard—whose vast resources would now be accessible, or so it seemed, with extensive opportunities for the siphoning and diversion of funds and goods far into the future, with no advance risk at all. "What an excellent idea," the Imperial Engineer declared at last. "It is clear, my dear Prince, that you have worked out your plan most thoroughly."

"Aye, indeed," Ninshub chimed in. "I would think that this proposal is extremely likely to increase our naval efficiency."

"And you, Father, if you have no objection . . . ?" Yezdigerd turned solicitously toward the musing emperor, whose nod of agreement seemed distracted and offhanded. "Good, then. I shall have proclamations drawn up and issue an order on the treasury." He arose, ever businesslike.

"In a way, it is fortunate," Nephet Ali was moved to remark as he stood up, "that the great god Tarim sends us minor vexations such as these cursed Vilayet pirates. They keep us alert—do they not, O Resplendent One?" he added with exaggerated respect, bowing before his pensive emperor. "And they force us to better ourselves. The best trial of any new naval force will be in destroying this rascal Amra!"

FOUR
Thieves' Port

Even at mid-morning, the Red Hand Inn was noisy and crowded. Several ships were in—most of them low, fast galleys whose hulls boasted no level decking, much less any shelter for exhausted oarsmen. These vessels were now drawn up askew on Djafur's broad, sandy beach, and the inn's common tavern and upper rooms teemed with life.

The lower floor echoed with warring, dissonant strains of zither and fife, snores and groans, drunken arguments in male and female accents of a dozen languages, the clank of fish kettles, and the loud, strained voices of bleary gamblers still vying their bets from the previous night.

The interior of the tavern, under the low, sagging timbers of its upper level, was cramped and dim. Even by hot, hazy island sunlight, the place remained cool and dank because of windows overlooking the harbor. There was also an open archway leading directly onto the wharf, where weary patrons sought peace, idling and dozing on kegs and crates or on the flat, worn planking. One of these guests, the Cimmerian best known as Amra, sat along the edge of the dock, idly spearing fish.

"Well, Captain," a gruff voice challenged, "when will you make your next treasure cruise?"

Knulf Shipbreaker, proprietor of the Red Hand, was also master of the trim pirate galley, the *Victrix*, which lay drawn up on the beach a mere dozen steps from the pier. The red-bearded Vanirman was stout and broad-chested; as he ambled near the low curb, Conan felt loose timbers shift beneath the man's solid weight.

"I know not, Captain." Conan half-turned to watch the Vanir's approach, less from courtesy than from a sneaking doubt whether his ancestral foe might try to fling him off the pier into the shark-infested harbor. Men of Vanaheim and those of Cimmeria had ever found differences; also, the captains of the Red Brotherhood who sheltered in this pirates' den of Djafur were less than easy allies, as experience had taught Conan. "I had thought to bide here," he said, "till some new ship arrives with tidings of trade and weather."

"Aye, a sensible course. Your men have not, in any case, drunk and gambled away the spoils of your last trip. So you are welcome." Easing down with a grunt, Knulf helped himself to a place on the wooden curb opposite his rival. "And there is the matter of your hostage, the fair Philope. Perhaps you are waiting for word from her family regarding your twenty talents of gold?"

" 'Tis too soon to expect payment," Conan muttered. "Or reprisal, either." He hated the notion of discussing personal business with a smug competitor like Knulf; on the other hand, there was no way of keeping such a thing secret in a small, gossip-filled port like Djafur. The whole town barely stretched from end to end of the cove, where its handful of galleys and twoscore fishing launches lay

beached. The place boasted but the one wharf of ram-
shackle timber and a broken-down stone jetty remaining
from the ancient fortress. The single, unpaved street of
brothels and doss houses swarmed with cats and flies, and
with slouching, staggering drunks, even at this hour of the
morning. The tidy fringe of fishermen's huts and trades-
men's villas climbed halfway up the hill, fenced by low
walls built of rubble from the ruined fortification at the
top.

Knulf, after sharing Conan's desultory glance up and
down the waterfront, resumed the conversation. "So you
must wait and hope, I suppose—" the Vanir smiled insin-
uatingly beneath his stained whiskers "—unless, of course,
you weary of the whole affair. Then you might sell the
hostage girl to me, at a discount . . . say, one-fourth of
your asking price, five golden talents. How does that
sound, Cimmerian? It would make you well-quit of the
deal and leave to me the risk of collecting payment. A
long chance, for a tidy profit . . . but such a gamble suits
my fancy! What say you, Cimmerian?"

"Nay, Knulf, and damn your mealy mouth for asking."
The Cimmerian growled out the words levelly, in a measured, businesslike curse. "I would rather hold out for the
full ransom . . . or not, as I please. 'Tis my name, after
all, and my oath that was given on the matter!"

"Aye, Captain. But you are green to these waters, less
feared and respected than I. You might soon move on to
other enterprises, unless you want to spend years building
up a reputation like mine!" Raising a scarred, grimy fist,
the pirate smugly thumped his drink-stained beard where
it lay across his barrel chest. "Anyway, I do not imagine
it has been easy keeping two women on a ship. Three
really, counting the dim-witted serving-maid. One wench
is hard enough to watch in a thieves' den like Djafur—"

"Enough! I will handle the business myself." As if to punctuate the remark, Conan's arm lashed powerfully, sending his short, thin lance angling down toward the waves. Where it struck, there commenced a frenzied splashing and swirling beneath the surface. But when Conan hauled taut the braided cord knotted to the lance, its barbed length floated free, trailing redness in the murky, gray-green water. As Conan drew up the lance and coiled the line, the splashing swirl receded but did not cease.

"A good cast," commented Knulf. "Must be sharks. They are hard to bring in . . . see there." He pointed a thick finger at triangular fins darting and circling through red-tinged harbor foam.

"Aye, a whole pack of the stripey devils," a gruff voice added. "They gather thickest near the haunts of men." The speaker was a bystander who had come forward to watch the flurry: a beached, decrepit-looking sailor who slouched from the shadows of the inn's eaves.

"I have speared a good many," Conan said, easing down watchfully on the curb. "But for every one I kill, two or three more seem to appear."

"Ha, Cimmerian!" Knulf chided him. "Do you not know it is the blood that draws them?"

"Aye, they prey on their own kind," the stranger cackled. "Like some humans I know."

The Vanirman laughed again, none too pleasantly. "No great loss. You would not want to catch and eat them knowing what else they eat!" He gestured to the beach shallows where, often as not, human skulls and bones could be seen washing among the pebbles and winkle-shells. Meanwhile, Knulf hove himself to his feet, making the planks creak. "Consider my offer, Conan. You and I have both sailed the turbulent Western Ocean, but the Vilayet is a tideless inland sea, where a captain needs wit and tact to survive.'' He turned on his heel. "Good hunting to you.''

"Good hunting, aye,'' Conan returned according to the etiquette of the Brotherhood.

When the Vanirman had passed through the kitchen doorway, the wharf idler spoke again. "Knulf is a canny fighter and navigator, but most of all, a sly conniver.''

"Aye,'' Conan grunted, "so I have heard. He polished his skills along with his breeches on the oar-bench of a Vanir dragonship, raiding as far south as Argos, and a hundred leagues up the Khorotas River.''

"I, too, have sailed the Western Sea,'' the pirate said. "I know your fame as Amra of the Black Corsairs . . . and as Conan the General, hero of the Shamla Pass and vanquisher of undead Natohk's sorcerous legions.''

Conan turned to peer at the wharf rat. The round face was pale and ill-shaven from a dissolute existence on the beach, the features puffy and shapeless with drink. "I do not know you, and I give no alms.''

"I am Ferdinald of Zingara, a smith and shipwright aforetimes, till I learned the higher craft of piracy. Know me as a man in search of a leader.''

Conan sized up the fellow further, assessing the wasted countenance, outweighed somewhat by the robust frame, the level stance and gaze. "Follow me, then. Will you have some drink . . . nay, some food in you, if the morning kettle is not empty?''

"If it is not emptied, it will be soon, with fivescore more mouths to feed.''

"What?'' Conan turned, following the Zingaran's gaze to scan the mirror-bright sea. There around the chalky headland came a high, trim galley, its black-painted hull highlighted by the flash of fast-stroking oars. " 'Tis a pirate craft, sure,'' the Cimmerian declared. "Under pursuit, or else putting the oar-crew through its paces. Looks like the *Tormentress*."

"Aye," Ferdinald affirmed, "Santhindrissa's cruiser. She and her pirate maids will make this place lively soon."

"Let us go inside, then," Conan said, arising from his seat. "I want my party to be ready for them."

After watching for a moment to make sure that no hostile ship chased the pirates, Conan turned and led the way inside. Any such pursuit was unlikely, he knew; it had been years since Imperial vessels had tried to blockade Djafur, much less attempted a raid. The place was too remote from Turanian harbors and too well hidden amid the ill-mapped shoals and treacherous currents of the surrounding Aetolian Isles. The pirate captains themselves, often as not, hired pilots from the native sea-tribes to guide them in and out through the maze of reefs.

These same tribes, deriving much of their wealth from the Red Brotherhood's activities, seemed willing to tolerate the presence of the Vilayet Sea's criminal dregs. They even joined in the Brotherhood's mainland raids with low, fast, crew-heavy ships of their own. Having no love for either the Turanian or Hyrkanian empires, the islanders would misguide Imperial ships onto the rocks or attack them with fire-skiffs in the narrow straits, rather than see them enter successfully. In these dangerous waters, the risk to foreign fleets was too great; thus the pirates continued to cruise with impunity out of Djafur and the lesser island ports.

Conan seated the beggar Ferdinald before a generous bowl of fish porridge. He turned to the inn's narrow, angular staircase just in time to watch his female entourage descend from their chambers. There came Philiope, looking calm and capable, if less regal than before, wearing one of her long, silk gowns shorn off at the knees for greater ease at shipboard maneuvering. Behind her was

Sulula the handmaid; having grievously neglected her appearance, she wore a shapeless plain tunic and walked with her eyes downcast beneath ill-kempt hair, frowning timidly. Last was Olivia in blouse and pantaloons, as beautiful as ever, but haughty, her face already made proof against the stares and catcalls she anticipated from the rabble.

Indeed, the rogues did stir and mutter upon the entrance of the women. But once their looks flashed to Conan, who scowled in his place below the stair, silence spread through the room like a fast-gnawing shipworm through a soft pine hull. Other females, in any event, were present: slack, slatternly barmaids and a pair of fisher-girls, variously buck-toothed and wall-eyed, who were quick to avail themselves of the interest generated among the tavern patrons by the unapproachable beauties.

"Captain Amra, good morn to you!" Philiope, calm and demure, came straight off the stair to Conan. Placing a hand on his shoulder, she raised up on tiptoe to kiss his smooth-shaven cheek. "You could have roused me up earlier . . . though I will say, I enjoyed the rest." Staying near him, she glanced about the watching pirates to mark the fact of her intimacy with their captain.

"Lady Philiope," Conan greeted her, smiling as ever at her forwardness. "Fair Sulula—" the young maid jerked her face fearfully aside "—and my hardy mate Olivia, good day!"

Conan's rough embrace, bolstered by a caress to her loose, dark hair and a firm clap to her rump, did not improve the dark-eyed Ophirean's humor. "No good day can follow an ill night," she retorted, pulling sharply away. "This smelly slum on its worm-eaten pilings rocks worse than a round-bellied merchant ship riding a gale! The lodging rooms are raucous at all hours with pirates' carousing and cursing

. . . and damnably cramped!'' She added this remark with a pointed look at her female companions.

"Olivia, love." Clasping an arm about her shoulders, Conan led all three women to a broad, round table. "If the men dallied late at their game of drafts, 'tis my fault," he explained, sitting down beside her. "Through ill luck or others' connivance, I went a hundred guilders in the hole. I had to stay up most of the night, and mash a few cheating fingers, to win it back."

"Oh . . . did you get adequate rest, then?" Olivia's eyes flashed too sternly to reflect tender solicitude.

"Aye, on yonder stairwell—" Conan nodded toward the upper landing "—with other seafarers even more sodden than I."

"Hmm." Olivia nodded pensively. "It must have been so, since you did not retire to my side." She sent another sharp glance at Philiope and her maid.

"Be assured, Olivia—" Conan lowered his voice to a murmur, casting a surly glance over the other men in the place "—I remained half-awake and vigilant. If any skulking rogue had tried to creep to your room—or to yours, good ladies—" he added to the two captive women, "I would have dealt severely with him."

"Poor Captain Amra!" Philiope said with a winning smile. "You must surely have a difficult time guarding the three of us from evil-doers! It was bad enough on shipboard, but here on land—"

"Aye, Captain. You spread yourself too thin," Olivia remarked with a dangerous look.

"It might be better," Philiope resumed, "if the four of us could share a single sleeping chamber. That would make it easier for Sulula, instead of having to run between two rooms to serve us . . . that is, of course, if dear Olivia would not mind—"

"Impossible!" Olivia interrupted her. "I could not bear it. As for your poor, terrified maid, she is clumsy and next to useless. You may have her back. But keep to your own rooms, if you please. Things are far too close here already."

"Aye," Conan allowed, "and they may be a good deal more crowded in a moment or two, when the *Tormentress* and her crew hit the beach."

"What, that pirate slut Santhindra—whatever her name is—and her vile pack?" Olivia shook her head in disbelief. "That does it! I will sleep aboard the *Hyacinth*, whether the cabin door is repaired or not!"

With a discreet glance around them, Conan leaned closer to his mistress. "I urge you, Olivia, to give a thought to what you say in company about Captain Drissa. Of all these scalawags and cutthroats, she is the one I might find it hardest to protect you from."

"You mean to say, the inn is going to be visited by a woman pirate?" Lady Philiope half-arose, craning her slender neck in eagerness toward the door. "Although I had heard tales of you, Captain Amra, there was no talk at home of such a marvel!"

"It may be that none who met her on the high seas has ever escaped to spread her renown," Conan said, helping Philiope to her feet.

Outside on the dock, Conan and his women joined the crowd that had formed to watch the trim, mastless craft put into port. It was a sleek bireme, longer than Conan's *Vixen* and somewhat broader in the beam, boasting a double row of oars closely interleaved on either side. At its prow, churning the water into a frothy wake that streamed alongside and astern, was a sharp, triple-barbed ram capable of pinning a ship in place or sending it to the bottom.

The *Tormentress* was well-commanded, as evidenced by the steady stroking of the oars, with never a missed beat or flurry of confusion down the rows. It moved at a fast clip and steered nicely, negotiating the turn around the last few unmarked rocks in the harbor mouth without a visible reduction in speed.

Of the two figures leaning on steering-oars astern, the taller, black-harnessed one was probably the captain. If ever anyone ran a tight ship, Santhindrissa did. Half of her crew, those manning the upper oar banks, were women—fierce, armed fighters who swarmed overside to seize the prizes her ship caught. The rest were male captives, taken at sea or on land raids. In and out of port, these slaves remained shackled in the lower benches to provide raw power—except, so it was rumored, when one or more of them was unchained at captain or crew's request, to perform some special service. Day and night, these men labored at a task that made their bodies flourish and their spirits wilt, toiling naked under the stinging lashes of their female overseers.

The *Tormentress*, like any bireme, had oar-benches set at two levels. Male pirates who had gone aboard told scandalously of how the men, confined to the lower seats, were made to work all day in Vilayet heat, their eyes on a level with the sparsely clad hips and shanks of the female pirates, who toiled above and paced the catwalk. Whether such a fate would make a man mad, or send him into an idiot's dumb raptures, Conan knew not. But in his talks with Vilayet pirates, he had heard of no successful escapes or mutinies aboard the *Tormentress*.

For security's sake, even so, Santhindrissa did not drive her ship up onto the beach. Instead, she deftly double-anchored just off the Red Hand's pier, a good deal closer in than the *Hyacinth*. After warping their ship around with a temporary line to one of the sturdier pilings, her crew stretched a long plank straight across from deck to pier.

Presumably, in the piratesses' absence, it would be with-drawn; the harbor sharks would then guard the captives as effectively as any sentries could.

Striding across the bobbing plank, the women were greeted with shouts of enthusiasm by the male brigands. Strong drink was brought out from the tavern and given to those arriving. Several bottles were slung through the air, so that before even stepping from their deck, some of the women were already half-drunk, frolicking perilously on the gangplank or wantonly dancing on their ship's rail.

Yet predictably, ere love had time to blossom, blood-shed did. A knife duel broke out on the pier, swirling swift and furious through the crowd. Before the bystanders could form a proper circle and lay bets, the loser—a male, one of Knulf's crew—was down. The deep gash to his hip, so it was judged, would probably bleed him or fever him to death in a week's time. The winner—a scrawny, pale, murky-haired pirate wench named Brylith, who wore a patch over one eye—held her bloody dagger high in the air, turning in a slow circle to acknowledge the crowd's cheers. Then she drank deep from the victory goblet that was brought forward, and did her fallen enemy the honor of pouring its purple dregs into his upturned, gasping mouth.

"Unship this plank!" Attention was drawn back to the bireme by a high, hoarse command. The ship's captain, the last female to come ashore, strode along the bouncing gang-way. Santhindrissa was an extraordinarily tall, slim, sharp-nosed woman, dark-tanned and sinewy—a Stygian, judging by her hawklike features and her straight black hair. Her shallow breasts were all but concealed by a harness of criss-crossed black strapping; her short leather kirtle rattled with weapons and manacle keys; her high-bound, black-leather sandals spiked the gangplank firmly. Raising one leather-wrapped fist on high, she gave a hoarse cry before setting foot on the dock. "All hail the Red Sisterhood!"

"Hail the Sisters!" the high-pitched cry came back, with a gruff underlayer of male voices joining in good-naturedly.

"A whole ship of women pirates," Philiope marveled, holding tightly to Conan's arm. "I never knew there could be such! Do they breed pirate babes, too?"

"Nay," Conan grunted. "Heavy work at the oars seems to prevent that. Or maybe it's Knulf's rotgut," he added, nodding toward a piratess who knelt over the side of the pier, already puking with land-sickness. "As a rule, they do not marry, but seem to prize their shipboard life."

"If you admire them so much, noble lady, you might join them!" Olivia spoke disdainfully, staying close though she refused to clasp Conan's free arm. "You, and your maidservant there, as well." She flicked a glance at Sulula, cowering by her mistress's side. "It would probably take only a small knifing to win each of you a seat at the oars."

"No," the noble girl thoughtfully replied, "I think not. The life of a sea-wench is, after all, somewhat less gracious than we are accustomed to."

"What? Why, you little baggage—" Olivia's retaliatory words were cut off by the jostle of bodies on the pier as Conan moved purposely to follow the mob back into the Red Hand.

Inside, the tavern was twice as raucous and crowded, with more idlers drawn in from the street by the excitement. Sullen, ill-kempt Ferdinald had somehow managed to keep possession of Conan's broad table, which now became a refuge for captains. The Cimmerian fell into conversation with a squat, broad-faced, mustached captain named Hrandulf, one of the chiefs of the sea-tribes, who always liked to stay abreast of the pirates' doings. Santhindrissa came to perch on the table's edge, and soon afterward the pirate-innkeeper Knulf ambled over, bringing with him a heavy ale jar for the party.

Their talk centered first on the *Tormentress's* successful cruise, which had netted medium-rich cargoes from two Zaporoskan trading sloops. Weather and Imperial patrols were discussed: There had been little of either in the Southern Sea. The only news, gained from one of the captured traders, was of some kind of naval proclamation in the distant Turanian port of Aghrapur, involving a competition, a vast prize . . . and rumors of sorcery. The account was unclear, gained third-hand from the mouths of sailors who tended to be superstitious, even under torture. Captain Drissa did not pretend to understand it; instead, she asked about the merchant cog anchored in the harbor, which led to talk of the *Vixen's* recent exploits, and of the hostages.

"Interesting," the female pirate told Conan, swiveling in her place to regard the women seated at the lower end of the table. "You still like them soft and delicate, I see."

Conan's female entourage ignored the remark; scowling Olivia fortunately hurled no insults, and Philiope wore a demure smile. Only the maid Sulula, cringing at her mistress's side, glanced up the table, then away, looking like a small creature trapped by Captain Drissa's bird-of-prey stare.

"That one . . . if you cannot get a fair ransom for her, sell her to me," the captainess declared in her softly husky voice.

If Sulula heard, she acknowledged it only by a tremor of her already-hunched shoulders. She had never yet had the courage to speak to anyone but her mistress, and then only in faint, anguished whispers.

" 'Tis no use bargaining with this mad Cimmerian, Drissa," Knulf Shipbreaker announced to his fellow captains. "I offered him a small fortune for the handsome Turanian there—" he leered at Philiope, who kept her face coolly averted "—but he would not hear of it, says his reputation is at stake! He prefers to weather the shoals and squalls of three women's temper, like a ship tossed between the reefs of the Aetolian Straits! It can be no easy matter—"

"Frankly, I cannot understand it either." Conan, leaning away from his womenfolk, put the best face on the matter before his fellow captains. "How do you Easterners manage it? There is not a pasha or a petty sharif along this coast but has several wives to his name, or a full harem—"

"Aye, a harem," Drissa agreed with him matter-of-factly. "There is much to be said for it."

Conan did not pause to ask whether she meant a female harem or a male one. "And yet," he went on, "thrice-blast all this strife and skirmishing! I always expected less warring in a household than on an embattled quarterdeck! But since a second woman and a third have come under my protection, there is no peace." He ruefully accepted the others' pitying laughs.

As the captains spoke on and the day progressed, the scene at the inn became even wilder, fueled by the unruly antics of the women. Pirates drank, gambled, and danced; they gambled at drinking and at dancing, and at their ability to dance while drinking. Fights erupted, most of them to be taken outside into the street, whence strident wagers and bloodthirsty cheers could be heard. On the pier, the sea-jigging was continuous, marked by the monotonous tweedling of flutes and brass whistles and the incessant thump of sea-boots, hard heels, and peglegs on worn timber.

Within the tavern, the gaiety consisted mainly of roaring, bawdy chanties and of hurling taunts and insults at rivals. Some female pirates lounged in the laps of their male counterparts in drunken, languorous undress; at the other extreme, one of Knulf's pirates was seen escaping a band of the *Tormentress*'s crew with his shirt and breeks shredded to ribbons by their daggers. The captains' table remained an isle of relative calm, though the less piratical females seated there were the inevitable object of leers and remarks from nearby brigands.

"Twenty talents, the captain is asking? I would wager she has more talents than that, if she could be made to show them off! Come here, lass, I'll trim your spanker for you!"

"And what about the little maid? What is she worth, a half-guilder? Why, I can pay the captain a higher ransom! Come over and fetch a pretty coin, missy, if you want to move up in the world!"

On the same rickety bench as the taunters there sprawled a female pirate, none other than Brylith, winner of the recent knife fight on the dock. In speech now slurred with drink, she mused aloud to the long-mustached Ilbarsi who cradled her head in his greasy lap. "I hear that in some of the great mainland towns, there are women who earn such a ransom for themselves every day—not as slaves or captives, but by sporting with different men, and giving pleasure to them. Now, there is something I would like to try!" Raising one listless hand, she caressed the stubbled cheek of the swarthy, sweaty pirate above her. "To receive money all the time, merely for letting men kiss and embrace me! That would be something!"

The Ilbarsi laughed, causing her lank-haired head to bounce in his lap. "Haw, are you jesting, Brylith?" He elbowed the ale-swilling Keshanian at his side, who guffawed in return. "What man in his right mind would pay a silver groat to roll and wallow with such as you? Who could believe such a thing?"

"Truly," the Keshanian grinned, " 'twould be a wonder fit to surpass the Golden-horned Bull of Luxur! Myself, I would never believe it!"

"Enough, now!" the girl Brylith protested. With her fighting spirit satiated and drowned in ale, she slapped only feebly at the Ilbarsi's bristled cheek and, floundering in his lap, raised her head halfway up his hairy chest. "It is base and heartless of you pigs to ridicule a young girl's romantic dreams! Just because I think of someday rising in this world and bettering myself—"

At that moment the conversation was interrupted by a hoarse, inarticulate scream—a cry violent and guttural enough to stand out even in the turmoil of the inn. While pirates glared around for its source, the serving-maid Sulula sprang up from her place at Philiope's side and darted away, through the back archway and out onto the pier. In a trice her mistress was up and after her, followed closely by Conan, who vaulted over a table to beat the noble girl to the exit.

Even so, he was late. Outside, pirates crowded to the pier's edge to watch a turmoil in the water below. In the sudden surcease of piping and dancing, they commented on the figure that had flashed through their midst.

"The lass had a hankering for a swim, so 'twould seem."

" 'Pears she found the company more to her liking."

Conan, stopping at the curb, drew out his heavy scimitar and cast it down on the planks. He was poised to leap off the pier when he felt Philiope lay hold of his arm, sobbing. While he tried to shake her off, another pair of arms twined about his neck, and Olivia remonstrated, "Conan, it is too late! Do you not see?"

Gazing down, he saw the harbor aswirl with sinister life of its own. A halfscore of the striped sharks, dog-sized, circled and darted into a patch of red foam. Others swam away in diverse directions, their wedge-shaped fins and pointed tails trailing red in the dirty water. Of the maid Sulula, no other sign remained.

"Why—what would make her do it?" Conan asked dully, shaking his head in wonder.

Philiope, wiping her damp face on Conan's sleeve, replied bitterly, "Maybe she thought it a better fate to be torn apart by sharks, kinder by far . . . than to remain a slave to cutthroats, whose highest aspiration might someday be to become prostitutes. But come away, please. I cannot bear to look!"

Inside the inn, over tankards of ale, Philiope elaborated further once her grief had subsided. "Sulula was far less used to a rough, subservient life than I was. She was delicate, never really very skilled as a maid, as your Olivia observed . . ." She nodded across the table to her frowning counterpart. "She even feared our transport to far-off Hyrkania, and the marriage that impended. For you see, she was in truth the noble lady, and I the servant."

"What? You mean it was an imposture?" Conan kept his voice low; this was a private discussion at a corner table separate from the other captains, and he sensed that the talk was becoming financial. "Why would you ever—"

"When your pirates stormed the *Hyacinth*'s decks, and we waited in fear below, my mistress made me swear to impersonate her. She had heard dreadful tales of Amra the Corsair; she feared you would rape her and ruin her for life, perhaps even kill her. So I played the noble Philiope and threw myself in your way to distract you, while she disguised herself as the poor, cringing maidservant. Sulula is my real name—it is Zamoran. I was a slave taken in a border raid by Imperials.''

"So," Olivia said, her eyes bright with discovery, "I knew you were no aristocrat. Smart little imposter!''

"Aye." Conan nodded admiringly. "A clever ploy, most bold indeed." He looked quizzically at the girl. "But why admit to it now, at the risk of your life?''

"I know you well enough to trust you, Captain Amra . . . I think." The Zamoran kept her gaze fixed firmly on Conan. "This tragedy, untimely as it is, will also affect your business dealings. I would not want it to cause a debacle and get us all slain. And, in truth, I have no great desire to return to Turan as a slave . . . and be punished, like as not, for my mistress's death. This pirate life is harsh, but I prefer it to a kitchen or a harem.''

"Oh, really?" Olivia asked spitefully. "It will not be so easy for you now, though perhaps you will prove a more skillful servant than your predecessor.''

"Olivia, enough. Speak no more of it!" Conan leaned forward, keeping his eyes on the Zamoran maid. "To all those who know us, you will remain Philiope and continue to be treated as a captive noble. It will be safer that way. An alias can do you no harm in this business, anyway.'' He frowned in careful thought. "The nobleman Khalid Abdal knew of your ruse, I see now . . . but he does not know that his cousin is dead, and he would not care overly about it, I think. Both she and he tried to deceive me, which was sore unfair. So if he brings a ransom, I will have it anyway, be our hostage alive or dead!''

FIVE
The Hand of Tarim

"**A**nd so we aspire ever higher." Striding toward the broad, heavy iron portcullis set in the granite wall, Nephet Ali gestured. A guard atop the wall relayed his signal, and moments later, with a creaking of chain pulleys, the spiked metal curtain began to rise. Alaph the alchemist watched expectantly, wondering what magnificent opportunities lay beyond the portal.

"This defensive gate, according to our forward-looking design, is lifted by the force of counterweights in the tower above." The brisk little engineer gestured up at the gate-bastion, broadest of the towers set at intervals in the battlemented stone wall. "The weights, of course, are raised by slaves—but it is better to use muscle-power only at morning and eventide to raise the weights to the top, rather than to keep slaves idle all day to work the gate as loads of timber and shipwares arrive." He smiled at his guests. "For this little group of ours, a humble postern entry would have sufficed, of course. But I wanted to demonstrate the principle of efficiency that is so important to our naval operations."

As the cullis clanked to a halt overhead, the Imperial engineer led the way beneath it. "Here—" he waved a hand broadly before him "—is the Navy Yard, the heart of Turan's power and influence throughout the known world. These facilities will be at your disposal over the months to come."

He led the visitors clear of the dangling gate, which immediately began trundling down behind them, and stood surveying the broad expanse of docks, sheds, and ship-berths before them. None of the party spoke—neither Nephet Ali nor his half-dozen guests, the final qualifying applicants for the Naval Prize.

The contestants, for their part, gazed about with alert eyes, watching each other almost as intently as they observed the wonders of the Navy Yard. They comprised a sampling of the keenest thinkers in Aghrapur, ranging from respected astrologers and wizards to lowly alchemists and draftsmen; but each one present had some singular insight or attainment to recommend him to Prince Yezdigerd's discerning judgment.

Here was Tambur Pasha, the noted astronomer and philosopher, sleek and rotund in a dark blue cape, his matching turban atwinkle with star-bright jewels and pinned with a heavy, gold moon-crescent. Beside him stood the seer and hypnotist Zalbuvulus, the lordly Northern prophet and philosopher, clad in long, Corinthian-style robes whose whiteness and length matched that of his down-turned mustache and fierce, shaggy eyebrows.

Swarthy-complected, genial Mustafar was present as well. As the renowned designer of a repeating catapult already being tested by the Imperial Navy, he favored the rest of the group with his strong-toothed smiles and pen-etrating glances.

Also present was the lean, black-skinned foreigner known only as Crotalus, a tall, mysterious traveler from a far and barbarous clime. Zembabwan by origin, so it was said, he gave an impression of youth and brisk energy in spite of his bald, wrinkled dark skull and wry, vulpine expression. He was well-received in the capital, ever more so by virtue of the deft entrail-readings and confidential counsels he offered prosperous Turanians. His clientele was said to include high members of the Imperial Court.

Amid this distinguished company, young Alaph felt out of place. His status as a mere alchemist and tinkerer scarcely warranted mingling with such preeminent sages. Their knowledge of the arcane arts was far beyond his humble experience; yet even so, he felt that he might be able to contribute to the matter at hand, and possibly earn a share of the tremendous prize that had been offered.

Alaph, while carrying on his father's trade as a bun-maker, had always reserved his main enthusiasm for his private alchemical experiments. The notion of transmuting base metals such as lead and tin into pure, peerless gold had long enthralled him. Coincidentally, and luckily, the hearth and ovens used in his baking trade made it easy for him to conduct metallurgic trials in his shop after-hours. Indeed, years of such efforts, carried on since late boy-hood, had gained him a passing knowledge of metals and of related mineral smokes, stenches, and residues.

Yet his most intriguing discovery, made just recently, was not even remotely the result of his alchemic pursuits. It came instead from observing a copper teapot that he had hung by a string over the hearth, where it twirled and hissed madly, as if possessed by an angry *djinn*. The kettle had been dropped, as it happened, the accident bending its pouring-spout to one side and giving its lid a tighter fit. It did not take Alaph long to guess that the vessel's unnatural excitation came from water-spirits trapped within, vexed by the assault of fire-demons and striving to escape; exiting to one side, the ghostly vapors drove the kettle in a circular path, twisting it upon its string . . . until the last of the water-spirits escaped, allowing the pot to unwind and dangle loose.

Enthralled by this event, Alaph soon put his ingenuity to work. He soldered together pots with two and three bent spouts, mounted them on pivots and loose couplings, and made them whirl briskly over scorching coals. He invented a spinning top which, once heated over a fire and set moving with a twirl of its stem, would spin interminably on a hollow iron base amid ghostly spirals of vapor.

He learned, at his peril, the treacherous spite of the fleeing water-spirits, and how to salve and dress painful scalds; he also invented a spoutless, tight-sealed brass kettle which, when filled and heated, demolished itself and the oven around it with a deafening report.

His command of the water-spirits had gained him some minor notoriety among the philosophers and spell-casters of Aghrapur. Although none of his whirligigs toys had yet found any function more useful than driving a flue fan, they were nevertheless applauded as valuable proofs of the existence of *djinni* and demons. A high priest of Tarim had even approached him about the possibility of creating a spinning-dervish statue above the altar fire at the city's main temple.

It was this latter honor, perhaps—along with the slim scroll he had submitted to the city library detailing his experiments—that had brought him to the attention of the prince of the empire. A special palace messenger, the very same who had visited Zalbuvulus and Mustafar, brought him news of the contest—by Yezdigerd's personal commandment, he was assured.

But his head was not turned; even while reeling from this lofty recognition, he began to imagine ways in which his devices might be employed in the naval realm . . . for instance, a ship which, instead of rowers, contained a hearth of light bricks and a giant kettle whose spouts vented out at the sides, backward along the hull. Such a vessel, instead of spinning from its inner heat, might instead be driven forward through the water, propelled at untold speeds by the power of the escaping spirits. The notion was thrilling, and Alaph's account of it—rendered bashfully the previous morning to Prince Yezdigerd himself—had sufficed to gain him a chance at the prize, along with these others.

"This place is a marvel, far richer in its way than the city wharves with their merchant vessels and tradegoods."

The speaker was the astronomer Tambur Pasha; as heads turned to him, he waved a purple-robed arm toward the splendor of the military harbor: the heavy, triple-masted Imperial dromons plying the sound; the trim biremes swaying alongside the stone piers; the countless vessels drawn up onto the beach, or waiting unseen in lines of closed sheds beyond; the kegs, bales, and stacks of naval supplies and timber standing on the docks or sheltered under roofs and canopies; the troops of marines and gaggles of workers marching or standing ready on every hand; the thickets of pikes and forests of masts, the raw hulls under construction; the whistles, drumbeats, and shouted commands.

"Few land-dwellers ever set eyes on these docks," Corinthian prophet Zalbuvulus solemnly intoned. "Except, that is, at the beginning of a long, arduous journey."

Alaph, gazing about at the high stone walls, could well

agree that this was true. Yet were these land walls really necessary for defense, lying as they did within the taller and broader circuit of Aghrapur's city wall? Thoughtfully he examined the defenses, the guardposts and sheer inner bastions extending well out into the harbor; and the compound's largest building, the Naval Garrison, guarded by moat, drawbridge, and iron-grated windows. Eyeing the bands of slaves and conscript troops who filed to and from ships or performed various tasks ashore, the young alchemist decided that the walls were intended to keep people in rather than out.

"Yonder is the first model of my rapid-firing catapult," the inventor Mustafar enthusiastically informed those around him. Seizing hold of Nephet Ali's arm, he led the group down the cobbled rampway to the docks and out onto a short stone quay. At its end stood a tall, irregular object shrouded by a fresh tarpaulin. Undoing the bindings and dragging the canopy aside, Mustafar displayed his contrivance to the others.

The double crossbow mounted two heavy, recurved bows of wood and horn, one stacked atop the other. The double bowstock rested on a swivel post, with a rotating shaft up the middle and gear-wheels at either side. The whole stood on a circular platform raised knee-high off the ground; from beneath this platform radiated four poles of a capstan, upward-slanting. Chain wheels, driven by the turning of the capstan below, engaged the slides of both crossbows, furnishing them the power to draw the bowstrings taut.

"Here, you see," Mustafar said, stepping up onto the platform. "The archer stands aloft, free to point the weapon in any direction. Below, four men tread in a continuous circle, pushing the capstan poles to keep the carriage gears turning. The archer depresses this lever to loose the bow—'' he worked a trigger at the side of the pivot ''—and this one to draw it taut again, by re-engaging the slide.'' He touched another toggle arm. ''While the mechanism is forcing back one bow, the archer is free to load, aim, and discharge the other one.''

Laying hold of the double bow, he swung it smoothly, pointing it at imaginary targets. ''Nephet Ali, is there a bowstring handy, and some arrows? I would speed a few into yonder islet.'' He pointed out at one of the sandbars flanking the channel entry several hundred paces distant.

''Nay, Mustafar, I fear not. Extra-thick cables are still being woven, large-sized arrows fletched, and heavy iron darts forged as well.'' Nephet Ali spread his palms regretfully. ''The weapon trials may not be announced for some time yet, thought I, for one, plan to attend.'' He turned to the others. ''Let Mustafar's inventiveness be an inspiration to you all.''

''He is clever, obviously.'' Zalbuvulus, the white-robed sage, solemnly stroked his long beard. ''However, if I may pose a question . . . your contrivance occupies five men, consuming their entire effort to operate two bows. Is that really an efficiency, when compared to having all five of them plying crossbows or heavy, leg-drawn bows, and loosing simultaneously?''

The point struck Alaph as being an eminently sensible one; roused from his close, admiring examination of the mechanism, he turned and waited for the response.

''A most interesting question,'' Mustafar said, addressing his elder rival with the unruffled air of an academy tutor. ''Is there anyone else who would like to undertake to answer?'' Smiling around at the contestants' expectant looks and the Vizier Nephet Ali's magnanimous hand-flourish, he proceeded. ''Very well then, I will explain. What my weapon achieves is the height of efficiency . . .

namely, to magnify the power of a single man. The four who turn the windlass are not archers; they do not need training, nor to speak Turanian, nor even to possess tongues or ears in their heads. They provide only raw, dumb power. Indeed, even if my device should require the services of a sixth crewman to lay a lash across the backs of the four, it will still be an advance in efficiency, and terribly feared. It empowers one skilled fighter, an elite technician, to hurl death with the strength and speed of four! No common rabble of ill-trained bowmen can perform so efficently or to the purpose. This, my good friends, is where the future lies.''

His speech was greeted with handclaps from Nephet Ali and huzzahs from Tambur Pasha. Zalbuvulus did not seem impressed by the performance; he merely deepened the scowl-lines of his face, answering solemnly:

"I find your words most illuminating as to the direction of your efforts, Mustafar, granting that all our invention is based on the muscle-power and obedience of slaves and subjects. My own ideas are aimed at securing a higher level of performance from all crew members, skilled and unskilled alike. It will be interesting to see our relative successes."

"If it is efficiency you seek," Tambur Pasha proclaimed, "I have already solved that problem." The astrologer dug a hand into the broad blue sash circling his paunch and fished there a moment. "Here it is, designed by my stylus and tested on my own kitchen-slaves." His plump hand drew forth a short stick braided with leather thongs. "Five times the obedience guaranteed."

"What is it, a riding crop?" Mustafar asked. The philosopher Zalbuvulus eyed the object with a look of skeptical disdain.

"See here," Tambur Pasha said, separating the leather

braids between his plump fingers. "Instead of a single whiplash, it lays down five at once. Shorter and lighter than your standard cattle whip, and less clumsy to use in confined spaces. It yields quicker and more intense pain, but with far less permanent damage. It promotes better endurance, too, for both flogger and victim. I call it the Hand of Tarim, though some might find that blasphemous."

"A superb idea, under whatever name." The Vizier Nephet Ali accepted the whip from the hand of its inventor, proceeding to flick the knotted ends back and forth in the air. "Why, such an item could be in use throughout the fleet in the space of one year! We must work out some form of commission for you on its acceptance, as we have done with Mustafar's highly promising weapon. But come, my friends," he called, waving the supple Hand of Tarim overhead to beckon them back along the quay. "We must all go to the harbor master's garrison now, to make arrangements for our particular needs."

Alaph stayed behind to help Mustafar draw the canopy over his invention and retie it in place. Hurrying to catch the others, they found themselves at the rear of the group alongside Tambur Pasha, who resumed speaking as if there had been no interruption.

"It is a mere trifle, of course, this five-taloned whip of mine . . . just a petty household convenience of the sort I dream up incessantly." The astrologer patted his spangled turban straight with a self-satisfied air. "My idea for the contest, now . . . that will be something unique. I plan to command the wind itself, by means of an engine carried on the ship. In place of oars, the crew will operate a pair of giant bellows. In that way, a steady breeze can be directed against the sail at the commander's will, regardless of weather." He preened himself again confidently. "Now that the contest is underway, I fancy there can be no harm in talking of it. Prince Yezdigerd was dubious about the idea at first; he could not seem to see the merit in it. Fortunately, good Ninshub, the finance minister, was present; he has a keen mind for efficiencies and economies of this sort. Now it remains only to put my plan to work on a large scale, with adequate manpower to show its merit value.''

Alaph blinked in uncertainty. Something vaguely disturbed him about Tambur Pasha's idea . . . though he had faith, of course, in the famed astrologer's wisdom. He looked to Mustafar, who smiled bemusedly, rolled his eyes upward, and answered, ''My researches of late have involved finding a better means of throwing fire into enemy vessels.''

Alaph silently debated broaching the subject of his own invention. He hesitated out of fear that to these accomplished innovators, his steam-dervishes might seem wildly impractical, little more than children's toys. Then at once it was too late; the maw of the Naval Garrison loomed on either hand as the group followed Nephet Ali across the drawbridge into the vast pile. Their way wound through a set of defensive courts and alleys arrayed under the view of battlements and loopholes.

Within the fort, a narrow stair led up to a vaulted chartroom, three sides of which overlooked the harbor. Before the rows of lancet window stood lookouts watching ships in the harbor and recording their sightings with ready styluses and clay tablets. Along the rear wall was a broad map-table presided over by the seated harbor master, garbed in trim naval turban and tunic.

With this officer Nephet Ali conferred, drawing the contestants over one by one and discussing the requirements of goods, labor, and ship usage for each planned project.

Alaph could tell that most of the contestants were making forthright, extravagant demands—both by their gestures and by the pained attitude of the harbor master. Yet in each case he evidently gave in to the vizier's urgings . . . for Nephet Ali, on the contrary, seemed inclined to push forward and enlarge on the inventors' plans, regardless of cost.

Even so, the young alchemist felt sheepish and awkward as he set forth his own needs: a small or medium vessel of but a single oar-bank, a good quantity of light firebrick, and larger and costlier amounts of bronze or hammered copper, with suitable kettles and vats—plus solder, rivets, charcoal and so forth, and the services of smiths, ship-wrights, slaves, overseers, a pilot, and a trial crew. As he spoke, it all seemed impossible in view of his youth and low station.

"I see no problem, lad," Nephet Ali assured him. "It sounds most reasonable to me. Are you sure you will not need a larger ship to bear the weight of all that brick and metal?" He shot a glance to the frowning officer as he made out his list.

"No, sire. This should be enough to test out my idea." He stepped back bashfully. "If it works, of course, the device could possibly be refined and enlarged . . ."

"Very good, then. And what of you, Crotalus?" Nephet Ali looked past Alaph to the tall, lean Zembabwan. "You are the last one left, and we have heard no word from you this morning. What will you be needing for your plan?"

At this, the other contestants muted their talk, presumably out of curiosity. Alaph, too, stayed close by to hear the nature of the black seer's wants.

Looming near in his yellow-fringed, darkly embroidered robe, the shaven-headed prophet answered in a deeply accented voice, "I have need of a ship."

"Only a ship," Nephet Ali prompted, "and nothing to go into it?" He glanced to the harbor master, who made marks on his tablet. "How large a vessel do you want?"

"A ship to cross the Vilayet," came the strange accents from the dour, pursed mouth. "And a crew who will go where I tell them."

"You mean to undertake a voyage, then," the harbor master ventured. "That will require ship stores and guards as well. Exactly where will you fare to?"

"I cannot discuss such matters." The tall sorcerer's earnest, steady-eyed stare seemed to make the port official uneasy. "I will know when I arrive there. It lies across the sea."

"Take two ships for the mission you have described to me," Nephet Ali volunteered. "A light, fast rower and a well-armed escort." He glanced again to the harbor master, who shrugged to confirm the decision. "That should discourage pirate attacks."

"A voyage oversea," the harbor master mused aloud, "around the South Bight, I should imagine. That will call for some days' provisions between friendly ports—"

"I will not go south," Crotalus cut him off, "nor into port. I will go . . ." the hawk-nosed seer extended a long, knobby finger toward the eastern wall of bright-lit lancet windows . . . that way."

"East? East by north?" Nephet Ali shook his head uncertainly. "You mean straight across the Vilayet? Ships normally follow the coastline, my dear fellow, because of storms and other unknown hazards—"

"I will go that way," the prophet firmly declared, his bony finger unwavering. "There lies the object I seek."

SIX

Sails Out of the West

Djafur, notorious as a thieves' den, served also as a brokerage for information and for ill-gotten wares. Pirate captains and chieftains of the local sea-tribes, if their course took them near, found it advisable to put in there for news and barter and to quench their salt-rimed thirst in the Red Hand Inn's gloomy interior.

"Two vessels, you say; Turanian warships." Thoughtfully, Conan swirled the dregs of his ale, tilting the wooden jack on the scarred tabletop. "Bound into the north Vilayet, wouldst guess?"

"Aye, most certainly—an Imperial dromon and a light penteconter, with the smaller ship slacking off oars to let the heavy one keep up." The chieftain Hrandulf looked earnestly from Conan to the other captains around the table. "What was strangest about it was the course they followed. We stood almost out of sight of land, steering by the Aetolian peaks, but these two hove into view far a-seaward, where lies no island . . . as if they had rowed themselves straight across the water from Turan.''

"Hmm." Conan examined the silty dregs in his cup one last time, then tipped them out onto the floor. "The winds have been mild in recent days. They could well have made such a voyage.''

"Mild hereabouts, perhaps—" Knulf the Vanirman laughed gruffly "—but out there on the Vilayet's stormy bosom?" He smirked in disbelief "—where midsummer ice-squalls can blind a captain, and freeze the oars into their tholes and the rowers to their oars? Can you really inkle what weather the sea-gods may be conjuring just over the horizon?" The piratical innkeep shook his shaggy head. "Imperial ships have but seldom been known to shave corners and venture into pathless waters, even in the mild southern straits of Shangara. They fear to capsize in a storm, or to be broken apart on an anvil-wave—as you, too, must fear if you are a fit captain.''

Frowning, Conan shoved his cup forward to be filled by Philiope, who sat close within his reach. "On the Western Seas, we took greater risks than that.''

"Aye, he speaks true," the idler Ferdinald put in from an adjoining table. "There, to be sure, our ships were heavier-built, with higher, more weatherly poops and fo'castles. A line of low-cut oarports is an invitation to swamping. Whereas a strong, flat stern, fixed with gudgeon and pintle—''

"Enough, fellow," Conan growled aside to him. "What errand might these Turanians be on, I wonder, to strike so deeply into hostile waters?''

"Hmph." Knulf Shipbreaker shrugged. "Whatever it may be, 'tis of slight interest to us." The Vanir waved a hand to dismiss the matter. "Some diplomatic mission, most likely, bound for the northern Hyrkanian baronies.''

"Bearing rich bribes or armaments, perhaps," Conan pondered aloud, "to suborn their rebellion from the southern empire."

"I doubt it," Knulf said. "If any plunder is on board, it is too well-guarded."

"Aye, mayhap," Conan said. "But why, I ask you, two ships so ill matched?" He guzzled his ale contemplatively, then set down the mug. "The big one is too large to beach easily, if it is a true Imperial dromon, with five banks of rowers pulling three sets of oars on a side. But the penteconter is a shallow-draft vessel, good for working close inshore. If they mean to deliver or carry away some treasure, quite likely the two will have to separate. Where the little one goes, the big one cannot follow." He wiped ale-foam from his lips. "A penteconter holds but fifty oarsmen, no more than one of our galliots."

Knulf shook his head in disbelief. "What, then? You propose to set upon them and plunder a Turanian military squadron?"

"With a squadron of our own, why not?" Conan looked around at the assembled captains. "Follow them at least, and learn their business. It is time we of the Brotherhood began to hold sway in these waters! The dromon could never catch us anyway, not on open sea."

"Aye, 'tis true," Ferdinald volunteered, "and shadowing them unseen with two or more ships should not be difficult. A galliot could follow their sailtops with its mast unstepped, staying hull-down beneath the horizon, and the other ships might then follow the galliot."

"It is a good plan—aye, to be sure," Conan avowed. "At their destination, we could close in with a chance of seizing loot or hostages." The Cimmerian shrugged. "There has been little else worthwhile to do of late."

"Survival is always worthwhile, compared to reckless adventuring." The Vanirman turned away in his chair, scowling in businesslike disdain. "Amra, if you undertake this mad scheme, do not expect me and the *Victrix* to join in."

"Nor my *Tormentress*, either." Santhindrissa, who had listened in silence, sat unmoved in her masculine way, with one booted leg cocked over a bare knee, and black-gloved thumbs hooked through the straps of her leather halter. "There are easier, surer ways to lay hold of profits and captives."

Conan shrugged. "If need be, I will go alone with my two ships. Then I will not have to share out the spoils." He looked back to the man of the sea-tribes. "You say the Imperials stood off the south Aetolians at early dusk?"

"Aye." The chieftain nodded. "They would have laid up overnight—needing rest, and not knowing well the reefs hereabouts. If you take the North Strait this morning, you could catch them, though I advise against it—"

"Many thanks. Here, Ivanos!" Arising, Conan called across the tavern to the tall Corinthian, who was gambling near the door. "Assemble our crew on the beach without delay, and ready the *Vixen* to launch! Check on water, provisions, and weapons. Ferdinald, come with me." He smote the Zingaran on the shoulder. After nodding farewell to the other captains, he put an arm around Philiope and led the way out the inn's back archway onto the pier.

Tramping wordlessly to the end of the dock, the three lowered themselves into the *Hyacinth*'s launch. Conan and Ferdinald each took an oar, while the woman sat in the bows with a line. The cog lay but a short pull away, at anchor; in a matter of minutes, Philiope had tied up alongside and they were clambering over the rail.

"Dogs, look you lively! Olivia, we are going to make sail!" Crossing to the cabin door, stoutly if crudely repaired under Ferdinald's supervision, Conan thumped with a fist and heard bolts rattling inside.

The unpainted panel opened wide—on the Ophirean beauty in her morning disarray. She wore a loose, open nightdress, her hair pinned up partially, with but a few raven curls left dangling alongside her bosom. "Conan, you come to me so late!" she breathed sleepily to him. "What were you saying just now?" Her brown eyes, soft in the early light, looked past him to Philiope and at once flashed hard. Frowning, she drew her nightdress closed. "She has come with you, I see. The insolent slave-wench Sulula. Have you not sold her back to her rightful owners yet?"

"Olivia—" Conan shook his head with a laugh, moving forward "—it is too soon, and I can hardly leave such as her alone with drunken pirates! 'Tis hard for you, I know—"

"Yet you leave me here! Why favor her over me?" Turning from the door, she strode away on graceful bare feet, her silk-draped hips twitching in anger. "You do not care."

"Olivia, you are safest here on the *Hyacinth*, with a few picked men and a stout cabin door." He thumped the panel with his hand. "But you refuse to share these lodgings with Philiope, so I must watch her constantly—"

"It is a miserable life here, I tell you!" she interrupted him. "Your precious picked crew dares not speak a word to me, out of fear of your bloody scimitar!" With impulsive disdain, she tore the nightdress off over her head. Careless of her momentary nudity in the dim-lit cabin, she set about wriggling into a more substantial gown of Turanian design.

"Then come and drink with me for once . . . but nay, it does not matter now." Striding after her, Conan laid a consoling hand on her uncovered shoulder. "Olivia, I was delayed by news of a prize that has been sighted. We are putting to sea at once."

"A prize, you say?" Eyeing him suspiciously, she twisted free of his grasp. "Which ship will you take in pursuit? I will go with you only if you leave that little baggage behind. Promise me!''

''Leave her to be ravished, you mean, and break the oath I swore? I cannot do that, for her sake and for yours.''

''Then give her to Santhindrissa, by Ishtar's girdle! There she will fit in quite well, with other hussies of low birth.''

''A girl like Philiope? Those pirate harridans would slash her to ribbons in a day!'' Conan shook his head firmly. ''Nay, Olivia, we sail in both ships, and the two of you must come along. But if you insist, I will leave her aboard the *Hyacinth*. You may come with me in the *Vixen*, perilous as it may prove to be.''

''What?—and let her sail in luxury, while I wallow in bloody bilge water? Never, I tell you!'' At that moment Conan sidestepped, narrowly avoiding a perfume bottle that came flying past his head to shatter on the bulwark. ''You think I enjoy watching you waltz with death? Or that I like binding up your pirate cronies' bloody stumps, and rolling them overside when they croak their last? I have put up with it for love of you, but if that love is to be shared with a serving-wench . . . !''

More crockery came flying. Conan beat a retreat, pulling the cabin door shut upon the sound of strident complaints.

''Crom!'' he muttered to himself. ''I can see why women were but seldom allowed on shipboard in the Western Sea.''

Philiope looked on wide-eyed, only half-amused. Conan turned aside and muttered final instructions to his sailing-master Ferdinald regarding the voyage. Then he turned to the girl. ''I have ordered that you both be kept here safe, and separate for as long as possible. Olivia will recover from this fit, and I expect you to be kind to her.'' He paused, watching the Turanian girl's face.

"I will try," she told him with an earnest look. "If you want me to go with you in the fighting-ship—"

"No, remain here aboard. I will be in reach, so none will dare harm you." He placed a hand on her shoulder, stopping barely short of a kiss. "Farewell."

As he strode away across the deck, he sense the sail-hands smirking at his woman-troubles; a fierce sidelong glare quieted their snickers, wiping their faces to pale, respectful blankness.

Swinging down into the launch, he felt suddenly free, his shoulders loose and mobile. He took up the oars and pulled straight for shore, where a gaggle of pirates assembled next to the beached galliot.

"A fine lot of tavern-crawlers and trollop-bait!" he proclaimed as he dragged the launch ashore. "Where are the rest?"

Ivanos, ready with cudgel in hand to make sure none of the pirates bolted, said, "I have five sturdy knaves combing the gutters and brothels for our lads, and for enough others to fill in the empty benches. Here they come now," he added, indicating a mob of human flotsam that was being kicked and dragged along the beach from the lower end of town.

"Good work! I promise to pay any newcomers one hundredth part of half the spoils. For my regular crew, it will be a fiftieth, as before. Now, you men, wash yourselves in the good, clean Vilayet. Drink your fill of fresh water from yon bucket and spew up last night's sour dregs, for we soon shove off in pursuit of a prize."

Only a few of the pirates moved to comply, and those but slowly. "By Bel's sagging purse," one of the slackers complained, "why must you rouse us up so early? Fetch me back at noontide and I will row and fight for you in good spirit!"

"Not I. Count me out of this cruise," another declared,

half-joking. "I am too deep in debt to Mother Ulitha's girls to venture my life!"

"A prize ship, indeed!" a third spoke up. "I have heard what sort of prize they mean—a pair of swift, well-armed war galleys with no sign of treasure or cargo on board! Are we fools, to lift oars in such a chase?"

"What say you, dog?" Conan roared at last, choosing his target. In a single stride he was at the third complainer's side, dragging him up by the soiled collar. "Who feeds you such rot?—out with it, rogue!" He glared menacingly into his captive's face.

"Why, I heard it from none other than Captain Knulf Shipbreaker, who offered me a place in his crew!" The pirate gargled the words defiantly, his throat partly constricted by Conan's clutch. "What's more, 'tis said the ships are guided by sorcery!"

"Aye, sorcery," others muttered. "Mayhap it has something to do with the dark doings in Aghrapur's harbor."

"Aye, hiring witches and spell-casters to interfere with poor, honest pirates." The complaining voice was Diccolo's. "What an unfair business that is!"

"Mayhap it is but a trap, and these Turanian galleys are the bait!"

"Enough of this mutinous blather!" Conan declared, throwing down the troublemaking pirate. "I am your captain, and I say when to launch—"

"You may be a captain," unruly voices shouted out in defiance, "but we are a Brotherhood! We bow to no man, least of all to a northern hill-lubber!"

During the dispute, Ivanos and his crimps had worked the fringes of the mob more and more aggressively, prodding and threatening crewmen with their cudgels. Even so, the pirates looked ready to scatter. Glaring around him, Conan clutched at the hilt of his scimitar but thought better of it.

One of the shrillest voices was that of Diccolo, who now set up a chant, "Brotherhood or death!" But Conan, striding to the side of the beached galliot, thumped it hard with his fist, catching the pirates' attention.

"See this? This is my craft, I am its captain!" He ran his hand with pride of ownership up the smooth-mortised hull. "And this . . ." Reaching up with one swift move, he seized hold of an oar, hauled it clear of the thole-pins, and flung it one-handed straight into the crowd. "Here is your craft, Diccolo! May you captain it well!"

The heavy oar struck the unfortunate pirate and two or three of his sympathizers across the middle; the impact knocked them over backward onto the sand, where they floundered and gasped for breath. The deft stroke brought hoots and snarls of laughter from the standing pirates, breaking the tension momentarily.

"Now then, dogs, have I ever led you on an unsuccessful voyage? No!" Conan did not bother waiting for a chorus of agreement. "Have I ever lied to you? No! And is there a man of you who doubts that I will personally hunt down any slacker and take price of the passage out of his stripy, scabrous hide?" This time he waited for a reply, glaring around, and was rewarded with a few grudging murmurs of agreement.

"Months agone, when I slew your unrighteous captain Sergius, you took an oath to me. Since then, most of you have lived and prospered under my command. I now promise to do even better for you. Far better, with great things in the offing—but I want you to renew that oath!" Drawing his scimitar, he held it by the blade and raised it on high. "Swear by the hilt, Amra is your chief!"

Ivanos and his henchmen were the first to raise up their cudgel-hilts and swear; in due course, others joined in. Some vowed in the name of Amra, others by Conan, but their leader scanned the crowd closely to ensure that every man of them had at least muttered an oath of some sort, respectful or profane.

"Good, then," he declared. "Now, let's run this tub of ours into the sea!"

The pirates fell in behind Conan, and with a halfhearted cheer, they set about hauling the *Vixen* into the surf. After a few toilsome paces, the ship slid free and floated, its keel scuffing firm sand with the rise and fall of waves. At that point, the men leaped and scrambled up the sides, standing in the bows and using their oars to pole her out into the harbor. As they got underway, a good many pirates came out on the Red Hand's dock to see them off. Four well-wishers likewise watched from the beach: the crimps, waving their cudgels overhead in farewell.

Soon the galliot pulled alongside the *Hyacinth*. The sailship was already laying on canvas, making ready to warp out and raise anchor. Ivanos transferred aboard from the *Vixen*, returning the bigger ship's launch. Conan, having quizzed Ferdinald at length on his nautical skills, trusted his new sailing-master to keep the cog off a reef; he likewise trusted his lieutenant Ivanos to keep a close eye on the Zingaran, to keep order on board, and to prevent the crew from making off with his ship and his women.

The catapult had been transferred from the cog to the galliot, where it now rode amidships on the crossbraces built to support the oarship's mast. Keeping control of that weapon and a large preponderance of his crew, Conan felt sure of his ability to retake the cog in the event of mutiny.

Before long, with the *Hyacinth* adding sail behind them in the mild morning airs, the *Vixen*'s crew pulled out of Djafur harbor and Conan steered northward. The islands of the Aetolian chain clustered steep and rugged on either hand. Their rocky slopes afforded little space for agriculture or habitation, and shreds and tufts of sea-mist still clung to their shaded western sides.

The Vilayet, blue-green under a cloud-flecked sky, frothed white in places around saw-toothed rocks. Elsewhere, the deadly presence of hidden reefs was betrayed only by noiseless eddies of clear, dark water, or by the merest irregularities in the ranks of marching waves. In most passages through these isles, a ship without a skilled pilot was doomed; here in the broad strait, an experienced eye might be enough, if kept constantly open. Conan sent a man of the sea-tribes into the bows with a sounding line, and hoped that Ivanos behind him had the sense to do the same.

"Where is this prize ship of ours, then?" one of the oarsmen griped. "How far must we paddle before we collect our loot and get back to sleep?"

"Aye, and where is our mast and sail? A patch of canvas amidships would ease our labor better than yon spear-thrower."

Conan did not trouble to answer from his place at the steering-oar; it was obvious that no sail could be raised on this trip, if they wished to pursue unseen. Instead, he prodded old Yorkin with his foot, to step up his fluting and the oar-stroking as an alternative to further conversation.

Behind them, the *Hyacinth* hauled out into the strait—not too near, he was pleased to see, yet close enough to match his course between the isles. Luckily, the mild breeze lay westerly, abeam, so the sailing ship was able to follow without wide-ranging tacks and jibes. Yet even so, traveling at a brisk oarstroke, the *Vixen* pulled steadily ahead. Conan did not slacken pace; he hoped that by the time they reached open water, they could leave the cog hull-down over the sea's rim.

Before that came to pass, Conan was moved to alter course sharply. Across their forestem, just in advance of the cry from the bow lookout, he spied another vessel: From beyond the rocky headland of one of the northern-most Aetolian isles there emerged a black-sailed craft, its low hull aflash with stroking oars. "Port oars aback on my command! Ready—now!" He leaned hard on his heavy steering-oar. "Starboard oars double-time—stroke, stroke, and stroke! Good! Now pull stoutly, dogs, all ahead! Bow lookout, sing out your soundings!"

By steering his vessel sharp into the lee of the island, Conan endeavored to keep out of sight of the cruising penteconter. The black sailtop and purple pennon could still be glimpsed intermittently over the jagged rocks of the headland; yet he thought it unlikely that his own sail-less craft had been noticed from the deck of the military vessel, which stood a good way offshore, with a northerly heading. Now he bore in toward the rocky coast, keeping the landspit between the two vessels, meanwhile heeding the patient cries of the channel's depth from the lookout for'ard.

"No bottom here. Aye, no bottom yet. Reefs to starboard, but there looks to be a clear passage around them. Ten cubits here, but dropping away again. No bottom . . ."

Conan spared a glance astern. The *Hyacinth*, framed among the rugged cliffs of the islands, was quite likely visible to their quarry as well. But the Imperials did not slow or change course. Possibly they did not recognize the cog or regard her as a threat. In any case, if Conan had his way, they would not see her again.

Raising himself up on the galliot's low sternpost, Conan craned his neck across the headland and saw at last what he expected to see: some way behind the retreating pen-teconter, the broader sailtop of a full-sized warship. Its sun-bleached purple canvas was blazoned with the gold crescent moon of Turan, and strapped across with cordage to give it a weatherly shape. The dromon posed a greater risk of sighting them, and might even send lookouts to the mast-top from time to time; so Conan continued to bear in close to the rocks, reducing his oar-crew to half-strokes.

When next he could spy over the headland, the two ships had dwindled toward the horizon. Whether or not they noticed their pursuers, they seemed intent on some business lying away to northward. He let them go, keeping the galliot underway just enough to stay off the rocks, while the *Hyacinth* ghosted up through the mild airs of the island chain.

"Why then do we idle in such treacherous waters?" Pirate voices had begun to make impatient inquiries from the waist.

"Do we now run from our victims? Do we try to lure them onto the rocks, like sirens and shipwrecking maids of the sea-tribes?"

"There was a vessel ahead. I swear I saw one! Why steer shy of her now?"

To keep the men quiet, Conan began working clear of the reefs—a touchy business, requiring silent attentiveness, continual soundings, and some backwatering. By the time they rounded the headland, the penteconter was all but out of sight across choppy, open water. Only the dromon's large, square sail could be seen, and Conan set the oarstroke for brisk pursuit. Using the Vilayet pirates' crude flag signals, he ordered the looming *Hyacinth* to back sails for a time, then to follow.

The waves on the open sea were spirited. Even at a moderate pace, the exertion began to tell on the rowers. As the Aetolians dwindled astern and the sailtops ahead drew no nearer, the men resumed their grousing and grumbling. Conan speeded the stroke accordingly, though not enough to overhaul their quarry. Beside occupying the men, the orders achieved his secondary goal, that of carrying them out of sight of land.

By midafternoon, their place on the open main was marked only by two patches of sail on the northern horizon, and the taller masts of the *Hyacinth* trailing almost as far behind. The crew, though weary from its labor, was not yet jaded into dull obedience. The men were disgruntled and angry, and still spirited enough to question their captain. Now, if ever, was there a danger of mutiny.

"Where is our prize, then, and the easy pickings we were promised?"

"Our captain means to row across the Vilayet in pursuit of a will-o'-the-wisp! I, for one, will not abide it!"

" 'Tis as Knulf the Vanir said: These ships we stalk are lean, tough navy cruisers lacking cargo or plunder. 'Tis time to end this fool's voyage—"

"Knaves! Traitors! Be silent!" Conan, abandoning his steering-oar, leaped down from the poop and waded among the oar-benches. Seizing one of the dissenters by the throat, he yanked him out of his seat and flung him headfirst over the rail into the sea. "Rascal! If you want this voyage to end here, you can swim back to Djafur or ride on a shark! Stand aside, slaggards!" he told those half-rising to aid the drowning man, who now clutched for an oar blade.

"And you, you puling, miserable wretch—" He laid firm hold of a second ringleader. "Since you think the work is too hard, I'll ease the labor by using your guts to grease the tholes of our oars!" Reaching to his waist, he wrenched forth his heavy scimitar. "What say you to that?"

The oarsmen, uncomfortable at being out of landfall and winded by the long hours of rowing, lacked the spirit to stand against such an onslaught. Letting the ship wallow giddily in beam-on waves, they shrank from the lone mad-man in their midst. The boldest ones now gave voice to such weak plaints as, "That was hardly a fair thing," and, "Have some respect, Captain—" while the man in Conan's clutch grimaced and sweated with the pain of the iron grip on his shoulder. After glaring about him, Conan spoke again.

"Remember, dogs, on this very dawning you took an oath to me as your captain! It was a sacred vow before the sea-gods." His accusatory gaze met with few unflinching looks among them. "If you want to see land again, you will do as I say! If any of you want to give back your oath—" he waved his scimitar on high "—fine then, I will cut it out of your craw and offer it on a fishfork to Dagon!" He pointed the curving blade down at the shell of the ship, toward the weedy sailor's hell that every man of them feared. "Otherwise, you will obey." He raised the blade and sheathed it. "To those who follow bravely, I promise either riches or a glorious death!"

The crew, though still leery of their captain's wrath, began setting things in order. Some leaned on their oars to steady the hull against the giddy, sidelong motion of the waves; others helped haul the half-drowned pirate back into the ship. Conan returned to the poop, striding from one oar-bench to the next between cringing and sullen rowers. Telling old Yorkin to pipe up a brisk speed, he set about steering the *Vixen* on the course of the near-vanished square sails.

For three days the pursuit went on, longer than Conan had expected. At each dusk, the Imperial squadron would strike sails and heave to; the pirates, still out of sight of land, would drop anchor into the weed and sand of the Northern Vilayet and curl up on their oar-benches for an exhausted sleep. At first light, the pursuers would raise anchor, waiting for their quarry to make sail; then they would renew the chase, with the *Hyacinth* getting underway behind them.

Fortunately, the weather held, with no gales to swamp them or speed the sailships away out of sight. On the afternoon of the third day, land came into sight to eastward: a low, flat, featureless coastline with no shipping or signs of habitation. Conan had never voyaged this far northward, nor could any of his pirates tell him what to expect or where their quarry might be bound, other than toward the vast tundras of northern Hyrkania. The galliot's crew had fallen into a sullen torpor, accepting their captain's tyranny and their daily toil with glowering looks and superstitious murmurs.

The Imperial galleys followed the coast northward. Though they angled gradually toward shore, they showed no great eagerness to put in and search for food and water. The pirates eyed the swampy, uneven coast wistfully, yet knew better than to grouse to the captain about weariness or thirst. As night approached, a mist rose from the open sea, snaring and smothering the waning sun in rising gray tendrils. Before long, mists obscured the Imperial sails ahead; Conan slowed the oarstroke for fear of running onto rocks or passing their quarry unbeknownst. Losing sight of shore as well, the *Vixen*'s crew soon found itself in a murky, echoing gallery of fog, which swiftly darkened into night.

SEVEN
The Dead Land

When dawn came, the pirates uncurled their wet, cramped bodies from the oar-benches and blinked about them into smothering whiteness. The fog was so dense that Conan, from his place astern, could not see his own galliot's bows, nor indeed distinguish much beyond the sinister shrouded bulk of the catapult amidships. Waking at intervals during the previous night, he had glimpsed neither moon nor stars, nor heard any sound out of the emptiness. The waves passing under the keel were slack and listless, heaving themselves up and collapsing sluggishly in the sodden, windless air.

The ship's supply of drinking water was low. Some of the men, while gnawing their breakfast of hard biscuit, quenched their thirst by licking heavy droplets off the helves of their oars—but that source was impure, even if there had been some way of collecting it for later use. Lying here at anchor was eerie and troubling; it was also wasteful, and a dangerous spell of idleness for the men.

So Conan resolved to search for drinking water. Ordering the anchor raised, he went forward into the bows with two lookouts to peer into the fog and make depth soundings. By finding the coast and working northward along it, he hoped to resupply the ship and take up the pursuit.

He assigned two stout pirates to steer, instructing them to use the direction of the sea-swells as their guide. At his command, old Yorkin's bone flute struck up a low, rasping cadence. The dirge's sole accompaniment, as the crew began rowing, was the occasional creak of oars; its counterpoint was the slap of stray waves under the bow. The ship, lost in a universe that was the hue of corpse-windings, glided forward slowly toward an ever-receding wall of vapor.

In time, diminished depth readings confirmed their course. After a gray, featureless hour or so, they drew near land: first a series of jagged, unseen reefs, where surf hissed and gurgled warningly, turning them further northward; then a low mudbank crested with high, thick grass, having scarcely any beach or shingle at its foot. The margin of sand at the water's edge was too narrow to walk along, much less to draw up a ship on. The soundings here grew unreliable, even when done with poles; as the *Vixen* glided near enough inshore for them to examine the shoreline in the fog, Conan felt the keel balk against soft, miry bottom.

"The sea is dead calm," he remarked to no one in particular. "We must have rowed ourselves into an estuary. Good then, there may be fresh water nearby. And land-dwellers as well. Belay that ghoulish piping," he called to Yorkin in the stern. "We go in silence now. Steersman, ease off these mudbanks, but follow close along the shore."

Before their high fog-dripping keel, the grassy bank unfolded without much change. The dense grasses reared tall over Conan's head, even when he raised himself up on the rail alongside the forestem. No matter, since the fog precluded seeing for any distance. There was little reason to send men ashore and risk their loss or desertion; and Conan could not go far from the ship himself, lest his surly crew seize the opportunity to strand him. Thus far, there was no inlet or sign of a stream. He gazed down at the water, which looked dull and murky in the fog.

He jerked suddenly upright. "Avast rowing!" he hissed to his crew. "Quiet, all of you!"

Silence prevailed, broken only by the squeak of a steering-oar and the lapping of waves as the ship slowed to a halt.

"What is it, Captain?" one of the lookouts in the bow whispered.

"See those waves?" Conan gestured down at ripples spreading toward the keel. "Something has just now crossed our course . . . just ahead there in the fog, I would swear to it! A ship or . . . something."

His words passed quickly aft, relayed in muted, feverish whispers; for once none of the pirates dared move or raise his voice. When the lapping under the bows subsided, Conan gave a silent signal; then the rowing resumed more furtively than before. Conan crouched high on the bow, ready to order a halt on an instant's notice. Blank shoreline unfolded spectrally in the fog along the starboard rail, without any sign of human passage, or even of the presence of wild game. There was no vegetation except grass and sparse water-weed, and no audible sound of bird or insect.

"If a ship passed here," he muttered, "it was no heavy-hulled dromon. These waters are too shallow.'' Conan climbed down from the rail but continued watching the channel, sensing the galliot's progress through his bare soles. ''There is current here,'' he announced. ''Test the water's sweetness.''

A lookout lowered a pewter noggin on a string, raised it up to his lips, and spat overside. ''Not too salty, Captain, but brackish and foul.''

''Hmm. Likely there is a pure source upstream.''

''The fog is lifting, Captain.'' The second lookout touched his arm, pointing. ''There is land away to port . . . and more there, ahead!''

Indeed, a subtle paling of the early light was accompanied by an expansion of the visible world. There across the water loomed more grass-choked shoreline, a narrow channel, and a low spit of sodden mud. ''Bear in to starboard,'' Conan called back to his steersmen, keeping his voice low-pitched, ''and stay off that bar! We are amid a river's islets and meanderings. Avast rowing now, dogbrothers. Use your oars to pole us along the deepest channel.'' Taking a stout pole from along the bulwark, he waited ready to fend the ship off obstacles on either hand.

The sea-fog gradually retreated overhead to a low, mottled vault of cloud, but remained too murky and dense to allow for judging the sun's direction. The galliot's crew faced successive choices of route, through what turned out to be a labyrinth of estuaries, mudbanks, and tongues of grassland. Conan kept to the starboard channel whenever it appeared deep enough; on the few occasions when the chosen course dwindled to a stagnant mire, he and his pirates were obliged to pole the ship backward to a junction and take another direction. The water's current was but feeble in most places, far too inconsiderable to serve as a guide.

At one spot where the bank overhung the channel, Conan stepped ashore from the rail and tried to part the thick grass. The blades were impassable: as lofty as two men, and too razory-tough to hack through with a sword. There was no way to see over the tops, so he returned to the ship. Later, at his order, spry Diccolo was raised up on the end of an oar to survey the terrain; he claimed to see no hills or forests, only a limitless expanse of curving, nodding grasstops. Conan wished he had brought along the galliot's mast; from it, he might at least be able to spy the progress of another mast-top through the swampy wastes ahead.

The water, viewed in pallid gray daylight, was jet-black. When one dipped a hand in or tipped some out of a cup, it appeared deep red, almost the hue of wine or blood—a coloring so intense that at any significant depth, it shaded to inky opacity, making it impossible to see more than a finger's-width below the surface. One of the lookouts tasted it again, savoring a mouthful and swallowing it down, but said it left a vile after-reek on his palate.

The sluggish watercourse sustained no fish, so far as Conan could tell. He heard no bird-cries either, nor gutturals of frogs, though he thought the slick mudbanks showed faint, sinuous tracings of worm or serpent. An eerie deadness overhung this country, whose watchful silence somehow breathed the uncanny. It set Conan on his guard, making hairs tickle behind his neck; also, perhaps fortunately, it oppressed the crew, silencing the tumult of complaints they might otherwise have raised.

"Ahead there, Captain. A tree!"

Conan, trailing his pole in the water, raised his eyes from the bank, where, for the first time, he had recently spied dents and pole-marks in the mud, made before their coming. "Aye, so it is," he answered. "A tree."

The earnestness in the lookout's cry was almost laughable, stirred as it was by such a trivial cause. Yet the tree was, in truth, the first living thing they had seen other than grass; it was a broad, angular, willowlike shrub leaning far out over the channel just ahead, its leafy fronds trailing to the water in places. The branches looked to be limber and pliant, yet the upper sturdy ones would undoubtedly make a better vantage point than anything the pirates might improvise.

"Is there room to pass beneath?" the lookout nervously asked. "Mayhap we should take another channel."

"No," Conan growled. "We can clear it." Intent on the idea of catching the ship that must be somewhere ahead, he screened his face with a raised arm as the galliot's prow glided in under the hanging fronds. "Once we are well inside, we can send a man up aloft to have a look at the country—ahoy there, port lookout, fend us off that limb!"

Hurrying to lift his pole across the forestem, Conan jostled against the crewman. The lookout slid down openmouthed against the rail, rigid and lifeless—the same man who had swallowed the red-tainted water of the slough. "Set's biting devils!" the Cimmerian cried. "Crom!" He redoubled his oath as his pole-end caught in overhanging foliage. An instant later, the galliot's stem caught against the low-hanging bough. The ship turned and lost way, then came to an uneasy halt in the water.

The impact of the high prow caused a shiver in the branches overhead, from whence small objects began pattering down among the rowers. Dark, curled pods, Conan thought at first. But no, these pods moved . . . they must be grubs or insects of some sort. A pirate screamed in agony, clutching at his bare shoulder where one had fastened itself to his skin. He strained and tugged to pull it away, even two-handed; when he succeeded, a red rivulet of blood coursed down his bare chest from the wound it had made. At once there came more screams, stampings, and mad flailings as pirates tried to shake off and kill the vicious pests. Centipedes, the things were, with hard, segmented bodies, scores of scrabbling legs, and fierce, pinching mandibles. There was no telling whether the creatures were poisonous.

"Push ahead, rogues!" Conan thundered over the chaos. "Pole on through this greenery ere we are lost!" To set an example, he drove his pole into the river-muck and hove against it mightily. With muscles straining and tendons cracking, he felt the ship begin to edge forward beneath his taut legs, which were clenched hard against the crossbraces; he saw other pirates follow suit with poles and oars. Then a writhing weight struck his shoulder, and pincers sank into his skin with a fiery pain.

He brushed and smote frantically at his attacker as its mandibles flexed to bite deeper. It fell away into the bilge; though it writhed there slick with his blood, Conan could trouble over it no further. Instead, he lunged astern to recover his pole and resume laboring.

After endless, hellish moments, the ship's prow broke through the dangling fronds. The *Vixen* glided forth in pale daylight, into the broad pool that lay beyond the tree. There the pirates drifted while grubs were hunted out from under benches and carefully smashed; if flung overside alive, they merely swam away in a flurry of limbs, to reclimb the oars or the tree's trailing branches. The pirates' deep, ragged lacerations could not be cleansed, pure water being scarce at hand. But it appeared that, unlike the river beneath them, the tree-centipedes' bites were not fatal.

Only one pirate died of their attack, of blood leakage because the keen mandibles had nipped through an artery at the side of his neck.

The stream channel curved away ahead and, for the first time, a breeze stirred, ruffling the grasstops along the banks at either side. The pirates, though gory and shaken from the recent skirmish, were eager to pole forward out of the vicinity of the hell-tree and, amid this swampy maze, find a new route back to open sea. They toiled in earnest silence; it was some minutes before the former air of somber menace closed in again, sharpened by the uncertainty of ever finding their way.

Their captain, however, had a notion of what he sought; always Conan's eye scanned the streamside mud for marks of an earlier ship's passing. His terse commandments took them up long, devious channels, past more of the hellish trees hulking inland, and one overhanging the stream. Luckily, though, the channel beneath was broad, and they were able to skirt it, beating a score or more of the tree-grubs out of its remotest branches as they brushed past.

At length their winding course brought them to an uncanny sight. It loomed ahead for some while above the grassy banks, then unfolded massively before them as the ship nudged around a muddy promontory. There stood a great dead tree, stark and eldritch against the cloud-ribbed sky, its base as broad across as half the length of their galley, its branches bare and angular as the limbs of a bleached-white skeleton.

The enormous, monstrous shape was rooted in an islet at the center of a broad lagoon. The isle rose as white as the tree, covered over with what at first looked like fallen branches. But on closer view, as the galliot poled out onto the black pond—whose dark mirror threw back the vast, crazed webwork of the tree's pale branchings—its true composition became clear. The island consisted of bones, nothing else; large ones and small ones, human bones and greater-than-human, and lesser ones as well. They lay in furrows and heaps trailing away into the dark water, rising up in a sinister, mounded landscape around the vast, gnarled trunk and the pale, saurian knottings of its deep-sunk roots.

The bones, so it seemed from a distance, represented every sort of bird, beast, fish, and reptile in creation—or any that could conceivably have flown, walked, swum, or crawled to this forlorn place, to die and bleach under the evil tree's influence. It was a horror beyond understanding. The galliot's crew would have drowned sooner than row their craft under the loom of that baneful, skeletal tree—yet neither could they keep from craning their necks toward it in awe and dread. So they floated rapt, their brains becoming snared in the labyrinth of the great snag's twisted branches.

Conan, for his part, eyed the lone habitation that was in sight, made of the sole building material ready to hand: a low hut or shrine on the near side of the island, constructed crudely of bleaching bones. There was no sign of movement about the place; yet the presence of a bone raft, hauled up on the white-littered beach nearby, and the smudge of dark ashes raked around the dormant fire-midden heaped before the door, suggested that the place might even now be occupied.

"Oarsmen." The Cimmerian's voice was low and even, quietly certain of obedience. "You can ply oars here, for the lagoon is broad enough and deep. Row forward to yon beach. Then reverse seats so that you face the bows, and stand ready to pull clear again on my order."

The crew obeyed wordlessly, as if their turbulent pirate souls had already been drawn out of them by the sinister lure of the great tree. The ship glided on beneath the arching branches, the prow grated on the lagoon's unseen bottom, and Conan sprang down onto the islet with little fear of being marooned. Feeling loose bones crunch and shift under his boots, he strode toward the leaning, macabre pile of the hut. Sure enough, a pale wisp of smoke yet rose from the bone fire smoldering before its entry.

Within, however, the quaint tabernacle of ancient death enshrined death of a newer sort. The white, powdery floor was stained deep red, which flowed from the chest of an aged man who had propped himself up against one bone wall. A sword-wound had pierced into his side; he lived, yet could not remain alive much longer.

"Old hermit, who has done you this injury?" Kneeling by the victim's side, Conan peeled open the man's bloodstained robe to see the extent of the wound, then let the garment fall closed. "It could not have been many moments ago."

"Nay, 'twas not long ago," the old man gasped in a Hyrkanian dialect. "Turanian infidels, a shipful of them! They have gone off 'round the lake to steal the Tears of Thorus . . . some spell-caster has put them up to it, 'tis sure." The old, watery eyes focused on Conan's face. "You are a pirate, are you not? A Hyrkanian? Keep them from it if you can, son . . . the gems belong to us!"

"What gems?" Conan urged him, supporting his sagging, bony shoulder. "What is this strange place?"

"This is the mouth of the sacred river Yldrys, where all the dead of Hyrkania are swept, man and beast, in the hope of paradise! The bones come to rest here, beneath the great ancient tree. With them comes power."

"And the gems? What of those?"

"They are all-powerful, and sacred to this shrine." The old man reached up, his bone-thin fingers clutching at

Conan's forearm. "Keep them from the Turanians. Flee with them, if need be, and a great reward will be yours! But beware the Guardians . . ."

"What Guardians? Old man, what do you mean?" Conan braced up the hermit's lolling head, but it was too late. A red foam drooled from the elder's lips, and his yellow eyes rolled blankly in their sockets.

So be it. Lifting the frail old body and carrying it outside, Conan strode to the pond's edge, flung it in, and watched it sink swiftly from sight. That, presumably, would gain the old codger paradise. He walked to the galliot, still grounded on the bones, and sprang up into the bow.

"Ahoy, you craven rogues," he grated at them. "Push off and row! We have Turanians to fight and treasures to win!"

It would take diligent goading and abuse to knock the men free of the slack-jawed spell the giant tree seemed to have cast over them. On the other hand, he did not want to raise his voice, and their mute obedience was an advantage as long as enemies were present. By grunts and fierce gestures, Conan got them to pull free of the bone beach; then, shifting to the stern and stamping out an oar-rhythm with one booted foot on the deck, he steered the vessel around toward the back of the island.

As they rounded the hillocks of bone, a ship edged into view: the low, sleek penteconter, adrift in the lagoon, her black-and-gilt finish showing up trim in the dark water. No rowers lined the oar-benches; only helmeted Imperials were aboard, and those few seemed intent on doings ashore near the base of the giant tree. They did not turn and see the galliot approach.

The scene, as it unfolded to the fast-closing pirates, was of a shore party weirdly embattled. Several dozen Turanian marines—no mere oar-crew these, but full-armored Imperial troops—had been set ashore and were approaching the tree in a tight phalanx. These men had not, most likely, rowed across the Vilayet; they had been ferried in the larger dromon and kept at the peak of their fitness, to take their place on the oar-benches only when the smaller ship began its mission inshore. Now, superbly armed and trained, they moved toward their goal—but found themselves up against a hideous foe.

Giant black centipede-like things, ponderous relatives of the scourge that had dropped out of the trees onto Conan's men, blocked their path. These monsters, numbering a dozen and more, exceeded a full-sized warrior in length and girth. Rearing up on their hind sets of legs, they towered over the helmeted troopers. Their supple bodies flexed left and right with swift, darting motions, each one occupying several Turanians at once. The mandibles and leg-talons were proportionally huge and deadly, with the two claws next to the head prehensile and red-tipped, dripping venom. Their hard body-segments provided tight, natural armor against the flailing steel of their attackers.

The Imperials were caught in a standoff. Having moved partway up the bone escarpment and found their way barred by the giant creatures, they dared not break formation and rush past for fear of being isolated and dragged down.

Conan watched one of the Turanians come to grapples with a centipede; the armored man twisted and thrashed in its grip, unable to swing his sword or to inflict any damage with his dagger. Once the monster's mouth-parts sank home in the back of the man's neck, the victim writhed and screamed energetically, his struggles lasting long moments. The centipede pulsed greedily all down its length as if feeding; when at last the trooper fell away, his armor suit rattled and rebounded loosely on the bone scarp, a hollow carapace drained of all living substance.

Meanwhile, the skeleton force left aboard the penteconter watched rapt, and Conan's ship quietly closed with them. He steered to ram, but without sufficient speed; at the last moment, he sheered aside, motioning his pirates to draw in oars as the galliot thumped the Imperial ship and scraped to a halt alongside. The impact toppled the men standing in the penteconter, and the pirates, shaken out of their daze, knew at once what to do; they boarded all down the enemy's length and overwhelmed its crew, making swift and efficient work of the fight with their daggers. In the brief time the affair took, it was doubtful whether anyone ashore noticed the pirates' victory.

"Quickly now, dogs, make this ship ready for our escape. But I want two dozen men—you there, amidships— to row the *Vixen* ashore and help me snatch the treasure!"

In moments, the galliot nosed in toward the island, steering some distance away from the phalanx of soldiers. As soon as the prow grated on submerged bone, Conan sprang overside and bounded up toward the spectral tree. He saw advantage in being unarmored and light on his feet, especially in contest against enemies already pinned down and distracted in battle. Burdened only with a pirate's tools—the sword and the sack—he could outrace man or centipede, and the goal was plainly in sight.

Set in the base of the great tree, in an angular recess resembling an alcove, a cluster of gemlike amber droplets glinted in the wan daylight. Whether they were frozen globules of the dead tree's ancient sap, or amulets left behind by faithful worshipers, these baubles—hanging in the crevice like a bunch of oversized grapes—were clearly the objects sought after by the invaders and defended by the Guardians. If they were worth lives to either group, they plainly had value; on that theory, Conan made for them with his best speed.

The going was neither easy nor sure. The bones, brittle on the higher slope, crunched and shifted under his sandaled feet, and the tree's great roots wound and knotted like frozen serpents, providing uneven footing. When he was partway up the mound, a cry of alarm rose from the embattled Turanians; to Conan's quick glance, it seemed that the centipedes, too, had taken notice and begun to turn aside.

Now he was on the spreading base of the tree, leaping across dead bark that felt as course and tough as rhinocerous hide. Ahead rose the bleached, exposed flesh of the trunk, vaster even than it had seemed from below, enfolding the shadowy alcove. Straining his thews to keep up momentum, he sprang into the opening, steadied himself to reach in, and tugged at the hard amber spheres. They were held loosely in place by some tough, fibrous substance. Drawing his scimitar, he swung it wide and struck at the sinewy attachment; the gems pulled free in his hand, adhering together in a loose, rattling cluster, and went into his ready sack. Clenching the loot in one fist and his sword in the other, Conan turned and began leaping and sliding down the precipitous trunk.

His path was clear. Turanians and Guardians alike neglected their battle; both now moved belatedly to block his path, the centipedes creeping over the loose bones faster by virtue of their many legs. Yet he could make the waiting ship easily, much faster so than he had ascended. He bounded toward it, sliding downslope in places, scattering bones with careless strides in others—until he glimpsed agile movement in the dead branches above him.

Checking his headlong rush and scrabbling away upslope, he barely avoided what plummeted into his path: a full-sized, wriggling Guardian, dropping from above as its smaller cousins had done. It shattered dry bones with its impact, then instantly squirmed forward and reared high over him, its broad segments and taloned legs making it a tall, sizable tree in its own right.

Raising his scimitar, Conan struck mightily . . . and could almost feel the heavy blade dulled by the hardness of the monster's armored skeleton. Great mandibles, each one longer than Conan's curved sword, scythed down together at his head, the poison-claws squirting. He ducked and dove aside, fleeing as much from the beast's bug-eyed hideousness as from its bite.

Try as he might to win past, the centipede was nimble, cutting off Conan's lunges with scrapings and clashings of its serrated jaws. Each false effort gave the brother-Guardians and avenging Turanians time to move closer across the slope. Conan, unable to set down his treasure, tried a desperate one-handed overhead slash, straight down between the creature's gaping pincers. But his blade, rather than splitting the ogreish head, was clamped instantly in lightning-quick jaws. The Cimmerian, clinging to the hilt an instant too long, was borne over backward, with the full wriggling weight of the many-taloned body falling forward on top of him.

At once he felt himself splashed by gelatinous, foul-reeking ichor; the Guardian twitched massively aside, freeing him of its spiky weight. Its center segments, Conan saw as he scrambled to his feet, were shattered and trans-fixed by a long shaft: an arrow from the catapult mounted aboard the *Vixen*, two of whose pirate crew now leaped and hooted amidships.

The others waved their captain on, cheering from both ships in the lagoon. Recovering his sword and clutching his stolen gems, Conan dashed down the slope just ahead of the new detachment of clacking, racing centipedes.

The Turanians, however, now angled down toward the beach. As Conan sprinted for the galliot, the fleetest runner came between him and its bows.

The two fighters met in a clash of steel. Conan's downhill speed doubled the power of his stroke and drove the armored trooper over backward. The Imperial was fitted out in casque, greaves, and hauberk, with plate and chain attachments protecting his extremities; so he climbed to his feet patiently and deliberately, raising his lozenge-shaped shield with the certainty of warding off slashing blows from the heavy blade.

He could not have expected the long, curved scimitar to dart in under his shield like a light poniard, blindingly swift, yet powerful enough to drive though chain mail and rib cage alike, burying its point deep in his chest. Savage, piratical desperation, and an arm molded by death-grapples with northern savages and wild beasts, impelled the stroke that laid the Imperial marine dead in a clatter of armor.

Even so, others followed close behind. Conan sprang aboard the beached craft—whose half-dozen rowers had begun to push off, resigned to losing both captain and treasure—and instantly turned back to fight his pursuers. Mailed hands seized the bow, pinning the galliot to shore. A second heavy arrow spanged from the catapult, grazing the ship's prow; it missed the Turanians as well, losing itself ashore in a harmless scatter of bones. Armored troops now crossed the beach by the dozen, splashing into the water alongside the *Vixen*. Laying hold of the oar-tholes, they began dragging the stern of the vessel around toward shore. In spite of the heads and fingers Conan managed to crush and sever with his heavy blade, he knew that his boat crew was sorely outnumbered.

Then at once came a thudding impact astern. The second body of pirates out in the lagoon had finally gotten the captured penteconter underway, and now guided it inshore to aid their brothers and rescue the treasure. But few pirates from the larger ship leaped into the galliot to face the hordes of marines; instead, the movement was backward, the galley crew racing over the benches toward the penteconter to escape. As Conan retreated, he slashed the thick bowstring of the catapult with his scimitar, disabling the weapon.

As the last of the fugitives abandoned ship, a score of Imperials swarmed over the rocking galliot's side, their weapons raised to attack. But the pirates stood ready with oars, thrusting the captured vessel clear of the smaller one and stroking to gain speed.

"Bear to port! Port oars easy, starboard side pull hearty!" Conan barked out his commands even before he had climbed up onto the sterncastle and taken hold of a steering-oar. "Nicely now, dog-brothers, learn the feel of this fine ship." The oar-crew's differential stroke had already sent the penteconter out on a broad curve into the lagoon; now with the sweeps, he sculled it in a tighter circle. "To port, aye, again to port. Now both sides, gather speed!"

The penteconter was a fine ship indeed, more tautly built than the weathered old galliot and much better refined for its special purpose. Placing a hand on one of the heavy hemp cables strung from bow to stern along the rail, Conan felt it hum like the string of a well-tuned zither. The craft gained way rapidly under the crew's efforts, and the lagoon's dark water foamed redly in the wake of the oars.

Most of the Turanians were aboard the galliot readying oars, except for a dozen or so who maintained a last, defensive phalanx on the beach. A few looked up; even if they realized what was happening, there was little they could do. The galliot lay dead in the water, and the pentecouter still gathered way as it completed its circle and bore down on them.

"Now, dogs, all speed forward! Death to Imperial Turan and glory to the Red Brotherhood!"

The words were scarcely out of Conan's mouth before the shattering impact occurred. The pentecouter's keen bronze ram drove in through the galliot's hull. The blow knocked some Turanians off their benches, others clean overside.

"Now, sea-dogs, backwater oars! Push, I say, before they grab hold and try to board! Aye, there's the way, shove off! Let them row a swamped ship for their oar-drill! Let them mend her hull with grass and bones, if they can—they will not be racing after our stern! And what a send-off their leggy friends are giving them!"

Indeed, the enormous centipedes that had continued to harry the Turanian rearguard now flopped and writhed across the beach to the water's edge. The last Imperial troopers, retaining their three-sided defensive phalanx, waded backward into the lagoon. Some threw off helmets and armor to join their comrades who sat or clung aboard the half-sunken galliot. It could be poled or rowed to one of the grass islets to be repaired, Conan judged. Whether the hellish Guardians would enter the water or drop from the outermost branches of the death-tree was something he had no wish to wait and learn.

"Steady oars, now. Yorkin, pipe us a tune! With a new ship and treasure in our poke, it's homeward for us! Diccolo, shinny up the mast and spy out our way to the open sea!"

EIGHT
Sea-Trials

Mild sun warmed the harbor at Aghrapur. It blazoned
the bright angular sails of dhows, dahabiyahs, and merchant cogs out in the seaway, lending the Navy yard an
aspect of vigorous, bustling activity. The scene was a rare
one, for this was a day of sea-trials and contest adjudg-
ment. The docks and breakwaters buzzed with silk-clad
crowds of influential spectators—male and female alike,
the men fezzed or turbaned according to their station. All
were eager to see the the emperor's prize awarded; many
had gold or silver of their own staked on the outcome
through unofficial side bets.

Alaph the alchemist shared in the excited preparation.
At rare moments he even dared hoped that he might win
a portion of the gold—though of course, the more distinguished seers would precede him in demonstrating their
innovations. He felt nervous at the prospect of testing his
device before such a distinguished audience; Emperor

Yildiz himself was said to be in attendance, sheltering with some of his harem-wives and high counselors in a canopied pavilion set up along the main wharf. His royal son Yezdigerd, the contest's guiding spirit, had been glimpsed as well, strolling though the yards in the company of Nephet Ali and the other administrators.

The one unhappy circumstance—though in fact, Alaph guessed, it might be regarded as good fortune by some of the competitors—was the unaccounted absence of the prophet Crotalus. The black mage, as inscrutable and arrogant as befit his reputation in the court of Aghrapur, had sailed off into the Vilayet a fortnight before, at the project's very commencement. With him had gone a low, swift penteconter and a well-fitted dromon of the Imperial line, as well as crack oar-crews and a squad of elite marines—now all of them vanished without a trace in the hazy east.

Their course had been a risky one, straight across the trackless sea beyond sight of land. A blinding storm, a fog, or a mere navigational error could have delayed them many days. That was self-evident, even if one discounted the coastal sailors' superstitious warnings of floating sargassos and sudden, bottomless whirlpools on the high Vilayet—which menaces, after all, the arch-wizard Crotalus should have been able to deal with better than any ordinary man.

More to the point, in Alaph's judgment, the squadron had steered far outside the normal shipping routes, where their distress could have been observed and help offered. So they might reappear at any time, in his view. Imperial ships and troops were tough and resourceful, however untried their commander. They had not been given up as lost, but were still sought after by the empire's whole wide-ranging fleet.

In any event, rumor said, it had been deemed unwise

to postpone the sea-trials until Crotalus's return. After all, why call more public attention to what might yet become a famous sea tragedy? Debate and recrimination within the Admiralty and the Court had been firmly silenced, and a festive face put on the gathering. If Crotalus had forfeited the prize by his tardiness, why, so much the better.

Alaph, feverishly preparing for his own exhibition, was scarcely able to give heed as the Corinthian sage Zalbuvulus began displaying his work. The alchemist knew of it only when the expectant chatter of the crowd on the docks suddenly fell silent and heads turned toward the gate of the Naval Garrison. Of a sudden, the dockyard resounded with a familiar drumbeat, its steady thump scattering ragged echoes off walls, pilings, and ships' hulls.

Looking up from his work-crew's bustle, Alaph glimpsed a long double file of near-naked men—specially drilled rowers, decently breachclouted for this public expedition—marching out along the main dock.

The clever baker's-boy knew something of the Corinthian philosopher's highly innovative ideas. It would have been difficult not to, because for a fortnight past, the sound of bronze drums had throbbed continuously from the basement of the nearby jail.

There, by some form of spell-casting or conjuration, Zalbuvulus had worked to mold a hundred-odd convicts, captives, and pressed men into the perfect rowing crew. During that period, they had been induced to toil, eat, breathe, sleep, and perform every other action in unison, in time to steady, relentless drumming. Their hearts, it was rumored, followed the drumbeats as well; if the rhythm were to falter or cease for any length of time, they would all topple over dead. Employing shaven-headed Vendhyan drummers in shifts, the dour Corinthian had himself spent long hours with the rowers in their lockup and afloat, training in the harbor; Alaph did not doubt that the philosopher's stern personal manner, his steady, compelling gaze, and his powerful will had much to do with the evident success of the crew's conditioning.

That their discipline impressed the crowd was evident. Marching out along the dock and into their waiting bireme, the *Autarch*, led by their lean, white-robed master, the rowers trudged to the drumbeat in perfect accord, showing no discordant hint of individual identity. Zalbuvulus himself signaled approval with a satisfied twitch of his fierce gray mustache and eyebrows. Later, as the ship cast off and pulled away to sea, Alaph heard appreciative cheers; the trial crew's performance at the oars was evidently flawless. The alchemist had to acknowledge a twinge of dismay at his rival's instant popularity.

A display of inshore maneuvering was also well received; the ship's only balkiness seemed to be in medium turns, when half of the crew was called on to stop rowing while the other half labored to the drumbeat. But even so, the trials seemed to go off well; Alaph overheard a pair of turbaned courtiers speculating whether such drum-conditioning might be applied to land infantry as well, or even to slaves and Imperial subjects in their daily tasks. Alaph secretly dreaded the prospect, because of the noise it would make.

Once the bireme set out across the harbor on a lengthy endurance run, its drumbeat dwindling rapidly over the blue-green wavelets, attention shifted elsewhere—to Tambur Pasha in particular, and the wide-bellied galley he had fitted out to test his improvements to sailpower. As the craft was paddled out of its slip by bright-vested slaves, a new murmur of acclaim passed around the crowd lining the docks.

The galley's sail had been moved well forward of its

usual position. The new, shorter mast rose almost from the bows, where the silk-clad astrologer now presided, seated before a giant kettledrum. The craft's whole stern and middle sections aft of its low, broad sail were taken up by an enormous bellows. The low, tentlike enclosure of pleated cowhide stretched between long walls of railed planking to port and starboard. Between these planks and the ship's side-wales were long narrow benches, fore-and-aft ones rather than the customary oar-seats athwart the hull.

Along these benches sat the galley's crew. Fifty or so they numbered, fewer than such a vessel's normal complement, and most of them lacking oars. They sat facing inward, too, to the audible amusement of the crowd. Now, placing bare feet on the bellows' side planks and bracing their backs against the ships's rail, they thrust inward, to the sharp initial beats of Tambur Pasha's drum. Their legs straightened, driving the bellows' sides together to meet over the keel. A rushing exhalation sounded, and the white canopy of sail shivered, but it did not fill. The crew then drew back their legs and the bellows' sides with them. Their motion caused a loud, sputtering inhalation through the intake port at the back of the ship.

Alaph, once again acquainted with the general outlines of his competitor's work, could not spare the time from his own preparations to watch closely. Whether it was the uniqueness of the astrologer's invention, therefore, or its evident lack of success that caused the crowd to react with mirth was unclear to him.

For whatever reason, as the obtruncated galley lay in the water soughing and wheezing—puffing out its low sail intermittently like an ambitious bullfrog, yet producing neither a thunderous noise nor any progress in the water, with its crew flexing their lower bodies pathetically in time to Tambur Pasha's quickening drumbeats and shouted commands—the spectators' response was a torrent of laughter, jeers, and ill-aimed fruit, most of which rebounded from the bellows and sail and rolled into the scuppers. The drollery became all the more lively and universal once it was pointed out that the ship, rather than moving ahead, drifted slowly to the rear toward the dock pilings, possibly on account of the greedy, flatulent suction of the bellows' stern intake.

Alaph, though frankly embarrassed at the failure of the ebullient astrologer's scheme, was more troubled by the crowd's discourtesy. Beset by a new plague of doubts regarding his own invention, he wondered if his reception would be the same or worse. Turning away from his last-minute polishing and tidying, he looked on uneasily.

Fortunately, the dockyard officers, like good carnival mountebanks, were ready with a new act in lieu of the failed one. The sloop prepared by Mustafar the draftsman promptly sailed out from behind the wharf. It was an ordinary dhow, the same sort used for fishing or fleet communications, except for two objects mounted in the bows: a small ballista with an upright throwing-arm, and a spigot or siphon of some sort. From a short cable astern, the ship towed an even smaller craft: a quaint, mastless antique longboat with unmanned, trailing oars and a small, ornate cabin amidships—some kind of outmoded dispatch or ceremonial vessel, no doubt. Tacking out into view of the crowd, the crew of Mustafar's sloop cast the unmanned boat adrift, then luffed around to approach it bow-on, maintaining just enough headway to minimize their roll and pitch in the mild inshore breeze.

The sloop's crew of four, overseen by Mustafar at the helm, then busied itself with the war engines in the bow. After two crewmen labored together to wind back the arm of the ballista, one of them carefully placed a spherical shot or flask in the spoon-shaped terminus, holding it there two-handed. The second man cranked the whole assembly around on a turntable, while a third took a blazing torch from a smoldering fire bucket hanging in the forechains and touched it to the sphere. Whether from this action or by some unseen control, the torsion-arm lashed free and sent the round missile flying. Its path through the air, traced by a curving ribbon of black smoke, arched straight into the stern of the drifting longboat. There followed a flash and a sputtering explosion of flame, which engulfed the stern part of the boat and caused its brittle old paintwork to ignite and burn vigorously. The demonstration, after the initial silent awe it evoked, was greeted with wild cheers from the crowd.

Alaph, watching the burning hulk, wondered if the vessel might previously have been doused with lamp oil—but then decided that the bursting flask must have splashed some flammable humour over the old wood. A fiendishly effective device, that.

Mustafar's crew, meanwhile, turned its attention to the second object in the foresheets. It was another heavy bellows—not nearly so huge as the one installed by Tambur Pasha, but still oversized—hinged together at the front like the familiar blacksmith's tool, mounted on a pivot aforeships, and worked by a pair of long handles extending straight out to the rear. The long, thick snout of this implement was now directed astern and downward by the crew, its tip submerged in a keg secured to the mast. Then, with bellows parted wide, the men swiveled it around to point toward the burning longboat. Three of the crew, one at either side and one at the rear, forced the handles violently together with a swift, practiced movement. The result was a long, spouting column of fluid that squirted toward the burning hulk, some falling across the bows, most of it splashing into the water.

The bow section of the longboat was not yet aflame, and the liquid did not visibly add to its destruction. So the watching crowd made no applause—not until Mustafar himself, taking a blazing torch from a firepot astern, whirled it overhead and flung it in the same direction. The thick black fluid, which could still be seen floating sluggishly on the waves, caught the falling torch and burst into flame. It made a line of liquid fire, along which bright flames raced; reaching the vessel's side-wales, they leaped aboard. The target now burned with two distinct fires, and Mustafar's men set feverishly to work with the bellows, tracing more lines of living flame across the water and turning the longboat and its watery surroundings into a single, shapeless holocaust.

The cheers of the watchers were by then unrestrained. Alaph, quietly intrigued by the pyrotechnic display, noted that Mustafar's crew never used its torch to ignite the fuel as it left the bellows. That, presumably, would create a torrent of airborne fire, a terrifying sight indeed to an enemy. Yet it might also pose a danger to the ship and crew, or even to the onlookers. Likely, Mustafar was wise to refrain.

The alchemist's musings were cut short by the realization, from the energetic signaling of Nephet Ali near the emperor's pavilion, that he was expected to try his own experiment next. Hopping down into the bows of his ship and casting off, he ordered his crew to follow his example and shove free of the dock, out into the open harbor.

Alaph's ship, though just as large as Tambur Pasha's and lacking both mast and sail, had a complement of only two, including himself. It must have seemed odd to those standing ashore watching the small, heavy galley wallow on the waves with but a captain and a single crewman. Yet the man, a burly, tongueless Zamoran eunuch, set diligently to work, feeding the hearthfire to maintain heat. Young Captain Alaph went straight to the business of adjusting the brass steam cocks set low in the vessel's bilge.

Much of the space ordinarily occupied by oar-benches and crew was artfully filled in—first with a double layer of light earthen tiles, some of them specially molded to the contours of the hull. Aft were bins of fuel, fine-split hardwood that could be spread evenly through the firepit laid in the ship's bottom.

Then, nested over the keel and supported by strong metal braces athwartships, was the steam vat: a bronze vessel improvised, for lack of better resources, from a squarish metal sarcophagus looted out of the tomb of one of Turan's traditional enemy-kings. Carried home as Imperial treasure after a successful campaign, and stored in the palace gem-troves, it had only lately been adapted to this special purpose by drilling into its sides and forging shut the lid. The mortal contents were long since discarded, of course. Now the coffin made an efficient water-boiler, readily heated and well able to contain the substantial pressures that would be needed to effect Alaph's plan.

Leading from the sides of the sarcophagus, hammered metal tubes sealed by heavy turncocks continued straight out through holes cut in the planking of the hull at the waterline, stoutly reinforced and caulked. Once outside the hull, the tubes curved sharply back toward the ship's stern, like the bent spouts of the baker-boy's first teakettles. The nozzles, crowded with frantically escaping steam-devils from the boiler, were meant to provide the ship's forward motion. If this vessel was heavier than the ones that used to spin over his father's hearth—why, the boiling-vat was that much larger, and the volumes of water it held that much greater.

The heat was already substantial, as the hiss of scalding humours through the imperfect joints of the coffin-lid signaled to Alaph's ears. Now, with the fire banked up and flaming in its tiled enclosure, the energy of the trapped devils must be swiftly increasing. Hurriedly rounding his ship's rail, stooping and carefully avoiding the stray steam-jets, Alaph opened each turncock just halfway; then, peering overside, he was thrilled to see bubbles streaming out of the ends of the tubes and foaming at the surface in tiny puffs of steam.

Even so, he felt no hint of forward motion. The ship still rocked lightly in the harbor waves, floating near the shadow of the pier and its waiting occupants. The spouting devils, to his eye, lacked the fury they had shown in his kitchen hearth; it was as if, returned straight to their watery element, they lost all ambition. He looked to his crewman—no fault there, the burly fireman stroked the fire briskly, streaming with sweat. Impatient, Alaph walked around the ship again and opened all the cocks fully. The jets bubbled more profusely now alongside, yet the ship still did not get underway.

Shouts came from ashore. "Bun-boy, what are you doing? Brewing our morning tea?"

"Or is this a new way, perchance, of serving up boiled fish?"

The crowd had not waited long, and most had no idea of what was expected to happen, so the taunts were not savage, at least not yet. Alaph, while pained and baffled by his failure, caught himself sincerely hoping that the courtly mob had exhausted all its vegetables on the unlucky Tambur Pasha. Drifting dead in the water, he looked around desperately for a distraction. Luckily, he found one, at the same moment the restless crowd did.

It was the launch of the *Remorseless*, latest grand ship of the Imperial line. With the fitting-out and crewing just completed, this day had been chosen as an auspicious one for the maiden voyage . . . and now, in the face of Alaph's discreet failure, the Admiralty evidently felt the moment had come. The decireme, with its three unequal rows of oars on a side—the bottom oar-benches triple, the upper one quadruple-manned, causing it to be rated a "ten-ner"—typified the new class of larger ships, more powerful than dromons. It made a fine spectacle as it pulled away from the western pier to the throbbing of the drum, dwarfing the lesser ships that had been tried out that day. Stroking smoothly, with only occasional clashing and disarray among its oar-crew of several hundred, the high, broad ship gained speed quickly.

Another fast-stroking ship soon diverted the crowd's gaze: Zalbuvulus's bireme, with its specially conditioned crew, returning from its morning endurance run. The rowers still maintained their brisk pace, though presumably they had fared out all the way to the Ilbars River mouth; their early return seemed a highly favorable advertisement for the Corinthian's sorcerous skill. They came on briskly, with oars kicking up bright sprays of water and bubbles that streamed gaily over the submerged double ram. As the vessel drew in close, white-robed Zalbuvulus himself could be seen quite clearly between the two pairs of steersmen on the afterdeck—passing them brisk orders, it appeared, and then pacing forward to issue commands to the burly Vendhyan drummer who sat prominent at the break of the deck.

Obediently, the dark-skinned hortator ceased his drumming, crossing the heavy mallets on the bronze drumhead before him. Yet strangely, although his insistent thumping halted, the bireme's crew did not cease rowing. The oarsmen stroked on, their pace only slightly altered. It began to appear that there might be some danger of a collision with the new dromon *Remorseless* as it glided out into the cross-channel. Zalbuvulus was seen to bellow a command; he gesticulated angrily, without apparent result. Behind him, the steersmen struggled to turn their ship aside by paddling their two slim sweeps; they were hard-pressed to do so as long as the oarsmen drove ahead oblivious at brisk cruising speed.

Alaph, from his place in the smaller ship, at once understood the problem. It was the giant decireme, whose heavy drumbeats still rang out across the harbor. The ensorceled rowers, dazed by heavy labor and suddenly deprived of the drumming they had lived with night and day, now toiled instead to the beat of the larger ship's drum, which thumped nearer by the moment.

As the alchemist watched rapt, events confirmed his theory. The *Remorseless*'s officers, hoping to run clear of a collision, increased their rowers' tempo to full ramspeed; Zalbuvulus's crew, weary as they must be, likewise doubled speed. Surging forward with last-minute energy, they drove their bow straight into the big ship's forequarter. The impact, though not directly visible from the pier, could be judged from the groaning and rending of wood, the flying curtain of spray and broken oars, and the screams of maimed, trapped crewmen, which were soon matched by shouts and cries of alarm from the dockside spectators.

Alaph watched the scene, horror-struck by his first glimpse of naval combat. As the *Remorseless* settled in the harbor, filling and swamping, she likewise bore down Zalbuvulus's trapped ship, whose crew had finally ceased rowing.

All at once a new and nearer source of cries and alarms was heard. Mustafar, after setting his target launch afire, had turned to filling his bellows with seawater overside, using the weapon as a sprayer to drown most of the flames on the charred hulk. Yet he and his crew, stopping to watch the nearby collision, must have drifted afoul of one of the still-burning patches on the harbor, or made some other blunder. Now they swatted and bailed water at a lively fire amidships, trying to extinguish it before it spread to their kegs of burnable tar-oil.

Alaph, again unable to offer help, turned attention to his own launch. His fire-stoker, like himself, had been hopelessly distracted by the recent events. Even so, the fire under the boiling-vat still burned briskly, the flames having given way to hot, pinkish coals. Stepping to the starboard rail, Alaph examined the underwater nozzles. He saw no bubbles or steam-ghosts rising—nothing at all, even though the turncocks were fully open. Vapor hissed less strongly from the seams of the vat, he noted. The bronze sarcophagus looked rather strange to him, the heavy metal blushing reddish and bulging outward at its top and sides. An odd, vexatious, metallic squeaking issued from its hammered corners.

Then, of a sudden, he bethought himself. Shouting a warning, he turned and sprang to the galley's rail. As he dove overside, an impact struck his boot-soles. The fiery fist of a god smote him and hurled him headlong into the darkness beneath the pier and its surging, troubled waters.

Prince Yezdigerd, turning from the splashing chaos in the harbor and the strident emergency on the dock, strode along the main wharf. So swift and restless was his pace through the scattered, gawping crowd that his two body-guards had difficulty flanking him and shouldering aside unrecognized persons. Behind him in the tepid estuary, Turan's new flagship *Remorseless* lay swamped; her oars-men stood hip-deep, attempting to paddle the hulk back into the slips, while troopers on the raised decks stripped off their Imperial armor and swam ashore in dozens.

Of the various experimental craft, one bireme blundered about in the channel, her crew unable, for all intents and purposes, to turn; one was now a smoking, half-burned hulk abandoned by captain and crew; one wallowed help-less beside the dock, sucking and blowing futilely—Tambur Pasha's impromptu notion of reversing the great bronze in-take and outlet nozzles, so that the giant slave-operated bellows now jetted out air astern, had not yet produced any forward motion. And that was without considering the sorcerer Crotalus's ships, which had been lost at sea.

As for young Alaph's coffin-scow, it was nowhere to be seen . . . having rent itself to tiny fragments in a burst of smoke and noise, with considerable injury and panic both at sea and ashore. A great destructive force, to be sure, if only the empire could contrive to visit it on their enemy's ships rather than upon their own. If the little alchemist still lived, which seemed unlikely; no trace of him had been seen since the blast.

Yezdigerd, pushing with his seconds through the cordon of household guards, strode up to the Imperial pavilion. "Sir," he declared to the emperor on the instant, "you must not dismiss the whole enterprise because of the mischances of one ill-befallen day! A few misfortunes in a new undertaking do not mark the ideas as unworthy, any more than do the slips and stumbles of a tiny babe portend that the man will never walk. I entreat you, Father, do not abandon this endeavor—"

"What? Cancel the naval contest, you mean?" Emperor Yildiz, reclining in a capacious swinging seat with lush harem-maids seated close on either hand, turned his face up good-naturedly to his officious kin. "Just because of the loss of a few puny vessels, and some piddling damage to a large one? Or a few scorched turbans among my courtiers? Indeed, no, Yezdigerd. Why, naval ships are made to be battered about and handled roughly, are they not?" The monarch guffawed a little drunkenly. "This morning's display was most, ah, instructive. I would not think of putting an end to something that provides such capital entertainment. 'Tis the next best show to the Zamoran slave-fights! By Tarim, I have not laughed so hard in years as I did at the sight of these blundering, would-be admirals colliding and setting fire to themselves—have I, girls?"

His energetic hugs squeezed laughter out of his houris, and it was echoed by a fresh chortle of hilarity from his own round belly. "Nay, boy, by all means, go on with your naval dabbling. You may continue to offer the prize. Just see to it that I and your little mothers here are given a good seat at dockside to view the results."

Yezdigerd said no more. With a stiff nod, he turned away, pushing through the Imperial cordon and resuming his hard, forceful stride along the wharf. His bodyguards could not guess his destination, but kept pace in silence; from the sullen scowl on his face, they knew better than to trouble him with questions and risk the full force of his wrath.

NINE
Homevoyaging

"The fog is lifting," came the lookout's cry aloft. "Land ho, dead to port—it looks to be the Dragon's Beak."

"Curse the gods!" Captain Ivanos raised a thick, scarred hand to shade his eyes against the brightening blue-gray, studying the distinctive shape of the rocky headland. "That means we have drifted far south seeking those rogues."

"All the better." Ferdinald's quiet growl came from the tiller, where he presided as sailing-master. "We are of little use to Amra, if we know not where he is, or he us. It would not go well for us if we ran afoul of those Imperial oarships alone—or even the penteconter—undercrewed as we are."

Ivanos turned on him, scowling. "Was it not your plan, and our captain's, for us to follow at a distance and throw in with him on the attack? Now you have steered to south-ward. What if the Brothers are embattled, needing our aid?'' He shook his head ponderously, running thick fingers through his bushy beard. ''Do you want to be the one to explain our absence to Amra, if it costs him a victory?''

''The plan did not allow for a fog. I admit it.'' Ferdinald shrugged. ''Such is seafaring on this tepid Vilayet. Becalmed and befogged, we could do nothing—and Amra would like it no better if we lost the *Hyacinth* for him, and his women in the bargain.'' He nodded meaningfully toward Olivia, who appeared on the ladder at the break of the poop, with the captive girl Philiope climbing up behind her. ''Our safest course is to return to the shelter of the Aetolian Isles. Cruising here alone, we are prey to Imperials and shore pirates, or to any well-armed merchant that happens by.''

''We can outsail the Imperials . . . you can, or so you have boasted in the past.'' Ivanos shook his head, his scowl stubbornly set. ''I order you to turn northward and find the *Vixen*, as we were told to do.''

''Nay, Ivanos!'' Olivia, clad in short-hemmed silk pantaloons, light sandals, and a flimsy blouse suited to the warmth of the just-emerging sun, halted opposite the bearded pirates. She did not often parade on deck in such scanty garb, and her figure caught the men's attention; it rivaled that of the younger, leaner Philiope, who came up at her side, dressed in one of her short-trimmed gowns.

The effect of Olivia's winsome womanliness, though, was somewhat spoiled by the triple-bolted crossbow cradled loosely under one arm, its cable cranked back and ready. ''Lay your course for Djafur,'' she told the steersman. ''The time is past when we could help Conan on his treasure-hunt.''

''With all fitting respect, Olivia—'' Ivanos spoke evenly, appearing to ignore the hair-sprung weapon the maid of Ophir carried ''—I am Conan's lieutenant. He made me captain, and I ought to decide what course this ship sails—''

''If you are Conan's captain, then you are mine as well!'' Olivia showed no restraint, not troubling to keep the rancor from her voice. ''Know you, I am Conan's consort . . . his mistress . . . aye, even his master at times! If an error is made, I can account to him better than you or any raffish pirate. I say go south.''

''But what if Amra seeks us?'' Philiope's voice, soft and reedy compared to Olivia's, betrayed genuine concern. ''What if he puts himself at risk while searching? We should stay nearby, whatever the danger—''

''What are you snouting into this for?'' Olivia jerked her head impatiently aside at the younger woman, without altering the downward slant of her crossbow. ''You, a prisoner, whose only wish is to escape from us and see all pirates destroyed! Am I supposed to heed you?''

''Oh, but I do not feel that way!'' Philiope stopped, flustered. ''I mean, I am under Captain Amra's protection. I care for his safety—''

''Why should you?'' Olivia demanded. ''You are a hostage, with a cash value if delivered intact, nothing more! Why claim a right to speak in this matter? Are you telling us you are something other than a captive noblewoman, to be bartered away at the first opportunity?'' Olivia's eyes, from beneath her wind-tossed raven tresses, bore in darkly on the girl.

''No,'' Philiope answered at last, her brown eyes darting restlessly as if trapped.

''Well then, southward it is! We are through rattling about on Conan's tether, discommoded and endangered to no purpose . . . for this voyage, anyway. Agreed?'' She fixed Ivanos with her look until he yielded a grudging nod. ''Remember,'' she told him, ''if the *Hyacinth* changes course, I will know by the cant of the deck, just as well as any peg-footed sailor!'' Seizing hold of Philiope's wrist, she strode back toward the cabin hatch.

Ferdinald, leaning on the tiller, spoke idly to Ivanos as they watched the two depart. "Methinks we ought to change this cog's name—*Hyacinth* scarcely befits a fierce pirate cruiser.''

"Nay, fellow.'' The other pirate shook his head. " 'Tis ill luck of the worst sort to change a ship's birth-name. So it is rumored among men of the Vilayet at least, who will not fight their best on an ill-omened ship.'' Ivanos spat in disgust, watching the two women descend the ladder and disappear. "Anyway, *Hyacinth* is a pretty name. I am not sure our new captainess would permit any change!''

"Ahoy, there, lookout! Avast singing out depths. We are well out of the river shallows now. But stay in the bows with your line ready and your eyeballs peeled. Reefs lurk in this fog!''

"Aye, Captain,'' the muted cry drifted back astern.

Steering the captured penteconter. Conan found it worrisome to bellow orders at crewmen he could not see. The accurst fog stifled not only vision, but hearing. Their exit from the delta of Yldrys, the Hyrkanian river of death, had been swift and triumphal—with the dark currents hurrying them seaward, a man atop the mast to confirm their best course, and the cask of strange gems lashed to the stern rail, where even now Conan kept his foot propped on it. But when they left the coast and its perils behind, it had been to plunge into the looming fogbank, which had never lifted from the chill offshore waters. The wall of cottony grayness had been welcoming in a way, with its promise of concealment—in particular from the enemy warship they assumed to be waiting offshore. Yet the fog was dank and windless, a drain to the spirit . . . and it had its own peculiar dangers.

"Pipe up sharper, Yorkin. Your notes do not carry." Conan thumped a heel on the deck to get the weary old flutist's attention. "I can feel the for'ard oars lagging—but keep your pace slow, lest we drive ourselves onto a shoal."

"Captain, what is that sound? Do you hear it?"

"Avast rowing." The question had risen from several pirates along the starboard side; now in the cessation of oars, flute, and his own voice, Conan pinpointed the noise to starboard: a soft, rhythmic rushing, like surf washing across a beach—but faster, and drawing near.

"Rowers, oars ready, now stroke! Ram speed, do not idle! Yorkin, a tune!"

Under the wild, orgiastic lashing of the bone flute, the penteconter lurched forward; the taut, trim craft gained speed in a swift series of jerks that might have thrown Conan off his feet, had he not had been savagely plying the tiller. Meanwhile, out of the featureless mist to starboard, a menace quietly took shape: the high, recurved prow of an Imperial dromon, its oar-banks flexing like triple wings amid showering spray, its toothed beak drooling foam across the racing wave-tops.

For an instant it was there; then it was gone away astern, a dwindling surf-beat lost in the fog. The Cimmerian might have thought it a dream or a ghost-ship, had he not felt the fluke of his steering-sweep thwack hard against several of the fast-driven oars of the Imperial's upper starboard bank. Some of Conan's forward rowers may not even have seen the vessel rush past, but to him, the image memory was still sharp and vivid: in particular, the tall, dark-clad figure standing like a statue in the enemy's bows, with only his smirking face turning after the escaping prey.

"By gad, it was the dromon, charging us at ram speed!"

"But no drumbeat, nor a chant . . . do they always row that fast?"

"How did they find us in this fog? By our piping?"

"It was by your smell, Rufias! Bathe yourself and do us all a favor."

"Enough, you rogues! Quiet, lest they find us again! Yorkin, pipe a low, steady pace."

Conan let the oarsmen do their work, using his sweep to steer a course that he hoped would leave the enemy ship behind. Not that they could be found again by any reasonable chance, groping in this murky porridge of a fog. By the time the larger vessel could slow and turn, heavy and overmanned as it must be, the penteconter would be as remote and hard to find as if it had never been seen. Their near encounter with death must have been ill luck, a fluke, Conan told himself. Still, he remembered that menacing figure in the dromon's bow, waiting so patiently, and watching so quietly.

Even if found, the penteconter should easily be able to outrun the dromon. The fog perforce slowed Conan's pace, for safety's sake; so must it hamper the clumsier pursuer all the more. Even supposing the ship's helmsmen had some preternatural knowledge of the reefs in these strange waters . . . why, they could not see in any case. Conan might have considered turning the tables and ramming the dromon himself, if finding the target were not a virtual impossibility.

"Captain, I hear surging water away to port."

Conan's ears, too, had caught the sound, though this time it was slower and less rhythmic than before. Either the dromon had matched their course and slowed its pace—listening, perhaps—or else the sound was white-water breaking over a reef. Conan let the oars stroke to the muffled flute and kept his rudder straight, straining to tell whether the noise moved closer or farther away.

"Captain, astern!"

"Crom! How has he found us?"

The oarsmen, facing rearward, were quicker to sense it than their captain; but true enough, there at the faint rim of awareness was a thrashing noise that quickly built toward full-stroke, and the beginnings of a shape: the dromon's thin, feral prow. This time it came on less suddenly, because the penteconter's motion bore directly away. But the threat was, if anything, greater, since the smaller vessel could not dart sideways. The big ship's speed and momentum were more than great enough to smash in the smaller one's stern, and a turning maneuver would slow the penteconter even further and make it vulnerable to a side-on ram.

"Starboard oars double-speed, ready, stroke! Port oars full speed, every second stroke!" Conan's fog-damp mane threw off heavy droplets as he swiveled his head between his rowers and the menace astern. "Turn her to port, lads! We make for the reef!"

"What, for the reef? Our captain is mad!"

"He would run us to death on the rocks rather than lose his treasure!"

"Silence, dogs, and obey!" Conan's own roar and the mad wheedling of the bone flute belied any need for silence. "Remember, this bucket has a shallow draft!"

The penteconter was indeed a superb vessel, as light and tautly strung as any minstrel's lute. It rode steady on the waves, responding smartly to the strokes of the tiller and gaining speed smoothly into its forced turn. A pity to lose such a fine craft, Conan told himself as he watched the bronze-fanged warship loom steadily nearer, adjusting course to drive into the little ship's port stern quarter.

"Reefs ahead, Captain!" came the cry from for'ard. "Shoaling waters off the port bow!"

The lookout, situated farther away from the mad flute and the dromon's churning oars, could likely hear breakers that Conan could not. Even so, someone else must have heard, or seen. No sooner had the cry rung out than Conan's wish bore fruit; the Imperial ship began to sheer aside, the line of its keel shifting away to starboard, finally well astern of its prey.

"They are standing off the chase!"

"Aye, to watch us eat rocks! They are no fools."

"White-water to starboard, Conan! Reefs dead ahead!"

"Quiet! Back oars. Slow her, but do not let her drift. Keep up enough speed for steerage way!" This was the touchiest part, maneuvering a stiletto-thin craft into dead grayness, barely able to see the mainmast, swaddled and blindfolded by fog. Conan feathered his steering-sweep lightly to gauge the vessel's speed. "Enough! Ship oars and stand ready to fend off hazards!"

Thanks be to Crom, the befoggled sea was slack and torpid, a sloshing morass. At least they would not be hurled wholesale onto the rocks. Yet even so, the craft's uneasy pitching and the squat, ugly waves betold dangerous shallows.

"Shoaling water ahead, Captain! There are reefs to port and starboard alike! We drift to port."

"Tell me, lookout, is there a pass?" The crew lay silent, listening to the exchange.

"No, Captain, none I can see. We are in a box."

Aye, Conan thought . . . with the Imperial warship waiting for them to try to turn out of it. No need to question whether their enemies could find them in the fog. The dromon, or its sorcerous master, seemed to have little difficulty in doing that. A one-sided contest, in truth. He fishtailed his steering-oar to maintain speed.

"Lookout, what is the bottom here? Is it rough?"

"Sand, sir, or weed, I cannot tell. It is level here but shallow ahead, no more than a handspan."

"Well enough, then. Rowers, quarter-speed forward! Be ready to stand up and pole—or, if need be, to climb out and wade! These seas are not heavy, and we can manhandle a light tub like this over the shoal without breaking her back. Here is our best chance to escape this foul trap!" Conan reeled, staggering almost to his knees as the keel grounded with a series of hard, shuddering scrapes. "Ship oars! Briskly now, dogs, and overside, before we batter ourselves to pieces on this rock!" So saying, he leaped overboard into frigid, waist-deep water.

After long minutes of wet, chilly work, the penteconter was afloat again, the pirates dragging themselves in over the side-wales. Only one man was lost in the fog, having fallen into a hole, and another's foot had been crushed under the keel. The light hull took a pounding, yet sustained little damage. Pirates moaned and swore, wringing out their shirttails as Conan climbed dripping onto the poop.

"Now to oars, dog-brothers, and row! Yorkin, pipe up the pace at double-speed. Ready, stroke!"

"What, double-speed among these reefs? You must be mad!"

"Row, I say, and thrice-curse the reefs to Tartarus! Our best chance to escape the Imperials is with speed!"

"Fetch me the awl, wench . . . there, from the basket." Looking up from her work, Olivia waved an impatient hand at a kit of sailmaker's tools swaying on a hook on the forward bulkhead.

"I do not want you to call me that." Receiving no reply, Philiope at length arose from her chair and rummaged in the basket. Turning and maneuvering a little uncertainly across the cabin's rolling deck, she brought the tool to the central table, where Olivia worked at trimming a broad leather belt. The servant offered the awl to her, wooden handle first; but the seated woman did not take it, so she lay it down on the broad, cluttered table. "You might find your work easier if you did not keep that dart-shooter in your lap every moment."

"Nay, wench." The piratess did not deign to look up at her, but adjusted the angle of the triple arbalest across her knees. "I intend to carry it even nearer to me from now on. That is why am making this belt, to hang it safe at my side."

"But what is safe about it? It looks as if it could go off at any moment, without the least warning. Those sharp metal bolts might easily kill someone."

Olivia laughed harshly. "That is what makes me feel secure! Here on a ship crewed by fools, lechers, and cutthroats, such is a woman's only safety." She took up the blunt, richly engraved bowstock and waved it in the air, taking no special pains to avoid pointing it at Philiope. "It is a fine weapon, I thank you for it. If you or your late mistress had had the courage to use it when that cabin door flew open, you might not be here now."

"I would be dead, most likely—not that you would mind!" It was Philiope's turn to laugh, and she did so, bitterly. " 'Twas a gift to Milady from her cousin Khalid Abdal, given to defend her purity. He is a hard, relentless fighter, but she was not. Instead, she used me for protection."

"A poor choice, it seems, since your mistress now

sleeps with the sharks.'' Olivia made the observation coldly, without a glance.

''I did what I could,'' the noble maid answered in a hurt tone, ''for Milady, and for myself. A woman treads a harsh path in these domains of almighty Tarim . . . whether it be over stony deserts or tumbling waves.'' As she spoke, she steadied herself against the edge of the table. ''My poor mistress was delicate and nervous, alas . . . ill-suited for the strain of an eastern lord's household, much less the grosser upheavals that fate can bring.''

''The fortunes of women are no kinder in the western kingdoms,'' Olivia observed with some bitterness. ''I, a princess of Ophir, know it only too well.''

''And yet,'' Philiope said, ''here among the sea-rovers . . . with such a man as Amra, such a leader . . . there is hope at least, a promise of betterment.''

''Do you mean my husband Conan's fond, drunken dreams of glittering wealth? Impossible treasures to be wrested from the slopping bilge of some rat-infested merchant scow?'' Olivia kept her eyes on her work while stubbornly shaking her head. ''If you believe that, you are as much a fool as I ever was!''

''Why, no, not mere wealth.'' Philiope leaned forward in the swaying cabin, her hands on the unsteady tabletop, and spoke earnestly. ''Amra dreams of greater things, too—of gaining political sway—of welding these pirates and fisher-tribes into an island empire, and rearing up a sea-palace at Djafur—''

''A palace, ha!'' Olivia's voice lashed out humorless, sharp with resentment. ''Splendid dreams indeed for a savage freebooter, who would rather be untrammeled by women—or for a wayward snipe like yourself, with nowhere to go but up! I, too, have heard such maunderings . . . enough that I want no more of them!'' Her dark hair tossing with anger, she looked up to meet her cabin-mate's gaze at last, her eyes burning like oven coals. "If you think Conan will build you a castle on the surf-washed sands of the Vilayet, then you deserve to live with pirates!"

"But I . . . we . . . could help him accomplish those dreams. He needs our aid!" Philiope came forward around the table to beseech Olivia. "What if he is in danger now, adrift or wounded along the north coast, dying for lack of our help? We should be there at his side, not sailing back to Djafur without him."

The Ophirean laughed harshly. "If you know Conan, you know that no one cares less for his safety than he himself does. He is blind to danger. Yet likely no great harm will come to him. He can take care of himself, better than he does his luckless women. He has more lives in him than a deep-sea turtle."

"Olivia, you are wrong to think he does not care for you . . . for us." Rounding the table, Philiope confronted the Ophirean where she sat gazing up. "He has provided amply for you, I can see, and will continue to do so while he lives. Though he is wayward and fierce, there is much love in him, and kindness too—enough for both of us, I am sure."

"If only I am willing to share him with you, you mean." Olivia's black-eyed gaze rested on her, unwavering in the swaying light of the overhead oil lantern.

"Yes, and why not? Multiple wives, even harems, are the rule here in the eastern kingdoms. Perhaps such is not a custom where you were raised, in Ophir . . . but truly, such a household can be full of love. It is not really so bad." Reaching forward, she laid a hand on the seated woman's shoulder.

"Permit him his hankering for a younger, fairer maiden,

you mean.'' Letting go the stock of her crossbow, Olivia reached up to pat Philiope's hand where it rested on her shoulder. "Accept it graciously, then, and share Conan with you? No, never!''

With a spring-steel grip, she clutched the other woman's wrist and lunged to her feet, twisting savagely. Philiope, crying out in pain, was borne aside and down, to stagger hard against the bulkhead. Slighter than her attacker and less accustomed to the surging roll of the close-hauled ship, the noblemaid was soon overpowered; Olivia, working swiftly and expertly with a thong from the tabletop, bound her slender wrists together before her and cross-tied them firmly. Then, dragging the helpless woman across the cabin by the excess length of thong, paying no heed to her sobbing shrieks, she drew the cord over a stanchion high in the stern corner and made her fast there, wrists raised above her head.

A gruff voice was heard. "Ahoy the cabin . . . Mistress Olivia, is all well with you?'' Thumps and rattlings sounded from the door to the main deck. "I thought I heard a cry in there,'' came Ivanos's voice. "Is aught amiss?''

Striding back to the table, Olivia snatched up her crossbow and turned to the doorway. "Nay, Captain, all is well.'' Jerking aside three separate latches, she swung the door half-open so that its bulk obscured the wall of the room where Philiope hung gasping. With her weapon plainly visible at her side, Olivia confronted Ivanos and a second pirate through the hatchway. "I have matters under control here. Like any prisoner, this cheeky wench feels rebellious at times, and threatens escape. But it is in my power to discipline her.''

"Oh, Ivanos, help me, please!'' Philiope's cries were

broken by reedy sobs. "Cut me loose . . . protect me, and Amra will reward you!"

"Ha! Listen to her, will you?" Olivia sneered. "What wiles these noble girls can command! She'll soon be singing another tune."

"Mmm, so that is the way of it." Ivanos, flushed and uneasy-looking, craned his neck as if to peer around the door; but he had simultaneously to watch the prongs of Olivia's gang-bow idling down near his loins. "Conan does not want the girl killed or . . . hurt."

Olivia laughed again. "No, I would not slay the miserable wretch unnecessarily, though I do hope to be rid of her soon, for a fat ransom! Captain Ivanos, where do we now lie?"

"In the East Strait, Olivia." The burly pirate looked somewhat reassured. "We are nearing Djafur."

"Good, then! For the time—" she shot a meaningful glance sideways "—you may ignore any sounds you hear from this cabin. Pay them no heed. Try to listen at the doorjamb and you will get a knife blade through your ear! When we weather the cape, sail safe into harbor and drop anchor, but come to me before sending anyone ashore. Understood?"

"Aye." The pirate was still wagging his head in uncertainty as Olivia shut the door in his face. After latching it securely, she turned to Philiope.

"Now then, little hussy, what was I saying to you? Oh, yes!" Going to the worktable and laying down her crossbow, Olivia rummaged among the tools and scraps to find two items. One was a knife—a long, gleaming poniard, its blade a handspan in length and wickedly pointed. The other was a coarse, tapering braidwork of thongs, secured at the end with a thick knot—an arm-long horsewhip, frayed and shortened with rough use, but far from unserviceable. Clutching one implement in either hand, she turned from the table and stalked toward her bounds captive.

"So, a shameless slut like you intends to share equally in my husband's regard!" Raising the knife point to Philiope's nape, she slit through the neck of her gown, then dragged the blade-tip downward with a shredding noise, stripping the fabric away from her prisoner's back. The noblemaid's gasps and shrieks went unheeded, and her plunging efforts to dodge free, tethered as she was in the low corner with barely enough room to stand upright, availed her nothing. Again the blade tore at her garments, and again, till the captive's bright clothing lay in ribbons about her bare ankles and mere forlorn shreds remained to drape the girl's lithe, unmarked nakedness.

"Now, wench . . . you would worm your way into my husband's affections!" Raising her arm, Olivia brought the whip slashing down across the pale, creamy flesh. "Hang upon him with sighs and murmurs, would you, and ply his weak male brain with your melting looks!" Again the lash rose and fell, and again, branding its brilliant stripes across straining, dodging back, thighs, and buttocks. "You want his favor—let *this* show you the happiness he will bring, and *this* how well he protects his fair toys! Would that *he* were bound here under my lash right now instead of you, an ignorant trollop! I would fight you for his love, if it was worthwhile—but no, the day may come when I give him to you freely! For now, though, I give you *this*! And *this*, as was given me in my youth—Shah Amurath taught me *this*, and worse, much worse—but *this* will suffice for a low, coarse baggage like you!"

Hoarse and breathless from crying out, Philiope sagged on her knees, half-conscious against the wall. Her pale body, spasming with dry sobs and swaying with the fitful roll of the ship, was a welter of pink stripes crisscrossed from the flogging. Olivia, too, was winded; she steadied herself with her knife-hand against the bulkhead as the deck went through an uneven series of evolutions.

Drawing in breath, she listened; on the deck overhead were thumps and footfalls, and what sounded like a cry of the helmsman, abruptly cut off. She pushed herself upright and turned from Philiope—in time to see a booted foot kick open the hinged window in the stern wall of the cabin. Soon after it came the whole man: a tall, lean fighter clad in dark robes and a black silk turban, with a curving saber gripped in one fist.

"Who are you? Begone, or my crew will have your heart on a spit!" Clutching whip and knife in either hand, Olivia measured the distance to the table where her crossbow lay.

"Your crew, indeed?" The swarthy Turanian laughed harshly, cocking an ear upward toward the cries and thuds that continued on deck. " 'Tis their heads that will be spitted, and not many days hence, on the pickets of Emperor Yildiz's palace gate!"

"Liar! You are no Imperial officer!" Nervous, Olivia played for time, moving nearer the table. "Your manner is too suave and high-nosed. Have I not seen you before?"

"Aye . . . on the deck of this very ship, the free-trader *Hyacinth*!" Executing a sudden lunge, the intruder leaped forward and brought his blade down on the tabletop, and the crossbow, whose tough cable loosed rather than parted, sending its three darts thudding in a sloping line across the bulkhead timbers. "I am Khalid Abdal," he announced, turning on Olivia, "the high sharif whom you robbed and humiliated, come to slay the vile brigand Amra and recover what belongs to me! I am most interested," he added, casting his eye toward the naked captive, "to see the way you treat hostages held for ransom."

"Khalid, Milady Philiope is dead!" The breathy words, gasped from the throat of the beaten, exhausted girl, brought a new flood of tears to her eyes and choked her with fresh sobs.

"I have heard so. 'Tis no great surprise to me, alas, given her frail nature and the low brutality of her captors . . . hers and yours." Khalid Abdal turned his inscrutable, appraising glance from Olivia to the beaten girl. "While you . . . poor lowly Sulula, the maidservant . . . wisely or not, you mimicked high station to shield my cousin from her captor's lust. You wore her clothes, assumed noble manners, and engaged the attention of her pirate abductor . . . all most energetically and believably, I am told."

"Amra is not here," Olivia interrupted, standing defiant with her useless weapons. "There is no need to seek him, so you may as well be gone. He has other ships and other men, and will doubtless swoop down to take vengeance on you. So I warn you, it would be most unwise to harm me. Just leave here, while you can . . . and take this serving-maid with you!"

"Nay, Olivia." Khalid Abdal smiled to see her face pale slightly at his use of her name. " 'Tis not her I am interested in, but you." Turning to face her, Khalid Abdal lowered his sword-point to the level of his waist. "I have been intrigued since first I saw you treading these decks." Slowly and deliberately, he sheathed his blade in the scabbard that hung at his side. "You are a beautiful woman, Olivia, and strong-spirited. I do not suppose that your association with pirates was a willing one, or an easy one." Moving closer, he cast a glance aside at the limp, wet-eyed captive. "Plainly, you know how to treat an unruly servant, which is a virtue among women of noble rank."

"Keep back from me," Olivia warned him tautly, holding her ground, "or I will pierce you through with this dagger!"

"Now, now, my lively one." The Turanian continued forward, spreading out his hands empty at his sides. "Your pirate lord stole a woman from me. Is it not fitting that I should take one away from him? You would like my company better, I think. I have no other wives, not yet, and never would I place any before you."

He closed on her across the gently rolling deck, and she did not lash out at him. When he took her in an embrace, drawing her mouth up to his, she did not resist. Moments later, knife and whip fell from her careless grip; her hands twined instead around Khalid Abdal, kneading and caressing him passionately. He bore her backward against the cabin table and occupied himself for some moments with a cursory exploration of her charms. When at length they pulled apart, Olivia was flushed and open-mouthed, gazing up at him while absently straightening her garments.

"You will come away with me, then, at once? Good." He assisted her in standing upright on the unsteady deck. "What of the false Philiope?"

"Her? I want to see the last of her!" Making her way to a cupboard against the bulwark, Olivia flung it open. Rummaging inside, she raked clothing and belongings into a sack. Then, coming back and stooping at the Turanian's feet, she picked up her knife and turned toward the bound, wide-eyed girl.

"You are right, I suppose," Khalid Abdal affirmed, watching her in amusement. "After such experiences, she is forever ruined as a servant. No matter, I know someone hereabouts who may want her, if she lives.''

Olivia advanced on her prisoner, who watched fearfully as the knife raised up over her head. She shuddered and closed her eyes, racked with relief as her tormentor used the blade to saw at her bonds. In a moment the thongs were cut, and the girl sank to the floor.

''You may stay, wench,'' Olivia said. ''I wish you a happy life among the pirates, since you crave it so much. Here, cover your nakedness with this,'' she added, throwing down a flimsy dress taken from the cupboard. Bending low, she brushed a hand across the girl's wide-striped shoulder. ''Rest easy, there will be no scars . . . if you do not let the pirates doctor you with their brine and tar-oil, that is.''

Meanwhile, a brisk knocking sounded at the cabin door. ''Khalid Abdal! Are you well, Sharif? The ship has been cleared.''

''Aye, I am well—but, curse the luck, my enemy was not here!'' Striding to the door, he unbolted it and confronted his henchman. Olivia followed with but a single backward glance; then they were gone.

TEN
Traitor's Harbor

"These be strange gems . . . ne'er in my years of sea-thievin' 'ave I seen the like o' 'em." However much old Yorkin's toothless gums may have aided his fluting, they did not, to Conan's ear, improve his speech. The pirate-priest held one of the amber gems up to his rheumy eye, trying to catch the strange effect of something moving in its translucent depths; the Cimmerian watched him narrowly, well aware that a pirate's skill at sleight-of-hand did not necessarily decline with age.

"How, then, do we know that these Tears of Thorus are worth anything?" came the carping, predictable question from Diccolo. Since the penteconter was cruising in a sharp breeze under its broad purple sail, most of the crew were free to idle fore and aft as they chose.

Before answering, Conan respectfully took the gem from the old man's hand. He replaced it in the open wooden chest, where it added its yellow radiance to the cluster of a half-dozen similar though oddly angled stones. "If the Turanians saw fit to send a pair of warships across the Vilayet to seize them, they are of value to someone."

. "Aye enough," old Yorkin said. "Belike as charms o' sorcery . . . I can yet feel th' enchantment in 'em." He rubbed his thumb and fingertips together. "But would ye sell such to th' empire, an' swell up their noxious power all th' more?"

"Piracy is business," Conan declared, "and business is evenhanded. It cannot hurt us to offer them to Turan, even to the same dire wizard we snatched them away from. But when word gets out over the sea-lanes, we shall likely be offered higher bids by others who want to keep them from the Imperials—such as their former owners, the Hyrkanians." So saying, he closed the treasure chest, placed his foot on it, and leaned on the lashed steering-oar.

"Aye, then," Diccolo still groused, "this will turn into another waiting game, like the split of the ransom from our captain's fair hostage. If ever we see a guilder of that, I will use mine to stand you all drinks at the Red Hand!"

The penteconter under its lug sail made good speed through the North Strait, rendering oars all but useless. In due time, the lookout, straddling the yard atop the sail, sang down that the port of Djafur could be seen around the headland. Conan gazed forward over the flying spray, satisfying himself that no hostile ships loitered about the harbor mouth. The Imperial dromon, which he still superstitiously dreaded meeting, had not been seen since their close escape in the fog. Their progress since then had been swift; likely the vessel with its uncanny pilot was far behind, and no better able to navigate the Aetolian passages than any ordinary ship.

"Yonder lies the *Hyacinth* at anchor," came the call from the masthead.

Good, then; Ivanos had the sense to turn back to port once they were separated. Shading his eyes with keen interest, Conan watched the bare masts of the cog evolve slowly from behind the brushy point. She lay far out in the harbor, none too convenient to the dock of the Red Hand; doubtless Olivia had had a say in that, fearing to lie in too close to the rowdy pirates' lair lest the ship be harried or overrun. Again, maybe it was Ivanos showing unexpected initiative and good sense. He looked forward with a tinge of dread to finding out how his mistress and Philiope had fared.

"To oars, men. That headland will cut our breeze. We want to look sharp in port in our new ship, and not stagger in close-hauled. Yorkin, pipe us a brisk stroke around the cape."

Conan could see tiny figures scurrying on the beach and crowding the wharf, drawn by the approach of the pente-conter, which they might well think hostile. Before turning inshore, he steered for the *Hyacinth*, intending to collect his women and a pirate jack to fly from the mast. But the cog lay hove-to and quiet, possibly untenanted. In moments the oarship nudged the bobbing hull and Conan sprang aboard, stepping from the high sterncastle to the midships rail with his treasure tucked under one arm.

As he vaulted the rail and crossed toward the stern cabin, the door suddenly flew open, disgorging men. Snarling pirates boiled up from the cargo hatch, and others swarmed down the rigging from hiding places in the brailed-up mains'l. In two blinks of an eye, Conan was surrounded. Wrenching out his scimitar, he faced a painful choice between letting go his chest of jewels and fighting one-handed. He determined upon the latter, but before he could strike a single blow, a cargo net was hurled over him. Plunging and staggering amid a flailing fury of blades, cudgels, and marlinspikes, he was driven to his knees.

His oarsmen, meanwhile, tried to push off from the cog and get underway. But grapple-lines were cast down from the tall ship to hug the pentoconter close, and pirates leaned overside with pikes and crossbows, menacing any who moved to unhook them. After Conan was drubbed down and disarmed on the cog's deck, the two shipfuls of cutthroats ended in an uneasy standoff, waiting at bay while a dinghy sailed out to them from the dock of the Red Hand.

Knulf Shipbreaker, looking stout and prosperous, boarded over the far side of the cog. Strutting across the ship's waist and waving a salute to his men, he loomed over Conan wrapped in his net. The vanquished captain lay watchful. He was only moderately crippled and bloodied, the net's thick cordage having protected him from the worst of the clubbing and sword-slashing. He watched as Knulf opened the jewel-cask that was handed him, examined the contents, counted the gems, then closed the cask and held it at his side.

"So, there he sits: the might Amra, lord of a fleet and master of a multitude, the most infamous pirate on the Hyrkanian Main!" The Vanirman's noisy eloquence plainly was meant not just for Conan, but for the whole pirate assemblage. "How sad to tell you, O Great One, that your fame has recoiled upon you and that your dashing reign is ended. History has passed you by, O Admiral! Now you will be remembered only as an object lesson."

"What traitorous devilment is this?" Conan tried to sit up and was immediately leveled to the deck by the boot of one of the Vanir's henchmen.

"Did I not warn you, Cimmerian?" Knulf inquired in a more confidential tone. "About the perils of notoriety, and the risks of too easy success? Remember, too, that I urged you to deal through me in disposing of your Turanian hostages. I offered you a most generous buy-out, as

I recall!'' Knulf laughed heartily, echoed by some of his cronies who stood nearby. "When faced with your stubbornness, I was forced to seek an independent deal. Most luckily so, as it happened, in view of the magnificent opportunities that have now opened up.''

"You swine, what have you done with my women?'' Conan demanded, dodging a kick. "I mean to say, where are Olivia and the hostage girl? If you have hurt them—''

To a chorus of laughs, Knulf replied, "The noblewoman Philiope, you mean? It turned out, as you may know, that she was not quite what she was trumpeted to be. Since I am too honest to try to palm off counterfeit goods, I have invited her to cast in her humble lot with me and be a helpmeet to my personal needs. Today she felt indisposed, so I left her in my chambers at the inn. But do not worry, she is well guarded.''

"Dog, I will whet my steel on your gravelly gizzard! What of Olivia?''

The Vanir, amid fresh merriment, said, "Forgive me, O Amra, if I laugh—but things have gone so well, in spite of the collapse of any ransom payments, that I feel most sanguine about the future. In particular, I have enjoyed my dealings with the Turanian emissary, one Khalid Abdal, whom you may recall from your piratical adventurings.'' He winked down at his glowering captive. "It seems that your fair shipmate Olivia found his arguments equally persuasive; she has gone off with him to Aghrapur, freeing herself of any pirate ties and leaving you to face the guilt of your evil career.''

"Rogue! Liar!'' Conan lashed out in vain, struggling against the handful of pirates who held the net tight around him. "When I get free, I'll carve your slandering tongue out of your throat—''

"I hardly think so. Instead, you will be called to account for crimes without number. The court at Aghrapur is in a fever, I hear, over your well-advertised doings. Know you, with Amra's capture, piracy in the Eastern Vilayet has been brought to a virtual halt; so at least the Turanian people will be told. The ledger will now be balanced for the destruction of commerce, the rape of this fine ship *Hyacinth*, the insolent assault on an Imperial war-squadron—of which I have yet to learn the details—and a score of other scandalous deeds over the past dozen years . . . all of which, including my own, can be laid conveniently at your feet. Right now my biggest item of potential profit—other than brokering these fine gems, for which I thank you—'' he patted the cask under his arm ''—is selling your head to Imperial Turan for punishment. Or rather, your whole notorious body.''

"Do you know, by the way, how they deal with pirates in Aghrapur?'' The Vanirman exchanged gloating looks with his fellows. ''Our sort have considerable popularity, as you may imagine, in a great seaport town that relishes gruesome accounts of our doings.'' He smiled wistfully. ''The Admiralty's usual punishment is a tug-of-war—a festive event for the street mobs, complete with food, drink, and carnival games. Four heavy cables are furnished, one lashed firmly to each limb of the offender. Four teams of able-bodied pullers are recruited, the whistle is blown, and the game commences. Passersby can join in as the frenzy grows, with extra ropes being spliced on as needed!'' He shook his head in vicarious enjoyment of the prospect. ''Such a contest can be a great holiday, a joyous procession passing through all the main streets of town . . . though of course the four-way road junctions are best favored.'' He smiled beatifically. ''Urloff Blacktooth lasted a whole afternoon, 'tis said—bellowing all the while, even with a leg and an arm pulled off. The winner, of course, is the team that ends up with the head attached to its portion.''

"Dog! Scoundrel!'' Conan snarled futilely. "That will be mild compared to what I do to you—"

"Enough, men,'' Knulf said, shaking his head sadly. "I fear my fellow captain lacks imagination. Drag him over to the rail, so we can show his shipmates his sorry plight.''

"How is it,'' Conan demanded, being kicked and shoved across the deck while still bound in his net, "that one captain of the Brotherhood can turn on another— betray him, rob him, and hold him up for public mockery? Is this a part of our tradition?'' Conan guessed full well that it was, but he meant to hold his own against Knulf in oratory, at least.

"The Brotherhood?'' Knulf laughed over the rail, crowing for the benefit of both ships. "With you, the pirate Brotherhood is wiped out . . . nay, rather say it has left you behind,'' he amended himself. "We of the Red Brotherhood are now a power in our own right, rulers of this island domain of Djafur, privateers and partners of the mighty Turanian Empire! See here.'' From inside his greasy vest he pulled a rolled parchment adorned with purple ribbon and seal, waving it on high. "This decree, signed by an agent of the emperor himself, names Djafur a free, autonomous allied port—with myself, Knulf of Vanaheim, as high commissioner.''

At this, a clamor of applause went up, all of it from the deck of the *Hyacinth* and well-coached, by the look of things. Conan tried to speak, but his wind was cut off by the pressure of a brass boat hook against his throat.

"In return for our alliance with him in these hostile waters, the Turanian emperor promises us rich subsidies, merchant cargoes of food and tradestuffs that we will not have to raid, but that will be handed over to us!'' Again, enforced applause. "Also weapons, ships and stores, as if we were recruits in the Imperial Navy, but without uniforms and the tyranny of naval officers!" This brought wild hoots and cheers that spread even to the decks of the penteconter. "And what must we do for this bounty, I ask you? Why, do what we like best! Raid and pillage and harry commerce; but only Hyrkanian ships and towns, acting as licensees of the all-powerful Turanian realm." At this, the acclaim was near universal.

"Additionally, we are to be given other duties . . . such as the collection of fees and tariffs from independent traders, according to the Turanian Imperial standard, plus a reasonable surcharge—" at this, knowing laughs and elbow-digs "—and the suppression of unlicensed rogue pirates, like the one just captured—" As Knulf pointed down at Conan, there came a furious murmur of denunciation and dispute. "Most welcome, perhaps," he went on, "to all those offenders who join under me in good faith, this document grants full amnesty for past naval crimes, and exemption from Imperial punishment."

At this, there rose from both decks a veritable storm of jubilation and controversy, over which Knulf had to shout to be heard.

"Therefore I call you to arms," he proclaimed. "Together we can subdue those of the rebel sea-tribes who have not joined with us in the alliance! We can rule these isles and wipe out any chief or captain who opposes us, or else buy him out with our successes. Onward, lads, for the Red Brotherhood and for empire!"

Over the frenzy of applause that followed the Vanirman's exhortation, one stubborn voice—the carping, blessed voice of Diccolo—rose from the penteconter's deck. "When has the Brotherhood ever joined hands with fat Emperor Yildiz?" he demanded. "When are these Imperial treasures to come to us? Where are they now? And what will become of us outcasts, the downtrodden of the earth, when Turanian warships have been given the run of these straits? Where will we be, if not chained to an oar in the bottom scuppers?''

"Aye, 'tis so," other men of Conan's crew echoed, with old Yorkin's garbled accents raised among them "How do we know the emperor will play us fair, aye, or that Knulf will? What is our guarantee?"

"I guarantee this," Knulf Shipbreaker declared fiercely, ". . . that any man of you who does not swear fealty to me now will end up in chains, packed off to Turan with your pig-headed captain!"

His words unleashed a brawl, the one that had simmered through so many speeches. Oars swung and thumped at the sailing-ship's side, steel hissed from scabbards, and arrows darted home into wood and flesh. Part of Conan's crew rose up in revolt, hacking at the grapple-chains and at Knulf's men who leaped down to guard them; a good many others cowered between oar-benches, or turned on their fellows with curses and blows. Conan, bent over the rail with boat-spikes digging into his back, was helpless to join in.

And in due time, the rebels, forced apart into the bows of the oarship, gave up fighting. Disarmed and clubbed into submission, afraid to dive overside and face the harbor sharks, they were sent up onto the cog one by one to be shut in the hold.

" 'Tis just as well," Knulf proclaimed from his place amidships. "We need a good lot of prisoners to make a show for our allies . . . and to make sport for the mobs of Aghrapur! Now, the rest of you, swear allegiance to me." Reaching to his waist, he drew his cutlass and raised it on high. "Swear by the hilt—to Knulf, the Imperial commissioner, and to Djafur!"

The oath came gustily, enlivened by fighting spirits. Indeed, the cheering went on for some moments, almost drowning out the hail that a ship was approaching the harbor. At length, everyone's attention turned to it.

"It is the *Tormentress*!" one of Knulf's lieutenant's reported. "Santhindrissa is back from her treasure cruise."

"Aye, curse our luck," Knulf said. "Likely she has not heard of the changes here. We must try to lure her alongside, or up to the inn. Ungrapple that oarship and put some men in it, but quietly. We may have a battle on our hands, or a chase."

"Help, the prisoner! He is getting loose . . . ah, *aieee*!"

With the crew's attention momentarily distracted by the she-pirates' approach, Conan broke free of his captors. Of the pirates holding the net over him, some few he felled with savage kicks and elbow-thrusts. Others, those who were too stubbornly tenacious or too slow in disentangling themselves, the burly Cimmerian dragged along with him. Struggling at the center of a knot of men, he lunged for the rail and dove overside.

In the narrow gap between the drifting ships, four men struck the water in a tangle of netting. One of them fought his way strongly to the surface, sputtering and splashing; but as the brisk harbor-mouth swells brought the wood hulls bumping together, he was caught in between. Stunned to death, his head deformed to a quaint oblong, he slipped motionless into the blue underworld.

The other three drove in deep on the plunge. One of them, a Khauranian of the western hills, could not swim; he never succeeded in untangling himself from the heavy net. He was borne downward, writhing and thrashing, choking forth precious, fleeting pearls of air in the azure depths.

The remaining two pirates, both able swimmers, were ready with lungfuls of air. Kicking free of the net, they breasted their way through the glassy blue liquor. One of them, a scarfaced, shaven-headed Ilbarsi, drew a long dagger from his waist and set out in pursuit; the other stroked clear of the ships' bobbing shadows, his black mane spreading and jerking taut with the thrusts of his corded arms and powerful legs. Then he turned to meet his foe.

The two came together in an eerie, slow-motion grapple, twisting and tumbling in the weightless depths. Hands clutched at wrists, while shins sparred. One knee drove sharply home, sending a jet of iridescent bubbles racing toward the sea's glassy roof.

In the blow's writhing aftermath, the knife blade turned sharply inward. Driven by powerful, desperate hands, it met skin, opening a gash in its owner's thigh that trailed dim streamers of blood through the water.

As his adversary kicked free of the combat, the shaven-headed pirate looked after him, surprised: The cut was slight; he had lost his knife to his foe, but he still had a chestload of air. Nothing was resolved—what, after all, was one more scar? Was it breath his opponent lacked, or courage?

Then his eyes roved sideways toward fast-gliding shadows. A tiger-striped shape darted in ghostlike, fastening itself violently and agonizingly to the oozing limb. More shadows converged—circling, then striking with swift, razor-barbed jaws. The pirate convulsed amid writhing, lashing shapes, and spewed out ruby-tinged pearls in a last smothered scream. As ever, sharks lurked near anchored pirate ships, drawn to the scent of blood.

Conan bobbed to the surface some distance away. Filling his lungs with a mighty gasp, he dove again, heedless of the weapons striking the water around him. The boat that had brought Knulf Shipbreaker from shore was putting out from the cog, doubtless to search for him; he swam deep, heading toward the harbor mouth, where the *Tormentress* had come into view.

This breath of air lasted a shorter interval, but Conan judged he was out of spear-cast of the cog. Surfacing and taking time to fill his lungs again, he heard exultant cries behind; the launch was on his track, reaching toward him under sail in a quartering breeze. Santhindrissa's ship was inside the breakwater, but sheering off cautiously. Conan dove deep, making for the weedy gloom at the harbor's bottom.

The dinghy's crew consisted of three sun-bronzed toughs armed respectively with crossbow, harpoon, and boarding-ax. Without any great pretense of wanting their prey alive, they scanned the water keenly, shading their eyes and peering into the turquoise depths for a trace of the fugitive. Their skipper, too, one of Knulf's lieutenants, hunted overside from his place at the tiller. Intent as he was, he may not at first have noted the difficulty in steering that caused the craft to bear slightly to leeward. Of a certainty, he noticed it when the tiller, seized by burly arms underwater, wrenched free of his grasp, causing the boat to veer sharply downwind.

The resulting jibe made sail and boom swing hard across, neatly clearing the dinghy of all four occupants. As the boat meandered off on its new tack, Conan drew himself over the stern and took the helm, leaving Knulf's men splashing and floundering in his wake.

The swimmers could not hope to catch him; the pente-conter, with its untried crew, was slow in getting under-way. The *Tormentress*, standing well off from the evident turmoil, idled oars in patient curiosity at the approach of the small, harmless boat. In a trice, Conan was under the bireme's looming stern, hailing the leather-clad captainess and bargaining to come aboard.

ELEVEN
Machinations

In the days following the disaster at the Imperial Navy Yards, work resumed more feverishly than before. The competitors for the Naval Prize picked up the frayed, scattered threads of their experiments even as the port officials undertook repair and reconstruction.

Soon after the tragedy, the black seer Crotalus returned from his expedition to the Eastern Vilayet—empty-handed, it was said, and with only one of the two Imperial warships he had taken. The surviving ship and crew were dispatched immediately on an errand south to Khawarizm, presumably to keep any of the men from telling of their recent voyage. But on a ship in port, however briefly, rumors are harder to quarantine than plague-bearing rats. It was soon whispered that the Zembabwan, through a perverse whim of the gods, had suffered the worst of an encounter with the infamous pirate Amra.

Crotalus himself was granted an immediate interview

with Yezdigerd. The prince, by nature restless and gloomy, had been especially so since the ill-starred naval exhibition. The event was interpreted in some quarters as a humiliation to him, particularly with reference to his Imperial father. Yildiz made no secret of the fact that the public gathering and the naval contest itself were Yezidgerd's idea, allowed to him as a pet project by an indulgent parent. As a further irritant, rumors abounded that Emperor Yildiz, working through the Admiralty, had set in motion a scheme that would soon end the problem of the Vilayet pirates once and for all—more traditionally, by diplomatic means rather than through the star-gazing and sorcery of the gullible young prince.

Of these innuendoes and intrigues, Alaph the alchemist could not help but be aware. In spite of his youth and humble background, he heard things; even in spite of his isolation from courtly life, his single-minded absorption in his work, and the pangs of the injuries he had sustained during the naval calamity. As he put in long days at the trireme shed that was his workshop, Alaph the baker-boy— a small, fez-hatted figure, always preoccupied and walking now with a limp—had ample opportunity to reflect on these and other matters.

The revenge of his unruly water-demons had been fierce indeed. Alaph still smarted from his narrow escape; his loose galabiyah had been shredded and the calves of his legs blistered. Burns and lacerations to the more private parts of his anatomy made it difficult for him to sit, or even to bend over. But even so, he had to remind himself, he was far luckier than those on shore who had been sliced in two by flying remnants of his steam sarcophagus, or scorched and blinded by the intensity of the blast. By rights, if anyone was killed, it should have been he.

When fished half-conscious from beneath the shattered

pier, on seeing the devastation all around him, Alaph had been in a kind of brain-fever. His soul long reverberated from the magnitude of the havoc he had unwittingly wrought. Clearly, these water-*djinni*, the demons or elementals he toyed with, had many rules and foibles. Clearly, too, not all of them were amenable to mortal logic and justice; he would have to study them carefully for his self-protection. He must never, for instance, use sea-demons in his boiler, for the salty residues they left behind clogged the valves and led to catastrophe and death.

Yet in his deepest soul, Alaph had begun to feel that if great Tarim had spared his life while others perished, it was for a reason. Specifically, he was kept alive to pursue this new knowledge; the innocent deaths had occurred merely to show him its power. Accordingly, with but little consideration of the Imperial prize, he now redoubled his thought and effort toward his greater goal.

Fascinating, disturbing new possibilities had occurred to the alchemist. The bursting of the coffin-boiler, fierce and terrible in its potency, nevertheless showed tremendous power—a power which, if it could be harnessed under the proper conditions, might prove very effective in warfare. How this destructive force might be carried to the enemy—whether, say, in a flaming fireship containing a coffin that had already been vexed near to bursting, or perhaps through the heating of a tight metal steam-bottle, fitted with a sharp or massive stopper that would be shot out at the foe along with the escaping demons—these speculations were the subject of Alaph's current work. Yet there were other aspects of it as well.

Without knowing precisely why, the little alchemist sensed that the fury of the demons' release had to do with the intensity of the heat they were subjected to, as well as to the tightness of their confinement. Along these lines, in addition to improved metalworking, he turned his attention to fuels. Greatly impressed by Mustafar's volatile liquids, he paid a visit to the weaponeer's compound and wandered beyond the thump and rasp of the smithy to the storage shed for flammable humours.

He learned that tar-oils, pitches, and more secret things were blended together in making up the flame-missiles. Some of the ingredients Mustafar had on hand gave good promise of being hotter and more compact fuels than wood or charcoal. Even though their use on shipboard posed obvious risks, fire was an ever more frequent weapon in Imperial sea-battles—so precautions would have been needed in any case.

Mustafar, uninjured and undiscouraged by his mishap at the sea-trials, continued to oversee a number of projects. These included the enlargement of naval catapults and the fitting out of oars as fighting weapons; also the notion of a flying projectile that trailed burning ropes or streams of flammable liquid, able as it passed overhead to set more than one vessel afire. The arms-maker, for his part, expressed interest in Alaph's work; he questioned him in particular about the possibility of some form of steam-bomb or a spraying, scalding catapult dart.

"After all," the smiling, swarthy-faced inventor told Alaph, "our business is the same; to serve our emperor and sow death and confusion among his enemies." As he spoke, the armorer filed noisily at the barbs of a deeply channeled bronze dart that was supposed to punch holes through ships' hulls. "We are honest workmen, you and I, with no great love or need of gold. I respect you," he went on, laying down his iron rasp to clap the bun-maker on the shoulder, "because you are a tinkerer like me, not one of these courtly strutters and posturers. We have no need to resort to aloofness or secrecy against our colleagues!''

Mustafar's reference was likely to Tambur Pasha, who remained in the contest along with the others. Though the astrologer's bellows-driven sailship had shown no practical value, he nevertheless proclaimed himself winner of the first sea-trials—pointing out that his scheme, at least, had not caused disaster and loss of life. For his ship's obvious failure, he blamed faults in the manufacture of his bellows, as well as unfavorable planetary configurations on the date of the event, which he also claimed to have warned against.

Even so, in spite of his refusal to admit to any flaws in his original concept, Tambur Pasha had shifted his researches to another means of naval propulsion. This involved an unfailing and self-perpetuating system, one that made rowers unnecessary. Its exact nature, though, was unclear. For once, the astrologer would not discuss his business; he refused visitors, and even kept his workers locked inside the shed at night to maintain secrecy.

''You speak truly enough, Mustafar,'' Alaph conceded to his host. ''My one real passion is simply to understand why things work. I know I will never have the stature of men like Tambur Pasha, so I feel overawed by them.'' The little alchemist leaned on his colleague's worktable in lieu of seating his scorched nether quarters on the rough bench beside him. ''The philosopher Zalbuvulus, now there is a formidable fellow!''

''Aye, he is a sour pomegranate,'' Mustafar agreed, filing away at his point. ''He has grown even more ill-favored of late . . .''

They went on to discuss the Corinthian expatriate, who, angered by the bad luck of his collision with the decireme, now carried forward his researches with a sullen vengeance. He retained the same oar-crew he had used before, holding each man individually responsible for the mishap. Still, he worked in secrecy, sequestered from the other contestants and Navy Yard personnel.

"At least we do not have the incessant beating of drums to plague us anymore," Alaph remarked.

Mustafar frowned, glancing to the stone-walled compound that hulked near his shed. "I would much prefer drums to the sounds I heard from the Corinthian's compound by night—screams, piteous pleadings, and those odd, rasping words growled out in a tongue no one around here seems to understand. I find such sorcery every bit as nerve racking."

"Zalbuvulus's abiding interest would seem to be the human spirit," Alaph said. "Perfecting it, making it ever stronger and more enduring . . ."

"Aye, and more subservient." Mustafar shook his head in distaste. "He is a strange one, not unlike the mage Crotalus. What that wizard's game is, nobody can tell."

"He has not bowed out of the competition, from what I hear." Alaph, weary of standing, eyed the bench longingly, yet did not dare lower himself onto it. "Whatever he required from the east, word is that he expects to receive it soon, regardless of his ill voyage. He was heard to say as much to Yezdigerd, shortly before the prince postponed the date of the new sea-trials."

"That may be so." Mustafar paused to thump his rasp clean on the edge of the table. "As for his part in the contest, he has already commenced work. He was allotted a gang of shipwrights, and a compound across the harbor, in the swamp. They began laying the keel of a ship, a special new design, just this morning."

"Hmm," Alaph mused. "I did not know. Well then,

Crotalus must indeed be confident of getting what he requires . . . and Prince Yezdigerd believes him."

"So much the worse," the weapons-maker said. "What these courtly favorites cannot have for the asking, while you and I, as honest workmen, can demand little!" He threw down his metal implements on the table. "Would Tambur Pasha dirty his hands like this? Never! But then, 'tis all patronage and interest."

"What do you mean?" Alaph, weary of standing, leaned an elbow on the worktable to rest his sore hamstrings.

"I mean the high courtly patrons. Tell me, whom do you receive your disbursements from?"

"Why," Alaph said, "funds and materials are released to me on an order stamped by Prince Yezdigerd himself."

"As I thought. You are lucky, you and the mystic voyager, Crotalus. Myself, I must apply under the seal of High Admiral Quub. For Tambur Pasha, it is Finance Minister Ninshub, or so I have heard. And Zalbuvulus's secret sponsor is our Imperial engineer, Nephet Ali."

"They are the ones at court who recruited us." Alaph shrugged. "What does it matter? We are all equal in the contest, are we not?"

Mustafar smiled, laying an arm on his colleague's shoulder. "And do you think that what you receive in subsidy is the full amount that is laid out from the Navy Yard's funds?" He glanced around, making sure his voice was covered from overhearing by the rasping and hammering of metal. "Yours is, quite likely—and Crotalus's, since I do not think Yezdigerd needs to steal from his own Imperial family. At least not yet! But in my case and the others, a large share of the profit goes into the pockets of our highly placed backers." Mustafar smiled bitterly. "That is part of the deal that launched this contest, the grease that smoothed its slide down the shipways, so to speak.''

The baker-boy shook his head in puzzlement. ''So you mean that some of us are favored over the others?''

''Aye, to be sure.'' Mustafar's eyes roved the shed watchfully. ''It was not meant to be that way at first, very likely. 'Twas just a harmless, temporary siphoning of the Ministry of Conquest's till. But as the source of supply grows larger, so does the need. And the potential future gains are so vast, far more than a mere five hundred golden talents for the winning invention. An illicit share of any new naval building and recruiting could be claimed as a consequence of it. Now, with the stakes so high, the backers are beginning to put greater pressure on their candidates. Dangerous pressure.''

''You mean that it could lead to more accidents?'' Alaph asked. ''Or to some kind of cheating?''

''I mean, baker-boy, be careful! Watch your back if you want to survive this.''

TWELVE

Master of the *Tormentress*

"So, that miserable newt has struck a deal with the Turanians! He declares himself Imperial governor of Djafur, or some such title. But does he have Imperial troops to back him?"

Captain Santhindrissa angled her spare, supple frame across the steering-bench to lean on the bireme's rail. One lank arm rested, through evident habit, across the starboard sweep, whose thick helve was steadied in place by tackles strung from the rail to the high, overhanging stern post. She lounged opposite Conan, who squatted on a keg that had been brought up as a makeshift seat.

Before them, along the ship's port and starboard rails, the *Tormentress*'s crew of female pirates plied oars to the slow, steady throb of a brazen chime. Farther down, between and beneath the files of sparsely clad women, flashed the blank faces of the male slaves chained to the lower oar-benches. They could be seen there rocking forward and back to the same slow rhythm, expressionlessly watching what transpired on the afterdeck. Conan found their dull, stolid gaze disconcerting, even more so than the women's scornful, appraising looks. It took a positive effort to turn his mind to business.

"Nay, Drissa, I saw no Turanian troops guarding Knulf, nor any Imperial ships in the harbor—none other than the one I stole, only to have it treacherously snatched by that blackguard!" Conan shook his head in indignation, his wet mane slapping his meaty shoulders. "Knulf did not boast of any Turanian garrison, as he surely would have done if he had one."

"Aye, then mark me, he does not have full agreement from the sea-tribes either. Not enough, anyway, to let foreign ships in among these isles." Santhindrissa's slender, callused hand touched the thick shaft of the steering-oar thoughtfully, sensing through its length the evenness of her rowers' stroke, Conan could well guess. "The chieftains are a contentious lot," she continued, "unlikely to unite behind Knulf without long skirmishing and infighting. We must parley with them first."

The Cimmerian, ever mindful of himself as the only unchained male aboard the *Tormentress*, watched his pirate hostess with wary interest. Her provocative manner—lounging bare-limbed before him in scanty leather breeks and halter, with clanking cutlass and dagger substituted for more effeminate jewelry—might be seen as a rough sort of invitation, so he judged. Or else a trap.

"But say, Captain," she cried, "we have neglected you! Your beaker is empty. Wine here, at once!" Clapping imperious palms, she summoned a youthful, half-clad boy up from below deck; the lad filled Conan's cup from an earthen pitcher, with scarcely an upward glance at his guest's solemn face.

"The sea-chief Hrandulf has never trusted our friend Knulf, any more than I have," Santhindrissa went on. "It is to his harbor we steer. He will help us resist this Imperial coup. Likely he is already summoning up his outlying clans. The sea-folk war against one another lightly and often, it keeps them in trim to fight outsiders."

"We should move against Djafur soon," Conan remarked, "before Knulf has time to fortify the place, or smuggle in heavy armaments and a garrison from Turan."

"That is foolish," Santhindrissa ridiculed her guest. "Why should the Turanians strengthen him so much? They only want to sow dissension between our Sisterhood—or Brotherhood, as you'd have it—and the sea-tribes. But Knulf will always be a traitorous rogue, just as poor an ally for them as he was for us. They must know that."

"I would guess that the Turanians have plans for Djafur and these isles . . . . plans that reach far beyond Knulf and our pirate Brotherhood." Conan leaned forward from his keg seat and dribbled out an oblong spatter from his wine cup on the gently rocking deck between them. "Think, Drissa. A few days agone, an Imperial squadron sailed straight across the Vilayet, thus-wise—" He slashed through the trickle of wine with the tip of his dagger. "That voyage, though mystical in its commanding, was not the first such crossing we have heard of, nor will it be the last. Whether by wizardry, star-reading, or other sly tricks, the Turanians will attempt oversea routes oftener in the future, to shorten their sea-time and to avoid our brother pirates—or sisters, if you will—along the south coast."

"So think you, in truth?" Santhindrissa sat regarding Conan's fanciful lagoon with a skeptical eye and a well-practiced sneer.

"Aye. Now, where is Djafur? Here!" Flicking down his

dagger, he stuck its point into the starboard edge of the puddle. "Sheltering in the Aetolians, ours is the port that lies farthest out to westward, nearest to Turan. A perfect base for our corsairs to raid such cross-sea shipping. Or even better, a port for Turanian merchants to take on provisions and find shelter from foul weather, before or after making the crossing. Independent of the Hyrkanian Empire, in the bargain, and easy to defend from her warships! That is the empire's real interest in Djafur."

"Hmm. An interesting fancy." Santhindrissa turned for'ard, tightening one of the steering tackles to make a minor course adjustment. "Not that it makes a difference . . . we will have the place back for ourselves anyway, no matter what Yildiz plans for it. Meanwhile . . ." reclining again, the captain turned her gaze back to Conan ". . . it is a rare thing to have a free male aboard the *Tormentress*."

" 'Tis a rare thing for me to set foot on a slave-ship," Conan retorted, with a glance of distaste at the two-tiered oar section. "Except as its liberator."

Santhindrissa shrugged, looking aside, unimpressed. "Consider these men as war captives, not slaves." Then she faced Conan again with easy assurance. "Believe me, there are none below decks who have not asked for it—" she tossed a bare shoulder provocatively "—one way or another."

"And what of the boy there?" Conan nodded aside at the youth who sat waiting in attendance by the break of the deck. "Did he ask to be your footman?"

Santhindrissa snapped her fingers, bringing the lad hurrying to her side. "Arin, here? As ship's boy of the *Tormentress* . . ." she lay an arm across his bare shoulders, then reached up and tousled his blond-burnt hair, letting him gaze up at Conan with sullen mistrust ". . . he has the luck, be it good or ill, to be the most-mothered child in the Eastern Vilayet. No more than that, and no less; I make sure of it.''

Patting the boy lightly on the rump, she sent him on his way. Then she continued, with the trace of a smile, ''Anyway, I know this is not the first time you have taken passage on a ship captained by a woman. Belit . . . that was the name of your pirate maiden on the Western Sea, was it not?'' She watched his face closely. ''Did she not also keep a crew of male oarsmen?''

''They were warriors, brave men of Kush,'' Conan growled in protest, half-rising from his keg. ''Never did they touch a chain or shackle, not for themselves or for others! They sailed on the *Tigress* of their own free, savage will—as did I.''

''Yes, Belit had a way of commanding men's blind adoration, so the legends tell . . . for already she is legend.'' The captainess nodded in grudging respect. ''Yet from what I hear of the true woman, her ways were wanton and reckless, squandering both loot and life—an unfortunate lack of discipline.'' Santhindrissa smiled somewhat primly as her fingers, perhaps unthinkingly, brushed the leather quirt wound at her belt. ''Since you and your savage crew took no prisoners, you needed no chains. But some of us do not slaughter so freely.''

''You think it nobler,'' Conan demanded of her, ''to eke a lifetime of toil and humiliation out of your victims? Rather than slay them honestly?'' He could scarcely bear to glance aside at the stolid, work-numbed faces below decks.

''At least we do not send them forth to be butchered for our private gain,'' Santhindrissa countered. ''We treat our captives well. We even tend personally to some of their bodily needs . . . shaving in particular, since they cannot be trusted with blades, and male beards are an abomination.'' She eased her poniard out of its sheath at her waist, exposing a few fingers of gleaming-sharp steel. ''We pamper them a little, and they find ways to show their appreciation.''

''Perhaps there is something to what you say,'' Conan conceded, wrinkling his nose. ''Your ship smells better than most slave galleys.''

''Well, then.'' Santhindrissa shifted her posture on the bench, crossing her bare legs mannishly. ''Since you like it here so much, I might find a place for you.''

In spite of her rangy looks and rough manner, Conan felt a kindling of interest and thought he saw it mirrored in her eyes. ''Well,'' he ventured, ''since we are shipmates anyway, for the nonce . . .'' He leaned toward her, elbows on knees. It was easy now to ignore the silent, steadily laboring crew. ''Tell me, Captain Drissa, would my place be above or below decks?—aforeships or poop?''

The piratess met his gaze demurely. ''To tell the truth, Captain, I hardly trust my own crewmates on my quarterdeck, much less a man. I like men best toiling at the nether oars, leaving me free to steer.''

''Nay, I do not think so.'' The Cimmerian shook his head in mock dubiety. ''When I ply new and dangerous seas, I like to keep a firm grip on my helm.''

Santhindrissa regarded him with a smirk. ''True, these waters may prove stormy at times.'' She shifted restlessly in her seat again, her eyes on him as she stretched her sinewy, small-breasted frame inside the black-leather halter. ''Even so, if you want to dip your oar, I would urge you to try.''

Accepting her invitation, he arose from his keg and crossed to the bench where she sat. She watched as he did so, unsurprised. Settling close beside her, his bare thigh brushing hers, Conan raised a hand and stroked her sun-warm, muscular shoulder. She reached up to where he touched her, clasped his hand, and raked sharp fingernails across the back of it, drawing blood.

"Hmm." Scarcely feeling the pain, and caring nothing for the gaze of the watching rowers, Conan did not withdraw his hand. "You play rough, Captain," he observed.

"I do." As his face nuzzled close for a kiss, she swung her fist up, smiting him hard on the cheek. He pressed numbly forward to claim his reward; but after the briefest instant, she pushed violently free, elbowing him smartly in the chest.

"What is it, then? You are not in the mood just now?"

"I am, I am . . ." She murmured the words invitingly with her lips half-open, a flush playing upon her cheeks.

Since she retreated no farther, Conan slid toward her on the bench, raising both arms to take her in an embrace. Of a sudden, with an expert flick of her wrist, the whip came lashing up from her side, searing the flesh all down his arm and wrapping around to sting his shoulder like an adder's fang.

"Crom, woman!" With a lightning twist, he wrenched the quirt out of her grasp and hurled it far overside. "You tease me, tempt and invite me, but you do not make it easy—"

" 'Twas never easy—never for a woman!" Now Santhindrissa lashed as fiercely at him with her sea-captain's voice as she had with her whip. "Why, I ask you, should a man suffer any less in his lust than a woman does in its aftermath?—splitting open in childbirth, shrieking in pain?" Her voice was made suddenly harsher by the rasping of steel as she drew her cutlass out of its sheath. "For a woman, ever it has meant the risk of servitude, the risk of death! For a man, on this ship, it means the same!"

Whirling the cutlass high overhead, she slashed its gleaming blade at his neck. Conan, stooping low to wrench his stolen dagger out of the deck planking, dove into a roll beneath the whistling stroke. He came up crouching, holding the knife out at chest-height; it was serviceable, but not heavy enough to turn away the curved sword.

In a flash, Drissa was on him, thrusting her point at his crotch. He fended with the dagger, springing aside and kicking with his bare leg at her sword-arm: a close miss. He danced away into the middle of the deck, and she stalked after.

"What do you want, Drissa?" he challenged her. "To kiss me or kill me?" He circled warily. "Is this all part of a she-pirate's love play?"

"Aye, it is," she assured him. "I will kill you if you give me the chance. But I would rather only wound you." As she spoke, she pressed confidently toward him, forcing him back. "A small wound, especially one in a nonessential part of the male body, would not much interfere with your service at the oars. As to my womanly favors—" she lowered her hand and clasped one sinewy thigh suggestively "—you will not enjoy them, I promise, unless you best me in this fight!"

Santhindrissa's crew, to Conan's surprise, kept their oars stroking smoothly to the slow, steady chiming. He knew it would be easy for the women to take up arms and swarm astern if their captain was harmed. Scattered yells and sounds of encouragement came from the upper benches; obviously, the she-pirates had seen this type of contest before; obviously, they enjoyed it. The male rowers said nothing, though every eye on the lower benches was fixed on the quarterdeck.

Tormentress's captain attacked viciously, leaping and thrusting to try to trap her victim in the narrowing angle of the stern rails. Her stabs and upward-looping slashes at Conan's loins were particularly deft; they forced him to shift his center of gravity continuously, suggesting to him that most of her fighting experience had been against men. After circling away for some moments, Conan saw an opening and lunged at his opponent, pressing to get past her guard.

But it was a false weakness; her cutlass was swifter, propelled by a hard, wiry shoulder, and Conan had to jump away from a slash that fanned the skin of his midsection. Drissa's blade, too, was devilish quick in turning; Conan's dagger-feint at her exposed arm left him open to a returning slash, under which he dove and rolled away across the deck. Tumbling against the keg that had been his chair, he grunted and sprawled aside, unable to spring back to his feet.

"Kiyee!" With a birdlike, triumphant cry, Santhindrissa sprang after him, swinging her cutlass high overhead. The blade arched down, to strike home with a moist crunch, spattering both fighters with rich red droplets . . . bright Zamoran wine from the cask that Conan had raised up in his defense. The steel blade stuck between the shattered barrel staves, giving the Cimmerian his chance; hurling aside cask, dagger, and sword, he tumbled forward and tackled his adversary's bare, slat-hard midriff.

The fight then grew desperate. Knees, fists, and elbows battered the Cimmerian, ever thrusting toward his softer and more central parts. His opponent writhed in his grip like a hairless she-panther, fiercely agile and eager to fray at his unguarded limbs with ravening teeth and nails. Though slimmer, she was almost his equal in height and reach; it became a duel of desperate resourcefulness and leverage versus bulky, concentrated power. In one tumultuous instant, the woman flung herself atop him and threw on a headlock, stifling him in the heady taste of wine, sweat, and sea-spray; then he regained control, slowly and deliberately matching knee to knee, arm to arm, and face to dodging, foully cursing face. A fumbling, groping search revealed no hidden weapons . . . and even leather garments, so it seemed, could be torn loose.

Meanwhile, the ship wallowed oarless in the waves. Shouts, cries, and thrashings came from the rowers' benches, with the male voices in particular sounding lusty and frenzied. Conan expected armed women to come and beat him or chain him to the mast at any moment, yet he concentrated on the struggle, determined to make the captain of the *Tormentress* fulfill her promise.

On a balmy island eve well before moonrise—when Djafur's harbor lay dark and still, and only the hardiest gamblers continued their expense of wine and lamp-oil at the Red Hand Inn—Captain Drissa's ship *Tormentress* hove into port. Her gorgon-prow slid silent over the waves, the oars slapping softly in the windless lagoon.

Even so, the ship was marked and recognized by Captain Knulf's night-watch before entering the harbor. Pirate guards were mustered up from sport or sleep to arm themselves and troop out onto the pier, and light, fast boats were righted on the beach and readied for quick launch in case of a skirmish. Even the commissioner himself was roused from his slumbers, though he showed no sign of girding up and venturing forth from his chamber. His pursuit of the fair Turanian captive had been single-minded, keeping him up through weary hours of cajoling and fighting. Only in the last night or two had a dogged silence from the chamber hinted that he had won his way.

"What is it, an attack?" Knulf grumbled through the crack in his barred doorway.

"Most likely not, sir," his lieutenant said. " 'Tis the galley *Tormentress*, with but sixty or so armed women. There is little they can do against our night guard."

"Good, then. Go deal with them. A man who cannot handle a mere fistful of women is a sorry sculp!"

On the dock, a reflector lamp was fired up and its beam directed at the approaching ship. The vessel showed no particular readiness for combat, with both banks of oars stroking evenly and the tall, lean captainess steering astern; the only thing about it that seemed unusual was the bundle hanging suspended from one sailless yardarm. At hailing distance, the bireme feathered oars, gliding in at an oblique, cautious angle to the pier.

"Ahoy the *Tormentress*. Stand off and parley in the name of the Imperial commissioner!" Jalaf Shah's accents were already as stuffy and officious as any Turanian tariff inspector's. "What is your business here? And why do you come at night?"

"Our business is your business, Jalaf," came Santhindrissa's shouted response, "trading and salvage! We come by night to keep from attracting any Turanian warships that may be cruising in your Imperial waters. But on this night we bring an item of trade that should fetch a handsome price from your commander—namely, the rebel pirate Conan!"

Indeed, as the ship glided near, it became obvious that the parcel at the end of the yard was a human figure, suspended motionless by wrists and ankles in a scrap of netting, looking tattered and bloody, yet trim-built and shoulder-heavy enough to be none other than the fugitive captain.

"Do not expect much, Drissa!" In Jalaf Shah, as in any Easterner, the camel-trader ran even deeper than the pirate. "If he is dead or near-dead, Captain Knulf may not want him. Our profit from selling him to Turan would be scant at best, and he must have enough life in him to withstand that journey.''

''Well, then, no matter. I will cut him loose and give him to the sharks.'' Santhindrissa motioned to a rower in the waist, who raised a cutlass over the rope tied to the yardarm.

''Nay, wait! Even his head may be worth something, and I need to make certain it is he, after all. I will offer you a dozen guilders out of my own pocket. 'Tis a ridiculous sum, but we do owe you our thanks for bringing him back.''

''A ridiculous sum, to be sure,'' Santhindrissa countered. ''Three hundred guilders would be fairer.''

''What!'' The lieutenant choked, but managed to convert his consternation to laughter. ''Ah, I see, you jest! Our absolute top price would be fifty guilders. For that much, I would have to consult with my captain, of course.''

''Two fifty, not a coin less!'' The bargaining continued as the bireme drifted closer to the pier, carried in by the softly lapping waves. At Santhindrissa's command, the rowers on the landward side stepped their oars to a vertical position, making a glistening fence against the silver-foiled lamplight; between the palings, the female pirates posed and loitered, idly flirting with the men on the dock. The guards kept their lamps playing along the ship's side to light the women and detect any hostile intent; a few busied themselves with hurling clamshells and offal at the hunched, dangling figure, trying to rouse it to life.

''Hark, Lieutenant, something comes!'' One of the pirates near the end of the pier spoke up uncertainly and was barely heard.

''If I offer more than a hundred guilders for that sorry,

flayed carcass," Jalaf Shah was expounding, "my captain
will have me suffer a like fate . . . yes, what is it, fellow?
By Bel-Dagoth, to arms! We are attacked!"

The guards, long distracted by Santhindrissa's galley,
turned in alarm to find a dozen smaller vessels luffing up
and bumping against the unlit side of the pier. Dhows and
feluccas of the sea-tribes they were, their sails blackened
with soot, their crews darkened likewise, except for the
glint of clenched teeth and staring eyeballs as they hurled
their grappling-hooks and swarmed overside to assault the
pirates. In moments the dock was a frenzy of shouts,
screams, and sword-clashings as the fierce, nimble men of
the isles forced the defenders back toward the inn.

Then a second alarm was raised as the *Tormentress* finally bore into the pier, her side-wales bruising against
the pilings. Oars, raised high at port, swung down to trip
and belabor the defenders, while the pirate women drew
steel and stormed the wharf, keening a blood-chilling war
cry.

The defenders, unready and desperate, battled on both
flanks—when in their midst yet another menace erupted.
The dangling body of Conan, borne in overhead at the end
of the *Tormentress*'s yardarm, came suddenly to life and
twisted free of its bonds. Swinging down heels-over-head,
the half-naked figure turned in midair, thudding feet-first
onto the broad dock with a cutlass raised and swinging.
Before him, pirates scattered or sprawled to the timbers in
a bloody spray. The dock-guards' withdrawal toward shore
became a blind rout, with Conan, Drissa, and the sea-
chieftains leading a frenzied rush at their heels.

Ashore, meanwhile, more stealthy boats had disgorged
crews; fires and skirmishings flared up and down the
beach, even along the street frontage of the town. A halfhearted effort had been made to fortify the inn—but now,

before the swarming rush of pirates and invaders, the low palisade barring approach from the pier was broken down and trampled.

Arriving at the Red Hand's kitchen entry, Conan was able to kick one of the door panels wide, bowling over the sculleryman who tried to close it. Inside, two fleeing pirates turned to fight, but only briefly . . . until their bloody carcasses were flung back lifeless, one across the fish-cutting table, the other into the flaming hearth. The press of attackers from behind thrust Conan relentlessly onward amid a chaos of shouts, clanking pots, and flashing cutlery; shouting a challenge, he came at last to the tavern's inner stair. "Knulf, you blackguard, show yourself and die like a man! Philiope, if you yet live, I come for you!"

Clearing one spiritless defender from the stairs with a slash across the shoulder, and two more with a fierce look and a snarl, he mounted swiftly toward the top. The upper landing was cramped, never built to allow room for swordplay. Yet it would have to serve—for as Conan strode onto the level, the inn-master's door swung open. From it emerged the Vanirman; he bore the heavy scimitar propped on one shoulder, meanwhile stuffing a yellow silk shirttail into a red silken sash with his free hand. Pushing the door shut behind him, he squinted to see who called.

"Amra, you misbegotten cur!" he roared. "I go just now to buy back your miserable head. How much killing do you take, anyway?" Raising the scimitar two-handed, Knulf advanced with a surprisingly light step. "Has no one ever told you," he added, launching the weapon in a powerful swing, "that it does not befit a common pirate to live too long?"

The blow missed Conan's head, shearing instead a fist-sized chunk of hard oak from the baluster. Conan, swinging from a crouch, struck back; but his blade was countered by the scimitar's edge in a parry showing amazing agility on Knulf's part. Then came another whizzing slash, striking yet another splinter from the woodwork. Conan dodged and countered, his movement cramped by the nearness of the stair and rail.

"Thus, and thus!" the stout captain cried, hewing a tight, deadly rune-shape with his heavy sword. "Have you never fought in close quarters? I have killed Vendhyans in the hold of a Zaporoskan river barge. Never will you find a tighter, smellier coffin than that!" Lunging with a quick step, he beat at Conan's cutlass with a ringing blow, forcing his enemy back onto the stair. "You are too oversized and clumpish to fight on shipboard or in civilized haunts," the Vanir taunted. "You should've stuck to your Cimmerian crags and glaciers!"

"I would fight better if I had my own sword, traitorous thief!" Stabbing in under Knulf's guard, Conan menaced his thin-booted ankles and drove him back from the stairtop. "I will have it yet—" he snarled, surging forward to retake the stairsteps he had lost "—and with it my ships, my women, and your steaming entrails!"

"You may get the sword first." Darting forward as if springing a trap, feinting as busily as a spider in a blinding steel web, the stout captain launched a new flurry of tight, two-handed blows. One of them, angled with sly skill, drove Conan's sword aside against a doorjamb; the lighter blade snapped off near the hilt with the impact of the cutlass's heavy, curved point.

Conan, rendered all but weaponless, did the instinctive thing: he hurled himself forward inside the sweep of the cutlass, to seize hold of his enemy and inflict damage at close range. The Vanirman was bear-tough, with scarcely enough fat to cover his slabbed muscle. Even so, the blows of Conan's fist, knees, forehead, and ringed handguard were enough to bear him backward against his chamber door, though he hammered the while at the hard Cimmerian skull with his own hilt.

"Whelp, rascal! You think you can best me in a grapple? Before I was called Knulf Shipbreaker, they knew me as Knulf Mancrusher. Ah . . . ah . . . *arh-ugh!*"

Conan felt the massive body stiffen in his grip; then the stocky Imperial commissioner lurched and stumbled forward. As he did so, he left exposed a double handsbreadth of pointed, red-dripping steel, standing out from a crack in the doorjamb.

"Who is there? Philiope?" Even as the Vanirman sagged to his knees, Conan wrenched the scimitar from his slackening hands and raised it overhead. "Get clear of the door, girl!" Striking near the latch with the stout weapon, he chopped away splinters until the panel flew open—revealing the captive maid, who flew into his arms, sobbing.

"Amra, oh, Amra! He told me you were captured, slain, eaten by sharks! A thousand lies! I knew you would come back . . . but I feared for your life at his hands." She shivered in his clutch. "He was such a brute. When I saw that silk shirt pressed against the door, I knew Ishtar had given me my chance! I struck . . ." She pressed her face against Conan's chest in a torrent of sobs.

"Knulf was a villain among thieves." Holding Philiope close, Conan eyed the fallen captain, who lay motionless in the hall, his back covered by a spreading crimson stain. "Now you are free, do not worry," he told her. "I will find Olivia and rescue her, too."

"Do—do you really intend to do that?" She pulled back from him, her face composing itself through her tears.

"Why should you ask me? Do you know aught of her fate?"

"She went to Turan. I did not think—she may not want to come back." Philiope shook her head, turning her face away in sorrowful uncertainty.

"What is the matter, my lass? Was there trouble between you?" Conan quested after her elusive gaze, tugging her chin toward him with two fingers. "Did Olivia use you harshly in my absence?"

Philiope kept her face averted for a moment, then met his look sternly, her tearstained features set in a solemn frown. "Nothing that a woman might do to me could equal what that pig did," she told him at last, indicating the body in the hall. "I bear Olivia no grudge."

"Good," Conan affirmed. "Because she, like you, stands under my protection, and all Set's minions had better flock to the aid of the man who brings her to harm!" So saying, he swept the noble maid up in his arms and assailed her with kisses.

"A splendid fight, a victory!" voices cried from the common room. Conan arose with Philiope to see whose footsteps sounded on the stair.

"Djafur is ours!" Santhindrissa came into view, backed by several of her pirate women. "The turncoats are scattered, and the place is fallen to the sea-chiefs. There are few losses to speak of among my women, and by tomorrow, my lower oar-deck will be full!" She flashed a glance at Conan. "If you want a permanent place on the *Tormentress*, Captain, this might be your last chance."

Conan laughed heartily. " 'Tis a brave victory all around, then!" He stood with an arm clasping Philiope as the piratess strode onto the landing. "We should keep the men from sacking the town, come dawn. Djafur was our home, and will be again. Make them stop killing the faithless pirates, too. Any survivors are sure to rejoin us."

"I would not worry overly," Drissa replied. "Already this siege is much like any other port leave—hard on the wine and trollops, but wasting only a fair amount of blood." She looked wryly from Conan and Philiope to the body on the floor. "This looks to be a happy domestic scene. You have vanquished our betrayer . . . and with a most cunning swordstroke!"

"It was not my work. Philiope slew him," Conan explained humbly. "In doing so, she saved me a good deal of time."

"A lifetime, it would seem to me." Santhindrissa examined the broken cutlass that still hung at chest level, its blade hammered deep into the wood of the doorjamb. "If you want a place among my crew, young lady, say but a word," she told Philiope.

"Thank you, Drissa, no," the girl muttered, clinging tight to Conan as she watched the swaggering women.

"Well then." The she-pirate left the hacked remains of the hallway behind. "You might take up the business of hotel-keep, a fit occupation for a grieving gentle-widow."

"Aye, there is a happy inspiration." Conan looked at Philiope. "This place had better have an owner, else it will be taken down stick by stick and carried off as driftwood."

"Why, I would imagine perhaps . . ." She looked up to her companion. "If that would allow us to keep company . . ."

"Aye, to be certain," Conan told her. "Djafur will remain my home port. I have plans for the place. Of course Knulf had other belongings, treasure and ships, that Drissa and I will be sharing out—"

"I have no need for more ships. You may keep those," Santhindrissa replied quickly. "One vessel suits our style of living—does it not, girls?" she asked her mates to grunts of assent.

"Then you can take out the difference in treasure, once we break open the rascal's hoard." Conan turned, inspecting the opulent if ill-assorted furnishings of the master bedchamber. "If I get the ships, I will be needing most of the men to crew them. I will want back the crews Knulf stole from me. And there are the gems I brought down from Hyrkania—those too are mine, looted fairly under the law of the Red Brotherhood."

"He keeps his treasure in a safe-hole under the wash-stand," Philiope said.

"Aha, most clever indeed!" Conan strode across the room to the massive, square-framed marble tub, doubtless taken from some Imperial barge. "That would explain why he never used it to bathe himself." Bending his knees and seizing hold, he shifted the heavy fixture aside with a grunt. "Aha, look there." He pointed down at bulging sacks, loose ornaments, and rare vessels of gleaming gold. "Here are the gems," he said, bending and taking up the wooden cask. Opening it and looking inside, he remarked, "One of them is missing."

"Aye, Knulf sent it off to Aghrapur." Philiope knelt beside Conan, placing an arm on his shoulder as she gazed down at the trove.

"Alas." Conan shook his head. "Before letting any of them go, I would have liked to know just what mischief that sorcerer wanted them for."

"Knulf said he would sell the Turanians just one at first, to sharpen their appetite. He sent it off with the prisoners a fortnight ago."

"Prisoners? My men, you mean?"

"Aye." Philiope nodded. "The captured crewmen, the score or so who would not forswear you, he sent to Aghrapur in your stead. He said they were needed for some kind of public ceremony at the palace.''

''Ivanos, that would be! Ferdinald—old Yorkin, too, and the gadfly Diccolo!'' Conan threw his gem cask down into the vat of gold. ''That is too much, it cannot be borne!'' Rising up restless, he strode away across the room, then turned to face his comrades. ''I will have them back here, I tell you,'' he declared, clutching the hilt of the scimitar at his waist. ''My men, my treasure, and everything else that belongs to me!''

Santhindrissa stood facing him with a hand on each of her shipmates' shoulders. ''You mean, snatch them out of Imperial Aghrapur, if they are not yet dead or impaled?'' She twisted her mouth in a smirk at the idea. ''True, I might attempt it for my crewmates—but only if it were possible!''

''Those men are my friends! Rogues they may be, but they were loyal to me! And I need loyal men for what I have in mind.'' Clenching a scarred, scabbed fist in the air before him, Conan stood opposite the women. ''Drissa, I told you why the Turanians wanted Djafur, wanted it badly enough to pay a scoundrel like Knulf as its governor. Now I tell you: I want it for the same reason!''

He turned to Philiope, who stood a little apart from the others. ''Ships have crossed the Vilayet, straight from Aghrapur to these isles. More will be sailing direct instead of using the slow, dangerous southern route. Djafur, this harbor—he scuffed the floor underfoot with his booted heel ''—is the ideal base for raiding such commerce. More, it is the single best port to shelter and provision those ships. It could be a rich city someday, a rival to Aghrapur itself. Kept independent, it may become the seat of a sea-empire!''

Shifting his gaze from one face to another, Conan went

on sketching sea-castles in the air. "To control the waters around Djafur, I need ships . . . enough now, we have a fleet of them! And we have the sea-tribes to scout and bear messages for us." He shook his head. "But for those ships, I also need captains—men or women," he added with a nod to Santhindrissa, "who are loyal to me, or at least honest, and who will do what I say when out of my sight. That loyalty is a precious thing, which has to be nurtured and protected. Loyalty to the death is rare, especially among pirates.

"So you see," he finished, "it would be in your interest, Drissa, to help me rescue my friends. If you join me, more of the sea-chiefs will lend support."

"A raid on Aghrapur?" She shook her head cynically. "Aye, perhaps so, if you can hatch a plan that won't get us all killed."

"And you, Philiope? Are you with me in this?"

"I, Captain Amra?" The young woman moved to his side, embracing him and laying her head against his shoulder. "I will fight beside you, or steer for you . . . pull an oar for you, or captain one of your ships. Because you have given me what I never had before, and that is respect. My days of servitude are over. Now I stand with you in rebellion, and I say death to Turan's empire!"

THIRTEEN
Trial and Torment

Green tropical sunlight filtered through trees and vines high overhead. A glance skyward revealed tangles of jungle branches, cascades of lush, bright foliage, and a dazzling riot of fragrant blossoms, their hues and smells accented by flitting traces of butterfly splendor and monkey musk. Birdsongs chorused on every hand, while from the near distance came the gentle plash of water meandering through stony ponds.

Amid the verdure, on a pliant bench cunningly woven of living, leafing flower-vines, Prince Yezdigerd sat waiting. The thin, fez-hatted prince made an incongruous figure in the jungle shadows, sitting straight upright with his trousered legs crossed, fingers tapping his thigh. He sat restless as if waiting for the trumpeting of the hour from the grand minaret in central Aghrapur—as in fact he was. At his feet a small puppy frolicked, exploring among the exotic shoots set in the flower beds and around the bases of trees in their carefully anchored stone planters. When waiting made the prince thirsty, he had but to snap his fingers; a turbaned servant appeared, fetching him at his request a chilled lime beverage in a gold-chased tumbler.

Moments later, another servingman approached, bowing deeply before him. "Your Majesty, the mage Crotalus." A brisk nod from the prince was enough to make the man turn and disappear from sight.

From a distance, the wizard, his dark face illusory-looking in the flickering forest shadow, wandered slowly toward Yezdigerd's seat. "This place is remarkable," was his first comment. "I regret, O Prince, if I have caused you to wait. Tardiness seems to be a difficulty of mine of late."

"No matter." Yezdigerd spoke without arising or changing his posture, bending only to scratch the neck of the dog at his feet. "I thought my father's hanging garden would be an interesting site for our interview."

"Indeed, it puts me in mind of my native country. Zembabwei is a land of high mountains and vast plains, but on the rainy slopes of those mountains are broad, dense jungles much like this. I have had frequent occasion to visit them; they contain every manner of animal and plant, including many that I have used in my researches." Moving nearer, the tall, dark-robed wizard chose a place beside a man-thick tree and settled there, seating himself easily on the edge of the stone pot.

"I am glad to hear it; these gardens may then have some practical use, rather than being just another expense of gross indulgence—but wait." Raising a hand, Yezdigerd paused in an attitude of listening, counting the rhythmic blasts of a conch horn that came drifting through the trees from the remote distance. "There. By the water clock in the Grand Minaret, it is just the ninth hour. You were not late; rather, more punctual than I, who was early. And I would expect no less, Crotalus, from a man who can row a fleet across the high Vilayet in bold disregard of fog and storm. But go on, tell me more of your origins. When I meet a man of your exceptional powers and faculties, I want to learn further about his upbringing.''

''If you wish it, my Prince.'' Crotalus nodded solemnly. ''By my power, I take it you mean my far-seeing. for that is the greatest of my skills, the one on which the navigational feat you refer to was based. And it is, indeed, rooted in my origins.'' Finding that his sandaled toes had become the object of the puppy's affectionate scrutiny, he bent idly to stroke the animal's back. ''My origins are—'' the mage's rounded, noble features composed in thought ''—far behind me.'' Sitting upright again, he folded his slender hands, which were pale-skinned about the palms and fingernails, in his robed lap.

''At home in Zembabwei, as in most every place, there are many conjurers. They draw their magicks out of the earth, from the plants, stones, and bones of forest and plain. Some of them transfer their souls into the bodies of wild beasts, to fly or stalk through the jungle as shape-changers. Others study at working their will over a distance, as by hexing and hypnotic suggestion. Such was my own childhood training, in the commonplace skills of rural magic.

''Yet when I sent my spirit forth to roam the night wind, it may be that I fared farther than most. Or perhaps I was more keenly alert . . . to the faint resonances of larger sorceries, the more powerful webs and beacons of power emanating from distant places. I came to learn that there were skills and beliefs of a higher order than the crude nature-worship of my fathers. Across the broad world, especially in the great cities and civilizations, mystical power—like Imperial power, if my Prince will permit the comparison—could rise to heights undreamt of in my native land.

"So it was that I turned my back on the common tricks, the hexings and healings, the birthings and deathings, the tribal and religious ceremonies of low, coarse humans. I projected my mystic sight ever farther to find the whole knowledge and truest tokens of power; and, in time, I journeyed far in my body to gather them. In so doing, I gained skills that can make me useful even here in Imperial Aghrapur, the grandest up-piling of wealth and civilization on the map, to men who control the destiny of half the world."

"I see." Yezdigerd nodded in his concise, economical way. "It was your far-seeing, then, and your sensitivity to magical emanations that enabled you to fare across the Vilayet in quest of the missing ingredient for your spell . . . though you have not yet disclosed to me what that spell is to be."

"No indeed, my Prince." Crotalus's smile was polite and confident. " 'Twere better if I keep the exact nature of my enchantment a secret until I am able to put it into effect. Though, I promise you, it will be a formidable contender for the Naval Prize."

"That I continue to accept your word on it shows my faith in your abilities. They soon will be put to the test, now that the charm you sought has come to us via the southern trade routes." Absently the prince stroked the neck hairs of the puppy, which had crawled panting into his lap. "You had already heard of its arrival, I take it?"

Crotalus sat calm, his smile unchanged. "I knew it without hearing," he said.

"I believe you, though it would not have been hard for you to find out, given the ebb and flow of rumor in this port." Reaching into the waist pouch of his western-style pantaloons, he withdrew an object wrapped in a pale silk kerchief. Unrolling the parcel in his hand, he held up the oddly faceted stone before him in a ray of sunlight. "I know that wizards value certain gems, but I have never yet clearly understood why.'' He gazed closely at the gem, perhaps searching for the rumored traces of movement in its amber depths. "It seems strange that such an object, small as it is, should warrant pathfinding voyages across the sea, and exact a price tallied in ships and lives.''

"Quite so. Although that,'' Crotalus pointed out, "is only one of the group of gems I sought.''

"Is it enough for you, then?'' Yezdigerd asked.

"With one gem, I can win the naval contest.'' The wizard eyed the gleaming bauble in the prince's hand, showing admirable restraint in not standing and reaching out for it. "With the whole set, I can do more, much more.''

"Then it would seem that my father's tame initiative to buy out the so-called pirate Brotherhood was not wasted after all.'' Yezdigerd laid the gem back in the kerchief, rewrapping it carefully. "Quite likely we can obtain the rest of them, once you demonstrate their value. But first there is the question of the time remaining. With such notable progress being made on the diplomatic front, the new naval trials cannot be postponed much longer.''

"Time is no obstacle. I need only . . .'' Crotalus paused, then held up two pale-palmed hands with all ten fingers outspread ". . . this many days.''

"How can that be? Initially you requested a month and more after your return from sea.'' Yezdigerd finally held out the wrapped gem, causing the mage to arise from his seat.

"My task is simplified for the present, having only one stone to work with.'' Crotalus bowed graciously as he accepted the packet, which disappeared promptly into the folds of his dark robe. "Time, in any case, is not necessarily fixed and unvarying. It is mutable, subject to change . . . how can I express it?'' His eyes fell on the puppy panting in its master's lap. "That dog, O Prince . . . is it dear to you?''

Frowning at the question, Yezdigerd shrugged. "No, it is merely one of the palace pets. It is a good breed, but there are plenty others of its ilk. Do you mean to work an enchantment on it?" He gazed up into the wizard's somber, intent countenance. "I am ready to make small sacrifices to observe lessons of science."

Silently Crotalus seated himself on the bench beside Yezdigerd. Taking the puppy out of the prince's lap, he set it in his own. With deft hands, he stroked the small creature—or rather, he moved his fingertips at a distance without actually touching the dog, as if enfolding it in some kind of tangible but invisible barrier. The animal sat contented, with mouth open and tongue hanging slack, occasionally cocking its head as its eyes followed the puzzling orbits of the wizard's hands.

"You can see, O Prince, already it begins to age."

Yezdigerd looked closer. Indeed, a subtle change had begun to come over the beast. Its bearing was now more sedate and dignified, and its physical proportions did seem subtly altered. As the spell took hold, the dog did not grow; nor, indeed, did it become a miniature replica of a graceful adult hound, with limbs attenuated and elongated. As the changes progressed, the pup remained an odd sort of hybrid: still blunt-pawed and round-bodied, but with a seeming of maturity.

"Size as well as time are subject to the envelope of my will." Crotalus continued his mystical passes—more broadly and smoothly now, like a sculptor imparting a final rounding to his clay. "In this exceedingly simple case, since there is no growth, and no need to let the subject eat and drink, years can be compressed into mere moments. As you see, the respirations are not even accelerated."

True, the animal sat calm. Even so, there was a melancholy, questioning look in the dog's eyes as it gazed up from Crotalus to the prince. Feeling itself age, it may have sensed that something intangible and precious was being taken away. Its bearing was definitely more weary and sedate; the creature's breaths came more heavily, and its coat grew out coarser, lacking the former sheen of health. Now gray tinges sprouted around the dog's neck and whiskers, like winter frost on a dying stump. With an exhausted sigh, the strange, half-developed creature settled its blunt, puppyish head wearily on the sorcerer's knee.

"The process can go on and on, or be halted," Crotalus explained, ceasing his hand motions. "It does not have to end with the life of the subject."

Interested, Prince Yezdigerd reached down to stroke the dog. He gave a start at finding the animal inert and cool to his touch. It had been reduced to a mere lifeless mummy, rapidly stiffening and desiccating. The skin of its neck pelt tore slightly as he jerked his hand away.

With a gentle laugh, Crotalus brushed the flaking carcass from his lap into a flower bed. "So you see, O Prince, time is of no great importance to me . . . or should I say, of no great moment? Ten days will suffice for the physical processes I require, assuming that ship construction will continue smoothly."

"Ten days then, no more. I will announce a date for the sea-trials this midday." The prince's manner hinted at a new-found respect for the wizard, also at new caution. "I assume the facilities assigned to you by the Admiralty are sufficient?"

"Yes, though I will need a full crew of slaves or prisoners, a hundred men at least. Their ability, even their physical health, is of no great matter to me—" here the dignified Crotalus shot a sly glance to his ruler "—since they are likely to be expended in the labor."

"I understand . . . as much as I need to. It will be done." Yezdigerd arose briskly from his viny seat. "Crotalus, I depend on you to produce, ah, tangible results. So far, this undertaking, and the performance of the two highly promising candidates I supported, have been a disappointment to me. I had begun to doubt the merit of the idea . . . but your demonstration here today reassures me."

He extended a hand and after the merest hesitation, laid it on the robed magician's shoulder. "Whatever arcane spell you mean to use to transform that gem into naval propulsion, proceed with it. At this moment you are my best, brightest hope."

The announcement of the new date for judging the contest was the focus of widespread attention. This second spectacle was to be far grander than the first, with space on the harbor mole and mudflats offered free to the general populace, in addition to the invitations sent to high-ranking courtiers for choice places of vantage in the Navy Yards.

A public holiday was declared, with the added attraction of real, living pirates: captives brought from the Eastern Vilayet, to be condemned and done to death by public torments, with crowd participation welcomed. It was rumored that the arch-criminal Amra himself was to be among them; in any case, no city householder could afford to pass up such a memorable event, neither for its promise of boon festivity and fellowship, nor for the edification and warning of wives, slaves, and children.

It could be asked—and in some circles, it most emphatically was—why, after the unmitigated disaster of the first seatrials, such a great and public event was being made of the follow-up? The answers were various, and not necessarily consistent with each other: Emperor Yildiz, it was whispered, grew feebleminded, whether from overindulgence in wine or from the gassy, sickly humours of his mercury bed; consequently, there were those in high advisory positions who did not mind urging him along a disastrous course for the sake of undermining his power. Or, alternatively, sly Yildiz knew that his son Yezdigerd's name was the one linked primarily in the public mind to the naval contest. The canny old emperor did not begrudge a flagrant expense of wealth and state prestige to humble his overweening child; so he publicized the event in the positive hope that it would result in another laughable failure. Yezdigerd, for his part, sought a more public triumph to enhance his reputation, and so the stakes were raised on both sides.

For Alaph the alchemist, the prospect of another judging rekindled old hopes for success in the competition; it renewed his fears as well, in the light of previous disasters. Regarding the promised execution of pirates, Alaph had always dreaded such displays because of a fundamentally squeamish nature—though generally he had been forced to attend the gatherings regardless, to take advantage of the booming trade in buns. Now his bakery commerce was delegated to others; indeed, it throve better unburdened by the demands of his steam-demons. The alchemist, except for occasional cursory supervision of his bakers, was left to devote all of his worry to the contest.

His notions about the value of his work had grown broader and clearer during his recent labors. Mastery of the water-spirits was a great power, obviously; also it was a great risk, one requiring nerve and courage to sustain. If an adept was willing to face death and horrible burns, great rewards might be sought, such as the power to set steam-demons to work rowing oared galleys. Alaph had conceived a way this might be done by means of a heavy, greased beam, pushed forward in a bronze box by a rush of living steam, then pushed backward again from the far end by the shuttling of the racing *djinni* through pipes and valves into another similar box. Such a back-and-forth motion could easily be used to swing oars, even on existing ships refitted to its demands. It would limit the crew requirements to three or four men, enough to work the rudder, feed the fire, maintain pressure in the coffin-boiler and release any excess. It would also be necessary to vary the bite of the oars in the water on port and starboard sides by direction of the steersman.

A heady idea, this, and more elaborate than his original one of rear-facing jets. Yet it seemed crucial to keep the demons confined as long as possible to get them to do useful work. Alaph had ordered more metal and artisans from the Navy Yard for the project, and set to work overtime on it.

Another idea along the same line was the steam ram. Oarships frequently fenced and chased, as every Turanian knew, to achieve a successful ram, with victory often determined by a deft turn at close quarters or a last supreme effort at the oars. Accordingly, Alaph saw promise in a device that might be fitted to bow, stern, or both, once again at the end of a long wooden beam butted inside a metal-clad box. When, at the proper moment, steam-devils were loosed into the box, the bronze-sheathed ram must necessarily shoot forth through the water, spearing or smashing the enemy vessel from an unexpected distance.

Already Alaph had assigned a team of artisans to the design. Yet of late he found himself teased by a further thought: Why must the ram stop at all once it was hurled at the target? Might it not be freed of the ship entirely, to speed home to the enemy like a waterborne lance or catapult-ball? Was there some way the fevered *djinni* could be contained inside the projectile, working to propel it though water, even through sky?

Alaph's sounding board for such speculations was Mustafar, his fellow contestant. Countless times the genial ship-armorer had proposed physical means to enable him to try to implement one of his farfetched ideas. While Alaph's suggestions to his friend had less immediate practical value, Mustafar seemed to prize them as pointing out subjects for future inquiry.

"With our combined skill and inventiveness," the armorer boasted, "there is little doubt that we will corner the Naval Prize between us. I care nothing for the mumbo jumbo, spells, and star-readings of our opponents; I do not think Yezdigerd will either, in the final reckoning." The mustached draftsman favored Alaph with one of his confident smiles. "At all events, my craftsmanship assures me a well-paid place here at the Navy Yard. The real profit in this business lies in the fitting-out of ships. So even if I do not win the golden talents, I will not overmuch mind."

The occasion for their talk was an informal pretesting of several of the contest schemes. Alaph was there surveying his new steam-coffin, its polished-bronze rectangle gleaming from the stern of a low, trim galley. The redesigned boiler was to be heated by Mustafar's liquid pitch, carried through a feedpipe from a keg kept safe in the bows. The more intricate mechanics of Alaph's invention were not yet installed, but he hoped first to test this improved sarcophagus for strength and leakage.

Mustafar, for his part, stood with the alchemist on the low stone quay, readying his catapult and waiting for the waterway to clear. The machine was a standard one, not one of his rapid-fire or heavy, dart-shooting models. But he intended to use it in a novel way, to hurl an exploding firepot that would burst on the water, spreading flames as a floating barrier to deter ships from approaching. Such a device, mounted on a light merchant vessel, could conceivably be a positive deterrent to piracy. Had Alaph not liked and admired the armorer so, he might have been painfully envious of his cleverness.

"These horsetail binding-springs are blasted troublesome," the black-mustached craftsman complained, loosening pegs on the catapult frame. "They react to the sea's damp and to the sun's heat, and must be tuned daily. Nor can they be left long at full tautness, lest they stretch out of shape. I have often thought of using some harder substance, such as bone or metal, to draw the cable."

"You will have plenty of time, anyway," was Alaph's comment. "It will be noon before Tambur Pasha's waterchariot is clear of the harbor."

He referred to the astrologer's latest experiment in automotion, a small galley powered by two water-wheels instead of oars. The wheels, suspended over each side of the ship into the water, resembled oversized chariot wheels, but with a couple of differences. The rims, for one thing, were fitted with projecting wooden flanges; these were meant to push at the water like oar blades once the wheels were turning. Alaph found this idea interesting, thinking of how it might be applied to his own devices; but then, there would not·be time to work up such a design for the contest.

As another peculiarity, the spokes of the wheels were curved, running out straight from the hubs but intersecting the rims at a flat angle. Around each of these spokes was attached a sliding lead weight. This, as Alaph heard it explained, accomplished the following self-evident effect: On the ascending side of the wheel, the weights slid in close to the hub, and so exerted very little leverage. But on the descending side, the same weights slid out to the wheel-rim and so bore down more heavily on the spokes. Therefore it must happen that, with the falling side in effect heavier than the rising side, the wheel would keep turning of its own accord. The paddles would push water, and the craft would move forward without need of man-power, providing a form of self-perpetuating motion.

The idea seemed to Alaph almost too good to be true. So it proved in practice, out in the water, since the craft would not seem to gain any speed. The astrologer stood in the stern, working hard with his steering-oar to encourage forward motion across the quiet bay. The wheels creaked and turned sluggishly, but it was unclear whether this was a cause or a consequence of the craft's slow drifting—aided, perhaps, by the efforts of the two slaves in the waist who had been assigned to grease the lead weights and keep them sliding.

"When will that fat fool give up?" Mustafar muttered. "As many times as the dull-brained idea has failed on land, why should he think it would work any better at sea? Ah, there at last, he orders his slaves to use their oars. At least he was not fool enough to leave them ashore!"

"You will have longer to wait," Alaph observed, "if he is not out of the way before Zalbuvulus sets forth."

The two of them turned to the adjacent dock, where the Corinthian inventor even then herded his oar-crew out to their waiting galley. As Alaph watched, he felt a cold shifting in his vitals: There was something of nightmare in this scene. Whatever dark preparation the sour philosopher had put his men through this time, it had left them scarcely men.

The rowers slunk and scuttled pitifully, straggling along the pier like no crew of healthy slaves the alchemist had ever seen. Their aspect as they hurried by was that of cowed, broken things cringing away from the lash . . . even though their stern, frowning commander carried none. As they scuttled past, they gave off a strange, hoarse rasping or chattering, though none of their lips appeared to move. All of them, eerily enough, had become hunchbacks. Each man, under his coarse neck-to-knee robe, slouched along with spine or shoulder sharply elevated. Alaph recalled none of them having shown this defect before. Their necks now hung forward unnaturally, looking red and painfully lacerated. In all, the deformities were worse than abnormal; rather, they appeared supernatural in origin. Several times the alchemist thought he saw the odd-shaped lumps *moving* underneath the loose fabric of the robes, and once, where a tear in the coarse stuff shifted, he saw eyes peering out—luminous eyes set in a squat, fiendish face.

"Fie, a blight on all sorcerers!" Mustafar swore hoarsely in his friend's ear. "Of all the dark conjurings men stoop to, this western vice of philosophy must be the worst!"

"He has saddled them with some kind of incubi," Alaph marveled, "demons that bite and claw at them." He watched the last of the hurrying slaves scurry into the ship before their stern-faced master.

"Aye. Each man with a personal imp to shriek and chatter in his ear—when to lift oars, when to stroke, when to puke and when to die!" The armorer cursed again. "I would be doing them all a favor if I unleashed my weapon now and filled up their galley with cleansing fire!"

"Nay, do not say such things," Alaph soothed, putting a restraining hand on Mustafar's knotty shoulder. "With any luck, they will be out of the way soon."

But fortune did not make matters easy. The galley, once orders were given and the drumbeat commenced, set out at a clumsy, halting pace. Some oar blades skipped over water and clashed against one another awkwardly, while others dug in deeply, stroking at a too-frantic pace. The result was forward motion of an erratic kind—made far worse, so it seemed, by the consequences of failure, which included guttural, rasping admonitions in an alien tongue and high-pitched, agonized screaming. As one oar section and then another faltered and recovered, the ship meandered out toward the river channel in a pitiful fashion, the shrieks and pleadings of its crew gradually fading.

Alaph, though leg-weak from the spectacle, consented to test his ship. "Mine is a simple trial anyway, merely to fire the coffin. I do not intend to go cruising about the harbor and delay your test further."

He made sure to pole the craft a fair distance from the quay, to avoid innocent deaths in the event of an explosion. Then he ordered his slave in the bows to open the tap and start the trickle of flammable humours. He struck flint and steel into the trough himself, braving the scorching blast as the fumes ignited. Once burning, the flame stayed bright and even, Alaph having already determined that it would not follow the pipe forward to the supply kegs. He waited. It was not long before the bronze sarcophagus began to tick and redden with heat and the restlessness of the trapped demons.

When the flat surfaces of the coffin began to bulge, Alaph vented some of the elementals, first through a pipe he had attached astern below the waterline, then through another above. The experiment showed what he should have guessed earlier: The pipes shrieked and spurted furiously, sending forth jets of dissipating vapor, but they did not provide any forward motion. Once free, the alchemist saw, the steam-demons would not willingly work for him. It was necessary to keep them contained, teasing them with the promise of freedom . . . as long as one did not tease and delay too long.

To mark his position in the water, he watched the nearby quay. There Mustafar was ready with his catapult, Zalbuvulus's demon-ridden craft having by now cleared the harbor. Then at once the alchemist noticed something sinister.

An oily, black substance dripped from the gutters at the side of the quay, pooling on the surface of the water. His eye followed the stain upslope to the wagon where Mustafar's kegs of flammable supplies waited, well back from the catapult. He glimpsed furtive movement about the cart; one or more of the kegs must have tipped or ruptured, sending a stream of dark liquid down to the waterside, where the armorer and his slaves made ready to strike fire for the weapon test.

"Mustafar! Watch out!" Over the shrill noise of the steam vent, his cry went unheard. "Cut off the fuel!" Motioning frantically to his slave in the bows, Alaph bent and twisted shut the steam valve astern, causing the plaintive soughing to die out. Standing and drawing new breath to shout, he saw a flame wink to life on the pier—wink and blossom, then expand to a giant, black-maned fire-demon. The hungry beast swallowed the quay in an instant and ran its greedy tongue up to the supply wagon to find a fresh feast there.

Alaph's vessel survived unharmed, though it had rocked in the water with the force of the blast, and its maker's eyebrows had been singed away by the fire-*djinn*'s ferocious breath. Of Mustafar, his helpers, and his brave ideas, nothing remained after the holocaust but char and bone-ash.

No clue was found, either, as to how the mishap had occurred. Some called it the inevitable price of trafficking with fire elementals. But Alaph was certain it had been sabotage. He even thought of expressing his belief to the Admiralty officials. But then the tragedy was forgotten in the excitement over the appearance of the pirate fleet.

FOURTEEN
The Scented Trap

The fleet that rowed into the naval harbor at Aghrapur and boldly dropped anchor was a motley, rugged-looking assemblage. There were four biremes, two-deckers of the largest type used by the eastern pirate bands, all but the one of them ill-maintained and undermanned; a good half-dozen galliots and oar-cruisers of a similar size; a trim penteconter, still in black Imperial paint, closely resembling the warship lost by the wizard Crotalus to the pirates; and a score or more of smaller sail- and oarships, the dhows and feluccas common to eastern sea-islanders and coastal raiders.

Disreputable and treacherous as these intruders seemed, they were not attacked by the harbor catapult batteries or rammed by Imperial guardships—because, after all, even a sizable pirate fleet could scarcely be seen as a danger to the empire, stopping together here in the very hornet's-hive of Imperial naval power.

Furthermore, above the skull and crossed-saber flag of the pirate Brotherhood, the largest bireme flew the blue pennant of a Turanian military governor. A canopy had been raised on the flagship's afterdeck, concealing whatever official passengers the vessel carried. But in view of the negotiations currently underway with the trans-Vilayet islanders, it was deemed prudent to apprise Emperor Yildiz of the matter before any action was taken.

The emperor, as it happened, was in no hurry to resolve the mysterious arrival. Yildiz saw the foreign fleet as a public curiosity and a highly fortuitous embellishment to the impending naval spectacle. He expressed his hope—which, in high court circles, was tantamount to a command—that any agreement or punishment would be deferred for several days, so that the result might be shown off as a part of the naval pageant.

Thus it transpired that a small, lightly-manned Admiralty launch was the only vessel to respond to the pirate invasion. The boat's officer steered alongside the flagship and, when refused permission to board, did not press the matter. Instead, he conducted a polite colloquy over the bireme's rail with a tall, hawk-nosed, leather-clad female who claimed to be its captain.

With utmost courtesy she was invited to assemble a shore party and meet with Admiralty officials later that day for an early supper at the palace. She replied that Emperor Yildiz and his entourage were equally welcome aboard her galley, the *Tormentress*, to share her shipmates' common fare. In the end they agreed to meet on mutually acceptable ground, or rather, sea, in the open harbor. Accordingly, an Imperial reception barge was fitted out, victualled, and poled into place; that evening, on its broad deck, several of the more substantial pirates and sea-chiefs were wined and dined royally.

Meanwhile, Aghrapur seethed with rumor and with deli-
cious, half-serious dread of the pirates. Townspeople
thronged the public sections of wharf from which the ragtag
fleet could be seen, while private boats cruised the harbor
for a closer look. Some of these were dangerously overbur-
dened with sightseers, peddlers, and ladies of pleasure, offering a wide range of goods and services for pirate gold;
most of them were turned away by swift Imperial cutters
charged with preventing the spread of piracy and other social
ills. By Admiralty order, yellow quarantine flags were run
up on buoys and picket-boats stationed around the intruders,
proclaiming that no traffic would be allowed between shore
and ships.

Yet it was well known that for a modest bribe, customs
restrictions could be ignored. Consequently, during the ensuing days, ill-gotten goods were traded and information was
sold; pirates were entertained in villas and disreputable
houses ashore, and various outcasts and unfortunates who
found themselves at odds with the civic ideals of the Imperial
capital ventured aboard the pirate scows, many of them to
stay.

In the council rooms of the Imperial Palace, these and
related matters were topics of earnest debate. Seated before
the emperor and his advisers, Prince Yezdigerd declared,
"Even if they sail under your Turanian flag, Father, they are
still pirates. How can we be sure they even have the gems
with them? Or the captive Amra? They have yet to allow us
a glimpse of him, nor is there any sign of Captain Knulf, the
pirate leader who first accepted your commission."

"If I may make an observation . . ." Nephet Ali, always
cautious at these meetings, spoke from his seat below the
emperor's dais, where Yildiz lounged on a throne draped by
four harem-nymphs. "It seems unlikely that they would sail
across the Vilayet, into the very shadow of our seapower,

without bringing along the items we require. Clearly they seek our tolerance, and have offered us these things to cement their relations with the Turanian Empire.''

''Offered, indeed!'' Ninshub, the finance minister, obviously felt no compunction in challenging his old rival, the Imperial engineer. ''From the hints they have dropped, there bodes to be hard bargaining ahead. The prices they want to wring out of us are nothing short of piracy!''

''Even so.'' The emperor's mild voice caused both counselors, as well as his concubines, to turn to him respectfully. ''They themselves, and their fleet and possessions, are now in *our* possession. So you may, I suggest, dicker and barter freely without overmuch fear.''

''If you mean,'' Prince Yezdigerd addressed his father, ''that we will seize them, and seize their stolen ships and belongings, and put each and every one of them to the sword, torch, or rope regardless of any Imperial commissions or bargainings—why then, I heartily agree!'' The young noble smiled severely about the room, a look that Nephet Ali found keenly statesmanlike. ''My only question is, why postpone matters? Why allow these scoundrels to idle in port and do one further day's damage to our prestige? Strike now, at once, and let there be an end to it.''

Yildiz smiled benignly on his son, meanwhile stroking the plump knee of a houri who was flung across his lap. ''I accept your views, Yezdigerd. I accept them as the overeager, impetuous counsel of youth. To the contrary, let me point out that of all the varied array of pirate ships before us, we do not know which ship or ships contain the treasure and our captive. In the forced action you suggest, it would be entirely possible to lose both. How much better to have them safely in our grasp before attacking, and risk losing only gold.'' He waved a hand as if to show the simplicity of the point. ''More important is the use we plan to make of the pirates in the impending festivities. To this end, Ninshub—" he turned to his finance minister "—I would advise balking and stalling, holding open your negotiations till the last possible moment. Do not be overly willing to pay out gold, lest some of the knaves become suspicious and try to flee."

"With your permission, Majesty . . ." Ninshub nodded in acceptance of the sound advice, speaking now with a respectful air ". . . how important is it that we secure this Amra, anyway? Would not any burly rogue on the quarterer's block or impaler's spike serve us just as well?"

"Why, Ninshub, I am surprised that you, my Imperial treasurer, would ask such a thing! Are you not, Isdra? Aspasia?" he echoed for rhetorical effect to his fat nymphets. "You question the very basis of our Imperial honesty and fair dealing." Whether the emperor's amazement was genuine or feigned was the kind of uncertainty that Nephet Ali always found it hazardous to wonder about in Yildiz's presence. "For one thing, this Amra is a bold and rebellious rogue, who has not even troubled to hide or disguise his piracies. That is the most dangerous kind of outlawry, a political threat that must be wiped out. And it must be done with enough certainty to satisfy the public. If he should escape, or if any other pirate still lives who can lay claim to his name . . ." The emperor shook his head, frowning.

"You see, it is the name that is dangerous, because of the folk myths and legends such defiant acts nourish. The man and the name must be destroyed with equal public certainty. That is the bond of truthfulness an emperor owes his subjects." Yildiz glanced across to his son. "Fortunately, we have at least one reliable witness, Khalid Abdal, who has served as our agent in bringing this Amra to ground. He can identify him credibly, even if they are trying to palm off some false prisoner on us. These other pirates, too, may acknowledge him publicly once they are up for punishment. If we let any live, it will be as a sign of our mercy and our good-faith wish to stabilize the Eastern Vilayet.''

"But, Your Majesty . . ." Nephet Ali finally spoke up, couching his advice in a suitably meek, questioning tone. "Do I understand that you mean to arrest these pirates anyway, and give them to the mob for slaughter on the day of the sea-trials?" The engineer shook his head in eloquent regret. "I fear that such an act of naked force might not gain the approval of your subjects, or enlist their full cooperation, even at public mayhem. May I point out that their reception of these foreigners in Aghrapur has not been entirely hostile?"

He barely blinked aside to Yezdigerd and Ninshub as he spoke, assuming that they would not support his views. "There is always in the common mind some sympathy for the underling, some slight resentment at the grip of total power . . ."

"Exactly." Yildiz nodded freely, tickling the soft neck of his nearest wife. "They like a fair fight, or at least an appearance of fairness. As I do." He smiled complacently around the company. "That is why I had in mind, not a trap or a summary arrest, but something more along the lines of a sea-battle."

"A battle here in Aghrapur's harbor?" It was Yezdigerd who took the bait; he was, after all, the least-seasoned Imperial counselor present. "But would the pirate scum even fight against the home fleet? There is no semblance of fairness in that."

"True again." Yildiz smiled happily from his trollops to his counselors. "Of course we can always goad them to fight or flee, by some pretext if necessary. But it will be a fair match only if they face a limited foe, such as your contest ships—the ones that you experts have, after all, commissioned to destroy the Vilayet pirates."

Yezdigerd, for once at a loss, knit his dark brows in surprise. "You mean, send our ships in the sea-trials against the pirate fleet?"

The emperor laughed boisterously. "Yes, precisely, to sink the invaders and kill or enslave their traitorous crews! What better tryout could there be for a warship? What better way to test the value of my young son's ideas, and prove their value conclusively to the public? The crowds will love such a contest. Let it be so!"

Aboard one of the galleys—though not the flagship, lest they be caught too easily in a treacherous attack—the pirate captains parleyed. Santhindrissa, who had reluctantly taken on the role of spokeswoman before Yildiz's officers, voiced her bitter contempt.

"These Imperial maggots, swathed in silk like the worms they are, can never be trusted! It takes a rascal as perfidious as Knulf himself to deal with such and wiggle through the tangled skeins of their courtly ways. An honest pirate should never hope to outwit them." She paced the canvas-shaded planks and whirled, restless in the narrow confines, her hard, high sandals clashing in resentment against the scarcely rocking deck. "They tease and toy with us here, knowing that we face overwhelming odds."

She paced most likely to keep the air moving against the lean, muscular flesh, bare except for the leather-guarded areas of breasts and groin, for it was hot and close under the deck canopy. "Whenever the whim strikes, they will attack; then all their pledges and bargainings will have no more substance than the foam that drools over the waves."

Conan, sitting perched on the starboard rail where the overhang of the tent let in a cool sea-draft, answered calmly. "Our best approach is still the one we agreed on. Delay them and hold out for the best price. Then sell me ashore, or else and a raiding party to free our brothers. When the jailbreak comes, the whole harbor will be thrown into confusion, and we can safely escape.''

"But why delay?" Santhindrissa wheeled on Conan fiercely, yet impersonally in her way, betraying no real sign that they had been lovers. "It was your notion to sail down Yildiz's throat and snatch the prisoners from his crop—your poor, suffering pirate brethren, and your former mistress as well!" Angrily she turned, pacing toward the quarterdeck rail. "Therefore act without delay, and shorten our stay in these treacherous waters. Why idle here, when in just two days your friends will be executed . . . and us with them, I half believe, if smug Yildiz has his way!"

"Captain, you speak unfairly to Amra." From her bench-seat beside Conan, Philiope came to her protector's aid. "You give him no credit for good sense. What of his feat of sea-manship?" She stirred indignantly in her light, brief tunic, well suited to the day's heat. "Was it not a great triumph for him to lead us here, straight across the Vilayet from Aetolia to Aghrapur, without need of any landfalls on the way?"

"The best speed, skill, and luck at navigation are a fault," the captainess replied acidly, "if they bring a ship or a fleet into reckless danger."

"Have patience, Drissa." Conan leaned against the stern-post, unperturbed by the she-captain's nervous catlike wrath. "I have sent spies ashore; tonight I go myself to scout the lay of the land." He glanced to the others present—the sea-chief Hrandulf, and the former lieutenant, Jalaf Shah, who had gained the command of Knulf's flagship. "By taking our time, we force their price upward; just remember to sell them me, but not the jewels. As long as they want the gems but do not know where to lay hands on them, they dare not attack." He gestured at the motley fleet lying at anchor beyond the rail. "We would do better to sell the baubles back to the Hyrkanians, anyway. Likely, on hearing of our trip to Turan, they will offer us an emperor's ransom."

"Your plan may be sound—" Hrandulf spoke in gruff islander's accents from his place on the port rail "—if you can in truth escape, empty the Imperial prison, and rejoin our fleet. But if you fail, do not expect us to storm ashore and free you!"

"I see no difficulty in it." Conan shrugged. "I and a half-dozen picked rogues, sent ashore with hidden keys to our shackles, should easily be able to overcome our guards. Then, with the aid of our pirate brothers, we steal a boat . . . we owe it to them at least to try."

"Fine, try, but do not fail." Santhindrissa eyed him menacingly. "Do it soon or my ship, for one, will be gone."

Ashore, meanwhile, rumors stalked the port concerning the pirates' role in the impending sea-trials. It was whispered that companies of Imperial marines would be placed aboard the contest ships—whether for a mock battle or a real one, whether against pirates or against each other, none could say. Then word was passed to Alaph through Nephet Ali, unequivocally: Be ready to fight the sea-marauders.

The bun-maker regarded the prospect with an admixture of dread and mournful resignation. How far this competition had progressed . . . from an exuberant, lighthearted chance at wealth and fame to a grim, mortal combat. The person to consult about fitting out a fighting ship would have been brave Mustafar . . . had he not been burnt to cinders in the dock fire that struck so swiftly and suspiciously.

Now Alaph ventured but seldom outside his shed, having requested Admiralty guards to circle the place. He watched constantly for saboteurs and assassins, whom he feared would be sent by his competitors or one of their shadowy backers at court. Admiral Quub was said to be outraged that his personal candidate for the prize had been killed. Yet no crime had been publicly charged.

In part to silence the inner pleadings of anguish and remorse, Alaph worked day and night to perfect his experimental craft. His smiths and joiners toiled likewise without sleep. As a result, more of them suffered cruel burns and injuries while performing the unfamiliar and highly advanced processes he required. But as the bright, glowing metal components were hoisted hot from the forge and bolted into the ship's timber belly, it became obvious that something very formidable was taking shape. The task gradually assumed a life of its own. Like the intricate ritual movements of a high temple dance, it made the doubts and pangs of mortal life seem petty and inconsequential by comparison.

In Tambur Pasha's shed farther down the wharf, a similar last-minute exhilaration seemed to have taken hold. There issued from the place a din of pounding and scraping that rivaled Alaph's. Whether the astrologer's scheme could avail him anything was still unclear, but his attitude was definitely superior to the alchemist's.

By contrast with those two, the trireme shed assigned to Zalbuvulus loomed dark and silent—as much so as Mustafar's beside it, which now stood deserted. On the night of the fire, when the Corinthian philosopher's crew had rowed him back from a second jerky, tragicomedic voyage through the harbor, there had been fierce wrath and retribution—as evidenced by shouts, wails, and panicked shrieks issuing from the barnlike building housing the slaves. Since then, all had been quiet . . . though Zalbuvulus, glimpsed on the dock, looked less grim than usual. He arched his gray eyebrows and mustache less fiercely, so it was said, and expressed no wish to withdraw his ship from the sea-trials.

The other remaining contestant, the far-seeing Crotalus, was lodged in a timber-walled compound across the marshy estuary, far from the bustle of the wharves. His recent mission in search of magical gems, it was now said, had succeeded at least in part. The nature of his plan for naval improvement remained a mystery, but evidently his patron, Prince Yezdigerd, had faith in his powers.

To Alaph's mind, admittedly unschooled and untraveled, the wizard's use of gems suggested sorcery of the most arcane sort. As far as he could speculate, Crotalus's magicks might produce any conceivable result: a means of controlling wind and weather, perhaps, or an all-seeing glass in which to find enemies, or a curse to smite his rivals with ill luck or bench-blisters. Whatever it was, rumor said, it was dire, and its effects had to be tested on mortals, as the fate of the Zembabwan's slave-laborers proved.

They were Zaporoskans, so word had it, taken captive in some punitive expedition across the Vilayet. Small-built herdsmen, clannish and untrained in any civilized work, they spoke a jabbering language that no one in Aghrapur understood, and so could be directed only by pantomime and by punishment. Whether Crotalus took them on as shipbuilders, rowers, or both, was never certain. It had seemed likely that they were meant to be magically trained or ensorceled like Zalbuvulus's crew. But whatever their duty, it was evidently not an easy or pleasant one; dock guards told of desperate escapees caught fleeing through the swamp in a frenzy of fear, babbling and gesturing incomprehensibly before they were dragged back to their sorcerous master.

Crotalus's preparations sounded obscure and formidable. Heartless, as well—but then, the alchemist had found it necessary to harden himself to suffering. If his own experiment should fail, it would doubtless wreak fiery havoc and cost lives, his own included. Whereas if it should succeed, it would destroy many more lives: first those of the hapless pirates in the harbor, then among countless enemies of the

Turanian Empire all across the whole length and breadth of the Vilayet. Mortal happiness, so it appeared, was a vanishingly small part of the prospect.

Hooves scuffed and grated on the cobbles of the dark suburban lane. Elm trees, their limbs pollarded to keep them well clear of the tops of roadside walls, rose like bulbous-headed sentinels against the stars. Two black horses and their hooded riders, lacking a lamp, moved forward at a slow, careful walk, winding between the estates and villas of the rich. The hardware of both horsemen's saddles was muffled, and the pair exchanged no word.

Here on the outskirts of Aghrapur, near the center of the world's most stable and powerful domain, peasant uprisings and bandit raids had in recent centuries been rare. Here it was no longer seen as necessary for every important inhabitant to shelter inside a castle or behind a city's massive battlements. Prosperous gentry might safely enjoy their wealth in the open country, as long as they could afford the expense of a middling-sized wall, a locking gate, and guards or watchdogs to secure the premises. Such measures sufficed to keep out the occasional starving members of the landless classes who turned to theft. Local marauders, after all, generally acted furtively or on impulse, and then but singly or in small groups. The patrols of richly groomed Imperial cavalry stationed in the outlying hamlets were more than sufficient to apprehend and punish most such malefactors.

The two riders followed along a high wall, whose polished-marble face silhouetted their cloaked forms in dim, reflected starlight. The wall led them to a gate, a double grating of forged iron. Its black, beaten spear-points thrust some way above the taller rider's head, pointing up toward unwinking stars. There was no gate house, and the small, open kiosk flanking the inner side of the entry was, on close inspection, vacant. The gate's latch was a long bar that extended inside the kiosk, out of sight.

Reining to a near stop, the two edged their mounts alongside the gate, whose dark recess served to conceal them from view at any great distance. They whispered there a moment, with heads bent together; then the taller rider handed his reins to his companion. Standing in the stirrups, he set a foot in the seat of the saddle and climbed to the upper crossbar of the gate.

"I will return this way," his voice murmured, resonant though muted. "Wait here, but do not stay beyond moonrise."

Instead of trying to climb across the spear-points, he hooked a leg inside the iron trellis, reached up and grasped one of the poles two-handed just beneath its flattened blade. Straining, with the faintest creak of metal but without any groan or exhalation, he bent the shaft horizontal. After stretching his shoulders under his cloak, he reached up once again and with a slow, patient effort, bent a second bar similarly. Drawing himself up and stepping through the gap he had made, he dropped catlike to earth on the far side. There, like a stray shadow flitting, he disappeared toward the yellow-lit windows of the villa beyond.

The place was a low, spreading structure. Enlarged over the years in varying architectural styles, it had been spared by its outer wall from having to sustain the blank, inward-facing, fortress-like design of a town manor. Instead, terraces opened upon outlying courtyards. They shed their light outward through ornate grillework, slatted wooden screens and, on the upper story only, thin, gauzy draperies hanging listless in the mild, still night.

Framed within one such opening, seated in the glare of bright oil lamps that lit her hammered-silver dressing mirror, a delicate beauty sat combing out her long, dark hair. What she may have thought of the image reflected in the burnished metal was unguessable, for her face, as she worked, maintained a haughty immobility.

There was in it, to be sure, a cast of stern, dispassionate evaluation. Perhaps she weighed the cost to her beauty of countless leagues on the open sea, or searched about the eyes for the latest track of maturing years. Perhaps she disliked the healthy color that outdoor living had imparted to her flesh. For she was copper-hued, even to the rounded undersides of her half-exposed breasts, even to her inner thighs where they peeked from beneath her brief robe. Her face in the mirror affected a slight frown from moment to moment; but that may only have been annoyance at momentary tangles in the dark cataract of her long, gracefully flowing hair.

Her judgments, if damning, would have been laughably harsh in view of the haunting beauty of her face. But any such thoughts were lost as her sparkling blue eyes widened, flicking toward a face that appeared behind hers in the mirror's hazy upper edge.

"Olivia, do not cry out." Conan glided noiselessly forward to lay a hand on her half-draped shoulder. "I have horses waiting outside. Throw on something to disguise yourself and we'll be gone."

The woman turned and gazed up at him, where he towered over her low-backed chair in his long, loose cloak. "You have come then, Captain, to take me home to the sea?"

"Aye." Striding to the single door, which stood closed, pressing his ear to the panel, Conan answered just above a whisper. "We have a hoaxing to pull off here, and other friends to rescue. Then we sail, back across the Vilayet. Fear not, you'll be safe among the brothers even if I stay ashore."

"You want to resume our pirate life together?"

"Yes, Olivia. Our future knows no limit!" Latching the gilded hook on the door, he moved along the wall to a tall, ornately carved and inlaid wardrobe. "Knulf, that traitor, is dead. I mean to take his place and lead the Brotherhood—but boldly, and to a purpose! New trade routes are opening up, and with our islanders resolved to stand against Turan and Hyrkania both, why, wealth and power will drop into our hands like ripe fruit!" He pulled open the wardrobe and rummaged roughly inside, dragging forth a long, dark dress and beaded shawl. "Here, this will do. Although—" he patted a sword-hilt beneath his robe "—you may have to slit the dress to spread your legs over a saddle."

"What makes you think I want to go with you?" Olivia had made no move to rise; she still sat poised, scantly robed before her makeup table.

"What? Why, now is the best time to go, to avoid the harbor sentries and join the fleet. I could take you from the wharf in a day or two, maybe, but there would most likely be bloodletting." Taking a dagger from the table before the mirror, he commenced a deed of butchery on the costly garment.

"Conan, do you really think I want to go and live in squalor among lecherous half-wits, to share again your flirtations with death and other women?" His obtuseness had evidently angered her, for she pivoted impatiently in her chair, her color rising.

"Why, it is the life you chose to share with me," Conan muttered, looking hurt. "I saw to it that you never lacked for anything—"

"Nay, nothing but privacy, safety, and dignity!" She shook her head in exasperation. "Certainly I chose it over death by ravishment, or slow starvation in a swamp! But is a woman never permitted to seek anything better?" She waved a hand, indicating the chamber around her and its lavish contents. "Can you not see, I would be mad to leave what I have here—the wealth, the ease, the security—"

"You would trade the freedom of the seas for this per-fumed cage?" Conan sniffed the air, growing visibly irri-tated, but raised a hand for silence. "Quiet, or we'll rouse the household. I cannot bide here long." He threw the knife and mutilated dress onto the cluttered vanity, turned from her, and strode away past the broad, silk-lined bed to the terrace window. Parting the curtains with the back of one hand, he gazed out intently through the aperture for a mo-ment, then turned back to the woman. "Make your choice, Olivia! What you have here is nothing to what I can give you."

Arising from her chair, she faced him unashamed. "I made my choice in Djafur. I thought you, too, had already cho-sen."

After another swift glance through the window, he let go the drapery and moved back toward her. "Come, my girl! Remember your oath—to sail with me on blue seas or red." He reached out to gather her up in an embrace.

"You mean to win me back with pats and kisses?" she asked impassively, her face still frozen at close quarters.

"Win you . . . or lose you!" Lifting her to him, he forced a kiss on her mouth. The moment stretched, extended; her fisted, red-nailed hands began to unclasp against his shoul-ders. Then footsteps slammed on the terrace outside, and a crash sounded at the door.

"Here, guards!" a deep, triumphant voice rang out, "I knew he would come to us! Pirate, harm her at your peril! She is mine, and I take better care of her than you took of my poor dead cousin!"

"Khalid Abdal!" Conan backed toward the wall, dragging Olivia with him while he wrenched the scimitar from beneath his cloak. "I heard it was you, but I did not believe it!"

"Believe and surrender, brigand!" The tall Turanian

strode in through the doorway, letting two burly Imperial guards crowd in at his back. Stopping in the center of the room, he nodded at two others who pushed in from the terrace. "To struggle against me is useless. Anyway, the emperor would have you alive and unmarked."

"So you set me a trap." Looking to Olivia, Conan let go her hand. "And you, Olivia, served as bait!"

"And if I did?" the woman asked, her complexion burning as she stepped haughtily away from him. "Would it have taken any less to free me from you? Does it make the least bit of difference?"

"Aye, it might have saved your new boyfriend's life!" Growling this, Conan sprang at the nobleman, his scimitar swinging high to clang off the saber raised in Khalid Abdal's fist.

"Back off! Hold, I say!" The Turanian's words were hurled not at Conan, but at the cudgel-bearing guards who crowded forward to menace the fugitive. "Let me fight. I will not have to maim him to beat him!" Dueling in the elegant Imperial style, Khalid matched his attacker lunge for lunge, stroke for stroke. He gave ground but slowly, with parries and ripostes that rang deafeningly in the confined space.

What the Cimmerian may have lacked in finesse he made up in strength, swinging the heavy scimitar as if it were a much lighter weapon. He gave no sign of tiring—least of all when, raising his blade to fend off a thrust, he pressed his enemy's blade clear on up to the ceiling, driving the saber's point smartly into a gilded rafter. There the weapon stuck and hung, far out of reach of the disarmed Khalid, who was bowled back onto the silk-covered bed.

"Now, knave!" Recovering from his rush, Conan drew in his sword for a savage thrust. He launched it—straight at Olivia, who darted in from the side to fling her body across Khalid's and shield him. Conan's strength was fierce in attack, but also in restraint, as proven when he stayed the thrust. The point of the tulwar barely dimpled the sheer fabric of his former shipmate's robe, briefly imprinting a second navel next to her real one.

An instant later, the Imperial thugs swept in from either side, disarming Conan and wrestling him to the floor. They fought him down, grunting and cursing; then they produced ropes and commenced the slow, hazardous process of binding him.

Khalid Abdal, meanwhile, disengaged himself from his wife. After muttering embarrassed thanks to her, he knelt down beside Conan in a most firm and businesslike way. Knotting both hands in the Cimmerian's mane, he forced his captive's head up and held it immobile.

"You fight well, pirate—better than I do, with a gentleman's training." He shook his head almost in regret. "I would, if I could, permit you a gentleman's death. But it is not to be."

Olivia, meanwhile, had gone to the window and parted the curtain. "Your guide has taken alarm," she told Conan flatly. "The one who led you here . . . she is leaving."

She peered out the window after the faint noise of retreating hoofbeats. "What, only two horses? Would you have had me ride with her, then?" She let the curtain fall, emotionless. "Or would she have ridden in your lap?"

FIFTEEN
The Naval Garrison

By dawn's first light, Conan found himself roped astride a cavalry mount lacking pommel and stirrups, bound tightly enough around the arms and chest that he could scarcely breathe. So intent was he on maintaining his balance, to avoid hanging askew in the saddle or being dragged along the ground, that he had little chance to work at loosening his bonds.

Lucky it was that the hour was so early. Few Turanians were abroad in the streets of Aghrapur, and there was only minor turmoil as he was paraded from the gentry gate down toward the waterfront. Had there been more watchers alert enough to guess that he was one of the captives fated for execution on the morrow, it would have brought chaos. In view of his paltry escort of a half-dozen rural cavalry, and the eager anticipation displayed by the few townsfolk abroad, he might never have finished the ride.

As it happened, he was not mobbed or spontaneously torn to bits. The soldiers' watchful closeness prevented any chamber pots from being emptied on his head, though there were some near misses. Only a few of the stones, melons, and scraps of offal that were hurled at him struck their mark. And from unshuttered windows and roadside stoops, along with jibes and taunts, there came the occasional odd whistle or cheer. These reminded him that felons and pirates were not universally despised or misunderstood, not even here in the seat of empire.

The riders entered the grandest part of Imperial Aghrapur just as the morning's commerce was getting underway. Scuffing at a forced pace past the markets, the great temples, and the lofty bastions of palace and fort, they came at last to the naval fortress, which extended the citadel eastward along the riverfront. Once they reached the high, clanking portcullis in the curtain wall, the public clamor fell behind. Inside there was, if anything, more bustle, but of a disciplined and military nature, obviously focused on preparations for the great festival to be held.

Conan, hog-trussed and ill-mounted as he was, could not help but marvel at the vastness of the Navy Yards. Here among heaps of lumber and the spools of cordage lay the bones and sinews of great Turan, formidable enough to reach across the sea and snatch wealth and slaves from a dozen far-flung lands. All these forests of oars and masts, the throngs of toiling conscripts and mountains of naval stores, amounted to sheer power, a heady and dangerous concentration of it. Not for the first time, Conan wondered if he, a rebel, had been foolish to venture so near the wellsprings of tyranny.

The cavalry troopers, stopping occasionally to display written orders and justify their presence to strutting naval officers, cantered past a row of roofed launching sheds that were cordoned by Admiralty guards. They skirted the main wharf, where a work gang busily furnished a broad pavilion with tables, benches, and a cushioned dais. Conan felt a pang to see, out in the harbor amid barges, galleys, and sailships, his own motley assortment of pirate vessels bobbing at anchor. From this vantage point, they looked feeble and tiny; framed by snouts of catapults and the armored beaks of docked biremes, they seemed to dawdle in the very jaws of empire.

Ahead rose the hulking stone pile of the Naval Garrison. Of all the landmarks hereabouts, Conan had studied this one the most carefully, going by accounts from pirates who had escaped the Imperials, and by his own distant recollections of the port from his service in the Turanian Army. He had scanned the building from the harbor, and the landward view filled in his mental picture of the place: a broad, squarish fortress, furnished with lookout towers and catapults on its crenellated roof and seaward terraces. Port officials occupied the upper story, looking out over the harbor through broad-arched windows, with soldier quartered beneath. The lowest levels, surrounded by defensive walls and a slimy moat, were used as a prison to house naval offenders and captives brought in from far ports.

Crossing from the stone wharves by means of a thumping wooden ramp into the metal-toothed gateway of the garrison, the cavalry troop finally dismounted. Conan was dragged off his horse by a pair of them, his head roughly scraping the cobbles before he could get his rope-tangled feet underneath him. The pair and their captain marched him in through narrow, constricted defenses, past a dozen armed sentries, to an inner courtyard. There they turned him over to Admiralty officials.

"Cut those preposterous ropes off him," an officious, mustached lieutenant in a red-plumed turban declared. "We have no need of them here, and Admiralty guards do not maltreat their prisoners."

"This is bloody Amra himself, pirate terror of the Vilayet," the cavalry captain warned. "He would just as soon slit your throat as dine on candied figs."

"If I throw him into the dungeon bound up like this, his fellow prisoners will very likely kick him to death or drown him." The lieutenant watched his subordinate draw a knife and set to work on Conan's bonds. "We need him healthy for tomorrow's execution."

"A ringleader like this one will stir up trouble with his former cronies," the captain said, preparing to leave. "I advise you to put him in a separate cell."

"Not much chance of that," the lieutenant muttered to the departing cavalryman's back. "With all the burnings and torments planned for the naval show, our jail is crammed with ill-doers from every part of the empire."

Breathing deep drafts of stale courtyard air, Conan flexed his cramped, sore shoulders. He silently thanked Crom for his good luck. Having been ill-handled, he was minded to crack some heads and break for freedom here and now. Yet he knew that would be foolhardy; it would endanger everything.

As things stood, he told himself, all he had lost by being taken prisoner was his own blood price from the Turanian crown. Barring further ill luck, Philiope must have made it back to the pirate fleet by dawn. Drissa and the others would have been instructed to say that he had escaped them the night before, and to continue negotiations over the gems alone. For him to break free again and return to the pirates, so that they could sell him in turn to Yildiz, to be sent back here . . . no, it would never be believed. Better to accept his luck and watch for routes of escape.

The Admiralty guards conducted him down a ramp to a barred, rust-blistered portal that creaked inward at their approach. They ushered him inside, where, to his surprise, the door clanged shut, locking out his captors. As his eyes strove to adjust to the dark, a cudgel smote him on the back of the head, filling up his vision with bursting stars. A hard foot drove into the small of his back, sending him staggering down a damp, sloping corridor pervaded by an atrocious stench.

"Get along there, fellow. Keep moving! Do nothing clever . . . unless you want more of this!" The club struck again, shocking him above the ear; in the deepening blackness and rancid, eye-watering stink, it was impossible to sense what direction the blows were coming from. Conan had a vague impression of at least two forms pressing behind him, kicking and shoving relentlessly to keep him off balance. He half-turned, dizzily, to resist; then his brain partly cleared, and he remembered that he *wished* to be thrown into the dungeon. He gave ground, though reluctantly, another blow from the cudgel helping him along.

"There now, you can go in and join the rest." He heard the rasping, grating screech of another portal near at hand, saw the low archway, and ducked as he was propelled toward it. He staggered through—but he did not expect to find that beneath the wetness of the floor, there was no footing. He fell in with a splash, gasping and choking in a waist-deep cistern of chill, putrescent water.

"Who is it this time?" a voice grumbled nearby amid the scattered laughter. "Another qat-smuggler from far-off Akif?"

Coughing amid the hoots and guffaws, Conan found his voice. "It is Amra of the Red Brotherhood. Who wants to know?"

"What, Amra, the Vilayet pirate? Amra the Scourge of the Western Sea?" The ensuing cheers and outcries, though sustained by the echoes in the place, nevertheless sounded feeble and tubercular. The loudest, heartiest ones came from the doorway he had just passed through. Peering up, he saw a closed, crusted iron grille and a face leering through it—a round moon-face, poxy and self-satisfied, grinning at his captive. "Welcome, great Amra! How lucky we are to have such an honored guest!"

"Away, stenchard!" As Conan slung filthy water up at the grille, the face withdrew. Turning to his questioner, he continued in a low voice, "My pirate fleet waits at anchor in the harbor, and I do not plan to be here tomorrow."

"Huh!" The fellow, a hulking, swarthy-bearded Shemite, laughed bitterly. "None of us did, that is certain! But come . . . if you are indeed Amra, there are men of your crew among us. They will recognize you." Beckoning to the newcomer with a careful, convict's gesture, he led him away through the waist-deep water. "I am Vulpus, by the way, a river pirate by trade."

The naval fortress, Vulpus explained, had sunk into the Ilbars river mud from the weight of its stone vaultings and buttresses. Thus the dungeons always were submerged to varying depths, depending on the season. Usually the water level was no higher than this; only rarely, during a spring flood or a winter torrent, did it rise to the ceiling and drown the occupants.

Over the course of years, the central corridor had been filled in with stones to provide easier access to the cells. The dungeons themselves had not been raised, since the only light and ventilation inside them came through stone grilles that were wholly or partially submerged. Throughout the place there were a few ledges and perches where inmates could remain dry; these were reserved for the fiercest and most respected felons. The hardship was intense, but temporary, due to overcrowding, which would soon be alleviated by death. For now, the prisoners suffered abominably from ague, chills, and festering bites.

"Rats, you mean?" Conan asked as he waded toward the shallower end of the vault.

"No, crabs." Vulpus pointed to an oozing gash on one hairy arm. "At night they creep in from the harbor and try to eat us. In all this wetness, the pincer-wounds become inflamed and will not heal. Fortunately for us, the crabs themselves make tasty eating."

Among the dregs and flotsam of the jail were Yorkin, Ivanos, Ferdinald, and the rest of the captured brothers. Also present were pirates from the South Vilayet, provincial brigands, naval mutineers, and local cutthroats and smugglers. Conan's men had heard of the pirate fleet's arrival, and were cheered by his presence. Yet they had hoped to be bought or traded out of prison, not joined by their leader; after rotting for weeks in this hole, they could hardly join in Conan's blithe expectation of escape. Others placed hope in the idea of outside help, such as a rescue by Conan's fleet; he took care not to disabuse them of this false notion.

"We are going to die tomorrow, most all of us," Vulpus declared on behalf of the common prisoners. "If you mean to leave here, take us with you. We will fight for you. We have nothing to lose."

Conan had hoped for this, yet he made no promises. "What of those Admiralty guards? They are tough monkeys. How many of them are there?"

"Guards, what guards?" Vulpus puzzled. "No self-respecting Admiralty guard ever comes down here. Oh, you mean Rondo and his crew—they are not staff, they are inmates like ourselves, trusties!" He laughed, snorted, and spat into the ubiquitous pond, that here was less than knee-deep. "There are six in all, counting the ringleader himself."

"A real scum-eater, that one," Conan avowed. "What is his crime?"

"Better to ask what crime is not his!" Vulpus hawked again, but this time thought better of spitting. "The warders allow him the key and the run of the place. Rondo chooses only his former cronies as helpers.''

The prison was in the form of three separate galleries around three sides of the fort, connected by the raised, U-shaped central corridor. Some of Conan's men were in the other cells, and he, in his role as Amra the pirate leader, insisted that they be told of his arrival.

Communication between the rooms was possible only by tapping on the thinnest part of the stone wall. Since Conan was not in the central gallery, there were further delays while messages were relayed to and from the farthest room, also by tapping. Consequently, the necessary work of planning and debating took up the rest of the morning.

The day's meal arrived, shoved in through the grilled door in a deep, hollow trencher that could be floated the length of the gallery. Luckily, the food was repellently familiar and unappetizing, a pasty gruel of sour grain, with formless lumps of fish and gourd embedded in it. So it was not all taken by the strongest inmates; a good part remained for the weak and desperate.

The convicts filled in and elaborated the gruesome picture Knulf had painted of the torments set for the morrow. A long and varied set of executions was planned to follow the naval trials—impalings, burnings in floating hulks, and so forth, culminating in the dismemberment of dreaded Amra and a few others. The city, by all reports, was in a fever of anticipation.

''And what of this sea-contest?'' Conan asked. ''I heard that the first tryout was a failure, in spite of all the devilments and fiendish inventions Yildiz's wizards could muster.''

His cellmates apprised him of current gossip about events at the Navy Yard, gained mostly during cleanup and burial details outside the dungeon. The reputation of the contestants, the unfolding mystery of their planned efforts, and the play of rival forces at court were included in the speculation. Conan, having run afoul of the sorcerer Crotalus, and having equaled his rare feat of navigation, could well see how much was at stake.

"Of course you have heard," Vulpus told him, "that on trial-day all the wizards will be set loose against the pirate fleet, to wipe it out. That, anyway, is the rumor that is lately abroad. I assume you are prepared for it."

"Oh, aye, yes." Conan, wholly surprised by this news, judged it wise to conceal his ignorance. "With any luck we will be at sea by then."

"For myself," Vulpus resumed, "I cannot relish spending my life on board a ship. River pirating was a freebooting trade, with short voyages and few men to a boat, at most. Our rowdies came and went freely—we split our loot evenly, and spent it as we pleased. But all the seafarers I meet tell of long bouts of toil and hardship, and fierce punishments. You pirate chiefs sound like even worse tyrants than navy and merchant captains, or old Yildiz himself. Why should a free thief follow such a trade, I ask you?"

"Never was a man slower than I to bend his neck to tyranny." Conan, with an earnest wish to survive prison and a sea-captain's thirst to recruit men, chose his words carefully. "Aye, even so, there is much to be said for a ship's routine—for the creed of the Red Brotherhood, and for following a strong leader. Why, I myself, years agone, was but a lowly trooper in Emperor Yildiz's army. I passed through his tutelage and learned from it, to the point where I now seek to rival him." He had gradually broadened his speech to the inmates around him. "By yielding to mastery and bearing up under it, you too might rise to become a master of men. I ask no more of any sailor under my command than that."

The nearby convicts nodded, seeming inspired by Conan's words. Shortly afterward, he helped Vulpus float the empty food trough back down the gallery, to return it to the trusties. But without preamble, while Vulpus pounded on the gate grille, a mob of unsavory, long-bearded inmates flung themselves upon Conan and forced him underwater, doing their best to drown him.

"Scoundrel! Devil!" they shouted as they kicked and pummeled, forcing him under murky splashes. "You pirate scum are the bane of honest smugglers! Our shipload of qat from Vendhya was burned by you ignorant louts—else we could have bought our way out of this hole! Die, sea-thief! Perish in foul muck!"

"Warder! Warder!" Vulpus rattled the grille, shouting for aid. "There is a riot, come quickly! The Riverbottom Rogues are murdering the pirate Amra!"

The moon-face of the guard Rondo appeared beyond the grille, twisted in a cynical smirk. Then, as Conan fought his way to the surface by hurling two of his attackers against a wall, only to be forced back down again by the rest of them, a cloud of doubt passed over the trusty's brow. Turning, he shouted gruffly to his helpers.

"Here, lads! The warden wants that villain Amra alive! There will be the devil to pay if he dies. Come and break some skulls!" Slamming his key into the rusty lock, the warder wrenched open the grille and let in three cudgel-bearing men.

In an instant, the rioters turned on the guards. Conan and the smugglers sprang alike from the water, lunging to grapple with them, while Vulpus forced himself halfway through the open gate and huddled there, resisting a fury of kicking and clubbing by Rondo. More inmates, by pre-arrangement, swarmed out through the door. In moments the trusties were down, splashing and gurgling for help, their clubs flailing overhead in vengeful hands. Conan rushed the door, pushing up through it into the corridor, with Vulpus acting as an involuntary shield.

"Now, swine!" Brushing the Shemite aside, Conan laid hold of Rondo's cudgel in mid-swing and snatched it away like a twig. As the warder turned to bolt, Conan caught him by the collar and dragged him up against a wall. "Where is the key?"

"Where is it? Right here, Cap'n, sir!" Rondo reached to a lanyard at his belt and offered his captor a rusty iron key.

"Only one key?" Conan seized it, wrenching the thong loose from the trusty's clothing. They were being surrounded by a crowd of soggy, angry escapees from the dungeon. "Does this fit that door as well?" He nodded toward the upper ramp, where the gate was visible only as a small square of cross-barred light at the end of the corridor.

"Why no, Cap'n, I have no key to that door." Rondo shook his head, sweat running visibly down his round face in the dimness.

"Vulpus, does the wretch lie?" Conan demanded over his shoulder. "I thought you said he carried the key."

"Aye, to the cells, to be sure," the Shemite said, massaging his battered shoulders. "But in truth, I doubt the Admiralty would give the outer key to Rondo."

"Nay, Cap'n, they would never trust me with a key to the outside! I an' my boys would've been long gone!"

"Why, you—" Conan clapped a hand on the warder's neck and began to twist. Then, at the pathetic look of the man, he flung him aside. "All right, live, if you can stand to!" He turned to the others. "What if we begin to kill him slowly? Will they try to intervene?"

There was little hope of that, according to the convicts. When Conan went to peer out of the grille, he saw two armed Admiralty guards against the glare, standing well up near the archway at the top of the ramp.

"Sounds as if there is some trouble below," one of the men called down good-naturedly. "Never worry, you are not bothering us."

"They want to escape, no doubt," the other observed. "What is your hurry, anyway? You will be let out tomorrow!"

The naval troops seemed unlikely to fall for the same trick that had fooled Rondo. And the inmates, after ransacking the trusties' barren cots in the wardroom, still had nothing, no implements or steel weapons. Releasing the wet, clamoring prisoners from the other cells, they nevertheless found themselves trapped in the dank basement, lacking even material with which to build a fire of any size. They could not get a purchase on the steel door, which was set snugly in its stone jamb, and they had nothing to use as a battering-ram.

"We have two hundred good men, even so," Conan pointed out. "And we have the underpinnings of this fort to play with! By Bel-Dagoth, we will bring the place tumbling down about their ears!"

And so the convicts set about trying to undermine the Naval Garrison. Taking chains, which they had a fair amount of, they looped them around a pillar in the wardroom. By tying on blankets and lengths of thong from the cots, Conan made places for as many strong men as he could. The tow line extended out along the arched corridor—which, they hoped, would protect most of them from the ceiling's collapse.

Yet the stone blocks, pinned in place by the whole massive weight of the fortress above, refused to move. Instead, the crudely forged iron links stretched and parted, sending the convicts down in a bruising, cursing heap. Angered now, they embarked on the even more dangerous course of looping and doubling chains, thongs, and blankets around two adjacent pillars. By twisting this makeshift binding in the middle with cudgels and cot-rails, they endeavored to draw the two columns together and topple one of them. Their initial effort caused a section of stone to grate and shift in its place, to frenzied cheering. But the pillar came slowly; the inmates were soon again hampered by weak materials and lack of leverage, and their labors dragged on through the afternoon without further result.

At dusk, a delegation of three Admiralty officers came down to the main gate to parley through the grille. Conan was summoned as spokesman for the prisoners, with Vulpus as his second and a crowd of inmates listening in. The harbor master—judging so by his ermine cape—was present, and possibly the dungeon warden as well. But the speaker of the naval party was the dapper, plumed lieutenant who had received Conan into the fortress that morning.

"Come now, Captain Amra," the man said, not troubling with introductions. "It is pointless of you to raise a stir all night! We want you men fresh and well-rested for the festivities tomorrow. Is it not possible to come to some kind of agreement?"

"That depends." Conan scowled through the grating. "What are you ready to offer that will make any difference?"

"Why—" after a glance to his superiors, the lieutenant clasped his hands before him "—the most attractive thing possible to a man in your position: an easy death. If you persuade your henchmen to weather the night quietly, without rattling the foundations and raising any more turmoil, my superiors have authorized me to promise that you will be killed cleanly tomorrow . . . by hanging, instead of the more elaborate punishment that had been planned."

"Mmm." Conan kept his scowl immobile as befit a shrewd bargainer. "But if I keep my men quiet through the night, there is nothing to guarantee that you will live up to your promise. I cannot trust mere words. What can you offer me right now? Besides,'' he added, in response to prodding and whispers from behind him, ''what is in it for them? Offer my men something.''

The naval lieutenant turned and conferred at some length with his superiors. After considerable head-bobbing in the torchlit dusk, he turned back to the doorway. ''If you must have it so, the Admiralty is prepared to make this most generous offer: If you all return to your cells, surrender the keys, and let us lock you in, we will moderate the punishment of any twenty prisoners you specify—at least ease it enough to guarantee them a swift, merciful death. In addition, we will let you, Amra the pirate, go free, and execute another convict in your place.''

At this, Conan could scarcely believe his ears, but the officer was not finished. ''Of course, to conceal such an imposture from the mob when we have promised them Amra, we would have to exact certain guarantees from you. Cut out your tongue, for one thing—the tongue, yes—and lop off a hand. That would keep you from revealing our secret and resuming your piratical ways. But that could be done immediately, as you request—''

''Never,'' Conan answered without hesitation. ''I will not accept freedom if my shipmates and prisonmates are not going to share in it,'' he told the officer, to cheers and eager thumps on the back. ''Rather, I offer you this bargain: Free all these men now, and do what you want to me on the morrow. But they must be freed unharmed, and permitted to join the Red Brotherhood's fleet in the harbor if they so wish.''

Conan spoke confidently; he judged that it would be a good deal easier for him to escape the Turanians on his own than to drag a prisonful of unruly knaves along with him. "And the fleet must be allowed to sail, as soon as it wishes and without interference."

Amid the howls of applause from inside the dungeon, the lieutenant gave a brief, cursory glance to his commanders and turned back to Conan. "I fear we have reached an impasse," the mustached man declared. "Our proposals are too far apart to be settled in the time allowed. There is no point in talking further."

"Aye," Conan agreed. "So go about your business, and we will return to ours."

On that note, the parley ended. Conan turned to face the universal goodwill and congratulations of his fellow convicts. The dungeon had grown even blacker than before, with lamps and oil growing scarce; most of the men loitered in the yellow-lit wardroom, taking turns in the reckless attack on the pillars. The chains and blankets were giving out fast, the stone having budged less than two fingers' width. There was still planning to be done for a morning escape; but as hope faded, the convicts' mood grew listless.

Two iron doors led into the dungeon, one at either end of the U-shaped corridor. During the late, unmeasured hours, Conan went discreetly to the second and lesser-used one, summoned by the pirate appointed to watch there. He had no difficulty slipping away from the dozing, dispirited crew; the lookout had, evidently, been bribed to bring him quietly. Beyond the small grating, outlined in moonlight from the courtyard above, he could make out two cloaked figures waiting in the rampway.

"Yes?" he growled suspiciously. "What is it?"

"You are Amra . . . Conan, I mean?" From the soft, cultivated voice, the high, shaven brow, and the fragrance of perfumed oil wafting in through the grille, Conan judged the speaker to be a court eunuch.

"Better to ask, who is it who knows and links those names?" Conan stood a little shy of the door, wary of some kind of sorcerous or treacherous attack. "Who are you?"

"My name is of no consequence here." Doubtless himself fearing some unseen menace, the visitor likewise kept back from the door. "I am a functionary of the Imperial Palace. My place is to hear and facilitate requests for help, both official ones and . . . unofficial."

"So?" Conan told himself he trusted this one less than the three preening admirals. "Who is that behind you?" he demanded, peering at the second, inscrutable figure.

"I was asked to convey something to you." Ignoring Conan's question, the eunuch reached into the breast of his cowled robe. "The request came to me through long-established personal channels. Servants of the Imperial Palace, you may understand, have ties to servants of other offices and households, who sometimes seek favors, or repay them."

The man paused meaningfully, gazing at the darkness of the grille. "Servants care for one another's well-being, you may know, as do freemen and nobles." From his garments the visitor had extracted a small object, which he clutched in his fist. "My presence here may or may not have the approval of some higher personage, as well. There are constraints on what can be done by servants, even eunuchs of the Imperial court."

"Out with it, man!" Conan snarled impatiently. "Who sent it?"

"That, too, is of no great importance." The visitor extended his fingers in a careful, gingerly motion, passing what he held through one of the interstices of the grille. "Doubtless you will know what to do with it."

Conan grasped the object in his fingertips, wary of some trap. It felt like a key. When he drew it in, he found that it was looped to a string: a long, tough thong, whose end would not pass through the grating because of a small piece of wood or bone tied to it.

"Farewell, Amra." The eunuch, having turned away, was already starting up the ramp, his unknown companion beside him.

"Wait! What does this mean?" Fearing a trap, Conan would not stick his fingers through the grille to fumble with the obstacle. Instead, planting a foot against the door, he wrenched hard and felt the thong stretch, then break free.

"Who are you?" he called in an urgent whisper, bending back to the grille. Something in the quick, loose-hipped walk of the smaller hooded figure struck him as familiar. "Olivia?" But already the two were turning out of the rampway, gone.

The implement in his hand, held up against the light, was of heavy brass, cut away starkly: a skeleton key. Placing it in the keyhole of the door and twisting, he felt it catch and heard a faint, rusty grinding as the bolt began to slide. Then, at the scuffing of footfalls and a dreary exchange of hails from sentries in the courtyard above, he stopped and eased the key out of the lock. Catching the bright-eyed gaze of the lookout behind him, he grunted and drew the man back toward the wardroom for a conference.

SIXTEEN
Under the Skull-Jack

The prisoners stormed the courtyard at first light, streaming through both gates and up the rampways on the heels of Conan and Vulpus. The Admiralty guards who first met their rush were the lucky ones; they were beaten down with mere fists and cudgel-strokes, blows that battered at their turbans and light mail without necessarily killing them. Henceforward the escapees bore weapons snatched from the defenders as they fell, and most of them were not in a mood to grant life to any helpless Imperial trooper who begged it.

In spite of Conan's strictures against noise, the tumult of fighting in the inner court could not help but spread alarm through the garrison. Luckily, the place was built more to keep invaders out than to hold fugitives in. An open stairway led up to the fort's defensive bastions; by prearrangement, the leaders took their force over the dawn-gilded heights rather than trying to fight through narrow, crooked corridors toward the closely guarded gate.

As the convicts burst out onto the broad parapet, trumpets and chimes sounded to rouse the fort; simultaneously, standing guards from the night-watch converged on the courtyard stair. Conan, wielding a borrowed halberd, drove and feinted between the first two of them, tripping up both with his stave. He did not turn back to chop or brain them; the pirates and cutthroats swarming behind could be trusted to take care of such details. Instead, he drove on through the patchily forming line of guards, past even the gate towers and drawbridge, toward the seaward side of the garrison, with its flags and its catapult battery. With but two hardy pirates sprinting close behind him, he mounted the stair to the harbor battlement.

Instructing his henchmen to slash the catapult strings with their shared saber, he raced on. Along the battlement stood three tall flagpoles intended for signals, weather warnings, and the like. Conan went to the tallest one, grabbed the halyard, and unwound it from the cleat. Fishing beneath his shirt, he dragged forth the flag his pirates had daubed on a sheet of rough bedding: a skull, grimy-white on a soot-blackened field, grinning over crossed sabers sketched redly in damp blood. The crescent banner of Imperial Turan had not yet been raised today; in its stead, Conan tied the skull-jack and ran it up the mast, arm over arm. Partway along, he stopped and severed the slack halyard with his ax, leaving a dangling end of rope. Then, hauling the pennant as high as it would go, he reached overhead with the poleax and cut the long, trailing end as well, so that both lines hung well out of reach and the flag could not be lowered from the parapet.

He hoped someone was awake aboard the pirate fleet to see the agreed-upon signal. At the moment, his ships were a mere gray huddle of hulls and masts against the dawning watery-yellow of the eastern sky.

"Amra, guards are upon us!" One of his escort pointed to a crowd of troops straggling from a farther stair: turbanless garrison troops, unarmored and all but shirtless from their early awakening, holding up scabbardless swords and yelling a groggy challenge.

Rather than wait and fight, Conan fled, leading his pair of convicts back toward the main group. As he came to the downward stair, a lone guard barred his way, springing up from the narrow-railed passage and raising a short pike in his face. Feinting with his ax, Conan parried, tripped up the man's legs and smote him in the groin with the haft of his weapon. Then he charged straight ahead, fetching the turbaned head a thump against the stone baluster as he ran over him. Behind him sounded more clanks, scuffs, and grunts as his companions claimed the fallen guard's weapons and turned to beat back the pursuers.

Ahead, according to plan, the escapees had cleared the parapet and broken into the broad, double gate-tower that hulked along the outer battlement. The stout oaken doors stood open, with convicts swarming around and passing inside; from within came shouts, clanks of weapons, and muffled curses. Conan shoved his way forward, jostling in through the nearer door to survey the torch-lit interior.

The tower contained the drawbridge machinery; defensive slits, too, and broad machicolations looking down on the approach to the gate. The bridge was raised, and most of the clangor inside came from inmates trying to lower it. They hacked at the thick chains that held the heavy plank platform vertical, hoping to release it and span the shallow, muddy moat below. The only fighting was atop stairwells at each side of the double tower, where pirates drove back the Imperials trying to reenter the place.

Conan sized up the mechanism as he jostled among the escapees. The control to release the ramp was below in the gateyard, very likely; yet here at the head of the tower ranged the massive wooden gears, stone counterweights, and iron hardware. Taking careful aim at the flanged, iron-bound pivot half the size of a man's head, Conan chopped down hard at it with the ax-blade of his halberd. The tough oak barely dented; but on his second stroke, the pawl split in its metal binding, deforming under the pressure of the heavy gear teeth it restrained. With a grate and a shudder, wheels began turning and chain links uncoiled. A crack of wan daylight appeared along the top edge of the wooden ramp-bridge directly before them.

"Escape is ours, brothers! Follow if you dare!" The convict Vulpus, sliding his stolen sword into his ragged sash, swung nimbly down through one of the broad machicolations and clung to one of the heavy chains where it was cleated to the timbers. As the drawbridge gained speed in its descent, he yelped and hooted, eliciting cheers from the watchers in the tower. Then, when the ramp trundled past half-slope, he let go his hold and slid down the timbers to jump clear. As the bridge thudded to rest, he stood in the gateway brandishing his sword and challenging the guards.

In response to his cries, other convicts started down chains and grates that hung in either side of the archway. Meanwhile, the fighting at the stairs intensified as escapees battled their way downward toward freedom. Conan joined in, taking up one of the heavy, musty fieldstones kept on hand to bombard intruding horsemen or vehicles at the gate. Hefting it high, he cast it down onto the heads of the defenders in the spiral stair. In its thudding wake, he and the pirates were able to hasten to the bottom, slowed only by stunned and broken bodies littering the way.

The gateway was soon cleared of guards and filled with

escapees. Vulpus, after outflanking and menacing the defenders, had made it his business to threaten his fellow convicts even more fiercely, keeping the first arrivals from scattering across the bridge into the Navy Yard. Such random flight within the walled enclosure, as Conan had explained, would have bought the escapees short-lived freedom at best. Now, as a massed, coherent group, they were ready to move against any goal or obstacle, if only their leaders could keep them together. Once Conan bulled his way to the front of the mob, they started forth.

The harbor front beyond the drawbridge was already astir in the pale morning. As the planks thudding under Conan's feet gave way to the hard paves of the wharf, he was surprised to see work gangs, civil and harbor officials, and even bands of foppish, courtly citizens aboard. These latter, in particular, gaped in horror at the flood of filthy troglodytes emerging from the garrison. Indeed, given the convicts' matted beards and untrimmed hair, their sodden, grimy rags and dung-pit stench, there was no way that the bulk of them could have taken shelter among the townsfolk. The nobles—who, Conan realized, must be early arrivals come to find choice places for the naval show—scattered in fear before the racing swarm. Other, rougher folk gave ground more grudgingly, raising shouts of alarm and menace.

"Call out the guards! The prisoners have burst their cage!"

"That huge one must be the pirate Amra! Get a rope!"

"Nay, get four ropes! We will not so easily be cheated of this day's sport!"

Yet none, even the gaudy officials with their ceremonial swords, stood fast to oppose the felons; those who could not scatter quickly enough cowered away smartly from clouts and saber-slashes. With Vulpus, Ivanos, and his other lieutenants assigned either to bring up the rear or to stop at turns and bully the fugitives along the right path,

Conan was able to lead his dozen-score in a mass toward the docks.

"Come, you prison hounds!" he bellowed as the throng began to slow and separate. "Follow me to escape and glory!"

"But, Amra," one of the convicts complained, "the city gate is over there! This way lies the river, and few of us know how to swim!"

"Forget the Mitra-blasted city," Conan exhorted the prisoner, hauling him along by one shoulder. "We cannot breach another gate so easily now that the alarm is out. Anyway, Aghrapur is a vile trap, full of knaves who want to rend us limb from limb. Ahead lies our best hope, to find ourselves a ship!"

Just ahead, indeed, were the navy docks. Conan had seen some likely looking galleys waiting unmanned the day before. But since then, he saw, things had changed; the smaller and less prepossessing ships had been moved, most likely for the sake of the pageant. In their place floated but a single vessel: a high, long, splendid triple-decker, trim and newly painted, its approach cordoned off by a dozen smartly uniformed Imperial troops. It was an elite warship, a decireme at least; the name gilded onto the stern rail above the brightly painted steering-sweep was *Remorseless*.

"There you see it. Our ship awaits!" Unwilling to let the outlaw band's momentum falter, Conan ignored his misgivings and waved his men forward with redoubled energy. "Come, dogs, and help snatch her from these paltry few guards!" The shout the convicts raised in reply as they jogged forward was half a croak of enthusiasm, half a rumble of awe. Luckily, few of them knew anything about ships; for his part, Conan felt savagely elated at the prospect of seizing such a beautiful craft, whether or not his fewscore untrained men could handle it.

The guards stood valiantly across the head of the dock. They drew swords, waiting in nervous readiness . . . until the mass of yelling, weapons-flailing convicts hit. Then they were overrun, hacked down and trampled, some few of them hurled off the sides of the dock to flounder or sink helpless in the neck-deep harbor. The attackers were hardly delayed, scarcely injured. In a moment they swarmed out along the drumming planks toward the stately ship, whose vacant oars stood out at an upward angle to its benches like pale, graceful wings.

"Look there, the pirate fleet is aweigh!" Ivanos, reaching a place where the pier afforded a clear view of the harbor, pointed exuberantly to the straggle of ships that were raising sail and turning under oars in the distance.

"Aye. They head inshore as we agreed." Feeling fairly sure of the truth of this, Conan glanced back toward the square bulk of the naval garrison to see if his pennant still flew. It did, flapping languidly, its ropes trailing out over the battlements in the morning breeze. On the parapet directly beneath was an indistinguishable flurry of activity; the guards would be chopping down the flagpole, he guessed, as the quickest way of ridding themselves of his skull-jack.

The view closer at hand was less encouraging. Along the harbor front came hundreds of soldiers in pursuit, some of them marching in disciplined files under the purple banner of the Imperial Household Guard, others running and swarming ahead in the gray tunics of garrison troops. They would arrive at the pier in a matter of moments—certainly in a shorter time than it would take to board the ship and get underway. To make things worse, these harbor piers bristled with catapults. Pausing amid the flow of fugitives,

Conan waited for Vulpus, unsure whether the river pirate would accept his command.

"Vulpus, take some well-armed men and guard the base of the pier."

The brawny convict grunted, his face impassive. Then he nodded and turned, calling fighters to go with him.

Gratified, Conan started for the ship. "Hold them off as long as you can," he called over his shoulder. "I will be back to join you."

Springing from the pier to the ship's rail, ignoring the thronging gangplank, Conan found Ivanos already assigning the ragtag crew to their places. The layout of the vessel, a decireme, was fortunate; two of its three levels of oar-benches, staggered alongside a central gangway, seated three men apiece, while the upper one extended outboard to accommodate a fourth man. Consequently, each long oar needed only one crewman with a rower's skill to guide it, with two or three more men to add raw strength. With the crew he had, still numbering over two hundred, Conan could fill up two oar banks and little more. It would be far from the ship's most efficient strength, and a weak, lubberly crew at best. Even so, with one of Conan's pirates to command every oar, they might at least row the tub clear of the harbor.

"Good work, Ivanos!" he said as he worked his way forward. "Get underway as soon as you can! You and Ferdinald steer. I will cast off."

Getting to the forepart of the ship, he greeted deaf old Yorkin, who was hoisting his copy of the skull-jack to the top of the foremast. Then he climbed the rail, leaped down to the pier, and unlooped the mooring lines from the pilings.

Nearby stood a heavy spoon-style catapult, its stone weights already cranked high, with a trough of iron balls ready to load beside it. It was a land weapon, though, mounted on a metal pivot instead of caissons. Conan had seen engines like it before, had even served one himself as a soldier in Turan's provincial wars.

This one, however, would require several men to aim it. An iron bracket, furthermore, limited its traverse to keep it from sighting back along the dock, so it could not readily be turned against the Turanians. Accordingly, Conan slid the head of his halberd underneath the ammunition bin; straining upward against the thick haft, he levered the trough over on its side and allowed the heavy, trundling balls to roll off the dock into the harbor.

Then he headed back toward shore, breasting the stream of the last escapees running for the gangplank. Ahead of him Vulpus's men had gone to meet the enemy. Now they retreated, doubtless because Imperial archers took aim from the shoreline, making the landward end of the pier indefensible. A few stray arrows arched through the air after the escapees, and harsh commands were shouted as the pursuers swarmed out along the dock.

"Back, now," Conan called to his fellows. "Board the ship, take oars, and row clear of this place! Do not wait. I will rejoin you!"

He halted to meet Vulpus and his men, smiting the big Shemite on the shoulder as he sprinted for the *Remorseless*. Oars were beginning to clash together and thump against the dock as the shouting, cursing crew made ready. Then, turning with a murderous yell, he brandished his halberd high and went charging back along the pier toward the attackers.

It was a mad tactic, the one his foes least expected. The dock was wide enough for three men to stride abreast, or for one to defend with a long-hafted weapon. Now, as Conan drove into their midst, the Imperials were too surprised and too closely grouped to react well. Men scattered left and right, falling inevitably into the harbor; elsewise they fought stiffly, lacking room to fence as Conan's ax-bit hacked and thrust at them. The middle ranks, coming up against the backs of those who had stopped short, were still pushed by others advancing from behind, and lost many overside. By then, Conan, driving relentlessly forward, was close in among his foes, too much so to be safely picked off by arrows loosed from shore.

Some few Imperials fell, even so, from arrows ill-aimed at the darting, thrusting pirate. And the purple-clad Household Guards suffered worse because their armor, while too light to resist the blows of Conan's ravaging ax, was more than heavy enough to drag them underwater. Many drowned that day in the reeking mud of the harbor bottom.

Whether any mortal man less swift and powerful than Amra the Lion could have held the pier single-handed, the helpless watchers ashore doubted. As he fought, his fierce totem-beast seemed to hover at his shoulder, guarding him from death's reach, striking fear into his enemies with its roar and its carrion breath. Dressed only in rags, menaced and cut at by blades from three sides, he danced the swift, perilous dance of tongue between gnashing teeth . . . barely evading the sword's razored edge, scarcely managing to keep hold of his halberd, yet plying it to deadly effect on planks that grew heavy with bodies and sticky with blood.

Came the time when the fight was no longer equal . . . when the many, overawed and baffled by the savage destruction before them, began to jostle backward and retreat from the one. It was seen by all, and later denied by nearly all—to no consequence, since that was the moment Conan himself chose to turn and flee. With his weapon braced beside him, he bounded back along the pier, while furious shouts echoed at him from shore, and arrows struck and skipped along the planks at his heels.

A mighty warrior, yet his doom surely was sealed as the Imperial guards resumed their chase. Possibly his greed for victory and his too-great success had been but wry tricks of fate; for while he fought so fiercely, his stolen ship forsook the pier, and him with it. With the lower banks of oars splashing and clattering clumsily, and with nearly the whole top row still canted upward unmanned, the *Remorseless* had floundered out into the channel.

Now, with the shouts of sixty oar-captains resounding steadily over the clumping beat of the hortator's drum, the ship was well away from the pier and gaining speed each moment, soon to surpass the ablest swimmer's pace . . . pulling, as Conan could see, toward the ill-assorted pirate fleet that maneuvered inshore to meet it.

There was little hope in swimming, especially with rowboats setting out in pursuit and archers closing on his track. Small chance here of pulling off the ruse he had used in Djafur Bay. Instead, Conan sprinted to the catapult waiting ready at the end of the pier. Balancing carefully, he climbed out on the weapon's long, leg-thick beam and squatted in place on the throwing-spoon. Then, clenching knees against chin to form himself into a tight ball, he reached forward one-armed and chopped his ax blade down on the trigger mechanism.

There was a spine-jarring impact, a splitting crash, a scream of tortured air. Conan's weapon was wrenched out of his grip; his thus-freed arm jerked downward and caused him to spin, wildly with earth and sea flickering past his vision. He felt himself flailing, twisting, flying inverted. Then water struck, flaying at him like rawhide and grinding like gravel into his mouth, nostrils, eyes. Reality throbbed and faded . . . he heard grotesque noises, retchings, himself sputtering and drowning at the surface of the sea. He reached for life, kicked, sucked in air. Then he saw a mighty ship's ram foaming near, turning toward him.

The steersmen worked furiously at turning; half of the oars idled, causing the *Remorseless* to lose way—and Conan managed to swim a few strokes and clutch an oar blade, which was then drawn in so that he could be hauled aboard.

In the Imperial Palace, many routine activities and offices were suspended for the festive day of the sea-trials. Other functionaries, particularly the guards and servants, were already at a fever-pitch of activity, which was slow to be penetrated by stirrings of alarm from the Navy Yard.

"A thousand regrets for disturbing Your Radiance so early," Nephet Ali begged earnestly of Prince Yezdigerd, "but there is the problem of interrupting your Imperial father's morning slumbers. I thought he should hear the news without delay." He hastened after the long-legged prince, who strode down the ornate, perfumed corridor of Yildiz's apartments.

"Indeed he should," Yezdigerd agreed. "You need not fear to disturb me, Nephet. I rise ere dawn each morning. If I had heard the news from other lips before yours, I would already have roused him myself."

"It could mean a most awkward disruption of today's agenda," the Imperial engineer fretted. But as they approached the door to Emperor Yildiz's sleeping chamber, he fell silent.

"We must see the emperor at once," the prince announced, striding straight up to the pair of tall, pigtailed warrior-women who guarded the royal bedchamber. "It is an affair of the greatest importance, do not delay . . . I take it that I still have access to him!''

At the blond giantesses' insolent looks, Yezdigerd straightened his back and gazed sternly at the panels of the gilded door. Nephet Ali, for his part, could not take his eyes from the guardians' supercilious northern faces and their bronze-cupped breasts. After an uncertain moment, the heavy battle-axes uncrossed; wordlessly, one of them pushed open the door, allowing entry to the lavish room.

Within, half-draped on his bed of velvet cushions afloat in the mercury pool, Emperor Yildiz lay snoring. He looked old, slack-skinned, and drugged; one of his limp hands lolled off the edge of the bolster, floating on its back in the silver metal. The whole scene, with the paunchy old emperor at its center, appeared to shimmer yellowly in the lamplight, as if clouded by some thick but invisible vapor.

Upon entry of the two nobles, one of Yildiz's harem-wives came hurrying from the farther reaches of the chamber, averting her gaze respectfully from Yezdigerd. Keeping her fleshly charms decently screened inside a loose silk robe, she knelt beside the pool and drew the floating bed to its rim. After some spirited prodding, murmuring, and daubing with a wine-soaked handkerchief, the emperor came to slow, groggy wakefulness.

''Yes, what is it?'' he mumbled blearily. ''A visit from my son? What trouble portends, then? Have I slept through a war, or some high state crisis? Speak, boy!''

At Yezdigerd's mute but evident irritation, Nephet Ali ventured forward. ''Your Supremacy, there has been an escape from the Naval Garrison. Sometime during the night, the pirate Amra and his fellow prisoners overcame their guards and forced the gate of the prison. As word first came to me mere moments ago, his band was storming one of the piers in the Navy Yard . . . doubtless to steal a ship and rejoin his cronies in the harbor. It appears that the pirate fleet, too, is under oars.''

''It is a blatant mockery of our Imperial authority,'' Prince Yezdigerd added. ''If this escape is made good, or if it results in more damage to our fleet and reputation, the loss to our standing will be immense. On such a day as this, with half the population of Aghrapur assembled as witnesses . . .'' He broke off, shaking his head in exasperation.

''It will make a fine and memorable show for my subjects, that is certain.'' Emperor Yildiz did not seem in the least surprised or distressed by the news. Now, with the able help of his houri, he peeled himself up from his rumpled mattress and edged his old haunches onto the pool's marble curb. ''They will not complain, at least, that their emperor has failed to match the thrill of the previous sea-trials!''

''A costly show it may be,'' Yezdigerd retorted, ''if it makes our rule seem slack and ridiculous. There is no question, Father, but that these pirates and all their henchmen be crushed at once, and totally. The matter requires your prompt and decisive attention.''

''It has my attention,'' the querulous old emperor replied as he strained to ease a purple robe of ermine-trimmed silk over his pale, clammy shoulders. ''The brigands will be destroyed, most assuredly—'' he turned to his son ''—by you, Yezdigerd, with the aid of your Naval Prize contestants, as we previously discussed. If I were you, I would see to it at once.''

''But Father, things have come far past that! This is no case for half-measures, and certainly no mere show for the common herd's amusement. This requires real, irresistible force.''

246

"Your Majesty," Nephet Ali diffidently pointed out, 'too public a resolution of the matter might backfire as well. If the mob is deprived of its promised executions, it might seek to vent its disappointment in other ways."

"Rest assured, Nephet Ali . . ." Emperor Yildiz shook his head resignedly ". . . if the mob is dissatisfied, it will find someone to execute. Never doubt that. But I intend no half-measures. Indeed, no, I shall send against these marauders the saber-edge of our naval ability, the best and brightest weapons and minds Turan can offer . . . as you yourself have stated, Yezdigerd. After all, if these seers and fakirs are worth five hundred golden talents in our naval contest, certainly they can prove themselves by destroying a rabble of pirates!"

"But Father," Yezdigerd protested again, "these ideas are experimental, not meant to be thrust into premature application . . ." Abruptly the prince left off arguing. As he gazed on his Imperial father's countenance, his own face reflected a sudden coldness. "There is no alternative, then?"

"Indeed not," Yildiz replied with an obstinate headshake. "I hold the might of the Imperial Navy here, at the ready." He raised to his son a half-clenched fist, which, though splotchily pale, seemed surprisingly steady to the task. "If and when I think it necessary, I will unleash its power. Until then, I leave it to you to carry out the role I have previously assigned. Let it be a test of your fitness at command."

Without a word in reply, the prince turned on his heel and left. Nephet Ali, stuttering his respects and apologies, backed humbly away from Yildiz. Then he turned and hurried after the prince, hoping to have a say in the outcome. The emperor, impatient to be dressed for the public festival, clapped his hands and called for wine.

* * *

To Alaph in his boatshed, the alert came early, well before the Imperial ramship *Remorseless* had fallen to the pirates. It was hard, in truth, to ignore the violence and uproar occurring on the longshore almost directly in front of the naval contestants' stations. The fugitives stormed past onto the pier, and then, even as the clash of weapons sounded, a mounted Admiralty officer galloped by, stopping at each compound to warn of an impending pirate raid on the port. Minutes later, when the alchemist had alerted his crew and made his craft ready, a footman came dashing from the Imperial Palace itself. He carried Prince Yezdigerd's seal, and breathless orders to sail at once, without waiting for any Imperial marines.

The other contestants must have felt a similar inevitability. For days they had lived on the edge of battle, readying themselves and their vessels for this trial by ordeal. Now that the moment had come, it was almost a relief. As the stolen, poorly-manned behemoth *Remorseless* wallowed out into the channel, four smaller ships set out in pursuit.

Alaph's galley was the fleetest—fortunately, since his compound was the one farthest from the harbor mouth. His water-spirits served him better than he could have hoped, puffing and hissing tamely fore and aft in their turn from steam traps pointed out over the ship's rails. Their furious desire to escape the coffin-boiler and the two bronze steam cages made the metal-clad beam trundle back and forth in a steady, repeating motion. Meanwhile, the rows of oars, whose helves were linked to the beam by hinged bronze arms, dipped uniformly into the bay and swept astern; then they lifted and arched forward to renew their stroke, tirelessly repeating the motion and propelling the low, mastless ship through the water.

The effect, of course, was somewhat terrifying, with red flames licking the belly of the coffin amidships and dense smoke issuing from the oil pan beneath, laying down a sooty wake and accentuating the ghostly puffs of white steam from both sides. Also, the harsh, explosive roar of the escaping demons, combined with the heavy thump and clangor of wood and metal parts, was intimidating—enough so, perhaps, to be an asset in battle.

The reaction of the crowd ashore was a lively one, evidenced by shouting, pointing, even panic and fainting, all of which were reduced to a frenzied pantomime by the racket of the demon-boiler and the creaking oars. Some of the heavily armed soldiers on the dock vacated by the *Remorseless* even jostled back in fear as the coffin-ship passed close by, angling to starboard on its approach to the channel. With only four men aboard, including two steersmen and himself busy tending steam and fuel cocks amidst the welter of smoke astern, Alaph could not help but feel a thrill of power at his initial success.

His neighbor and competitor Tambur Pasha, by contrast, appeared to be having poor luck with his refitted vessel. The large, ungainly wheels on the sides, laughable for any form of water transport, now were equipped with trimmed sponges between the paddles instead of lead-weighted spokes. The astrologer had explained that given the power of a dry sponge to lift water upward, they could be made to weight the descending side of the wheel more heavily, thus perpetuating the ship's motion. To this end, he had assigned six hefty slaves with mallets to pound the wetness out of the sponges as they emerged from the sea astern, draining them so that they would pass dry over the tops of the wheels.

The paddles, however, did not turn with anything like the vigor of well-handled oars. The small vessel bobbed sluggishly in Alaph's wake, scarcely moving from the dock, with the dribbling of water and the squashing thump of mallets its only notable product. It occurred to Alaph to doubt, in all frankness, that the differential weight of the sponges as they soaked up water could move the ship forward at all. Most likely, any forward motion was a result of the heavy mallet blows driving the wheels around.

The only thing that dampened Alaph's sense of triumph over Tambur Pasha was the realization that while the sleek astrologer wallowed in failure at the shoreline, Alaph's highly successful demons bore him onward into mortal danger. What, then, if all but one of the contestants met their death in battling the pirates? Would the survivor collect the prize, he wondered? The potent and secret weapon he had built into his vessel would, he hoped, make the difference.

Alaph's coffin-ship stroked into position for a forced turn around the end of the pier. Here was another test of his mechanism, for the steersmen could achieve only a slow adjustment of the ship's course with their sweeps. Now, by swinging down a locking wooden bar that restrained the tops of the starboard oar-helves, he limited the quarter-circle sweep of the pivot arms that drove them. The oars continued to stroke along with the moving beam, but did not dip into the water and thrust. Meanwhile the craft, moved only by its port oars, executed a narrow turn to starboard. When the angle was roughly correct, Alaph slackened the control and signaled his steersmen to straighten out the ship's course. Had he unlocked the bar momentarily at the height of the stroke and allowed the pivot arms to cross over to the other side of the arc, the bank of oars would have dipped and rowed in reverse, turning the vessel even more sharply in place.

Drawing out into open water, the alchemist soon oberved that his was not the day's only notable success. On the landward side, he drew near—perilously near—to the two-decked galley of Zalbuvulus, who had evidently gotten under oars shortly after he did. Alaph was startled to see the larger vessel bearing down on him, its bronze ram cleaving the harbor before it. Remembering the fiend-haunted crew's history of collision and misadventure, he considered making a forced turn, or even reversing both oar-banks.

Instead, it was the Corinthian who executed a turn. Rowing smoothly and precisely, his men responded to orders as flawlessly as the best-trained Admiralty crew. While the turning ship lay momentarily close abeam, Alaph caught a glimpse of the gloomy philosopher astride his quarterdeck. Then, through his own trail of smoke and mist, he saw the upper row of oarsmen.

The sight brought a cold stirring of fear to his gut. It was unnerving because of something in the rowers' aspect, something subtle but undeniable. This time the wretched oarsmen did not look ensorceled or afraid; there was nothing unusual about the drumbeat, nor any sign of impish *djinni* riding and hounding the men. They toiled expressionlessly, with utter precision. Indeed, their set, slate-gray faces showed no flicker of any human emotion, nor any bestial one, not even a glance aside at the alchemist's own snorting, fire-breathing craft.

To Alaph, in that fleeting moment, it was suddenly clear that they were dead, defunct, lifeless. He understood that their Corinthian master had slain them all, most likely in a sullen rage over his latest naval embarrassment. How Zalbuvulus induced them to work thereafter, how he exacted obedience beyond death . . . that was an arcane mystery of the foreigner's dark philosophy. Yet his slaves' performance, freed of all feeling and mortal distraction, finally appeared to meet his high standards.

The zombie ship, slowed by its turning, fell thankfully astern. Then Alaph, keeping watch through the vapors, spied an even greater enigma away to port. Out toward the marshes, from the direction of Crotalus's compound, there cruised a long, low, single-banked ship. Evidently the Zembabwan seer had managed to perfect his unknown magicks in time. At the very least, he had contrived to train his ignorant foreign rowers—by less dire means, Alaph hoped, than Zalbuvulus had used. The ship came on smoothly, its oars moving in almost perfect unison, at a brisk pace. Of its crew and commander, nothing could be glimpsed because of a long, low shed that had been erected over the decks and benches.

Alaph's task was cut out for him, then. The competition looked to be fairly even, if only three-sided: demons versus dead men, versus . . . gods knew what. The outcome must therefore hinge on which contestant could ram and swamp the most pirate ships, meanwhile keeping his own oar-ports above water, until the Imperial Navy moved in to clean up the leavings.

Ahead, through the smoke and wavering flame of Alaph's boilers, the pirate fleet now maneuvered under oar and sail in the harbor. Close before him loomed the giant *Remorseless*, still plodding out of the estuary to join the others, under the efforts of its fugitive crew. An easy and valuable target; whether Alaph could overtake the big ship before it converged with its pirate allies, he was not yet skilled enough to judge.

He had a hidden advantage over his competitors, in any event. Along his heavy keel, beneath the fire-breathing apparatus that worked his oars, his ship bore a second demon-driven device, a steam-devil ram. Using water-spirits already vexed to madness in his boilers, readily diverted by the mere opening of a valve astern, he could unleash a metal-fisted ram that would thrust out a dozen paces from the bow with hull-smashing force. It would then retract steadily of its own inclination as the demons' fervor cooled.

This contrivance Alaph had tested repeatedly in recent days by smashing barrels and knocking down old pilings in the harbor. He expected it to afford a crucial battle advantage: It would enable him to ram his enemies swiftly and unexpectedly, even from a near stop in the water or by merely matching speeds with a fleeing vessel's stern. Where galleys customarily must swing wide, gather speed on the approach, and ram the target vessel's beam or quarter, he would be able to splinter hulls from any speed and angle, even while standing clear of a boarding party's desperate retaliation.

An odd destiny for a humble baker's-boy, so Alaph told himself, grim-lipped. Yet he felt more than reconciled to it as he hunched over his controls, his small figure peering sooty and demonic through the smoke and glare. While he planned, he adjusted fuel and steam cocks to secure the maximum speed from his demons; Zalbuvulus and Crotalus were closing with him on either side, and he wanted to be the first to reach the *Remorseless*.

"Row, dogs, Tarim curse you! Bend your backs and make your spindly tendons snap! If you think the Naval Garrison was wet and miserable, wait until you serve a term in Dagon the Sea God's watery locker! Ponder on that and row for your lives!"

Restlessly, Conan strode the catwalk. While exhorting the convicts, he kept one watchful eye on the disposition of Imperial ships in the naval port and estuary. His starboard eye was swollen half-shut, bruised and abraded along with half his body from his headlong flight into the harbor. Yet on the whole, he had regained his strength; from time to time he seized hold of one of the long upper-deck oars and plied it single-handed, vainly trying to improve the warship's speed, before thumping it down in annoyance.

Fortunate they were, at least, that the whole force of Turan's home fleet had not yet been sent to stave in their sides or bottle them up in the harbor. Several fair-sized warships lay idle in port, while others appeared to have withdrawn from the area completely . . . why it was so, Conan could not guess. He personally believed that the Brotherhood's ships could outmaneuver and outrun the Imperial fleet, even in these close confines, but not all his captains were so confident. If Yildiz was holding back strength, it might be that he judged the three sorcerous ships that had been sent out adequate to do the job—a proposition that Conan was in no position to argue, since he had no idea of what powers these mysterious vessels might have.

They looked fearsome enough, to be sure—in particular, the foremost and central one, seething with hell-fires and spewing forth smoke. A blazing fireship that never consumed itself, it raced forward with oars but no oarsmen, trailing a pall of gray over the water. Ill luck it was that the devil-ship bore down on them dead astern; if Conan's oarsmen could have seen it from their benches, it would have speeded up their exertions considerably.

The two ships closing from the sides were less unearthly, though still sinister in aspect. The trim bireme came on with scarcely a drumbeat, its rowers stroking together with unnatural speed and a symmetry that was far too perfect. The long, low-roofed galley on the other flank paced equally fast, its oars rippling in a pattern that looked eerily familiar, if hard to place. Assuming that the three ships could maintain such speeds, it would scarcely be possible to outrun them even with a full and robust crew, much less with Conan's ruffians. Their only alternative, whether acting alone or as a fleet, would be to turn and fight.

"Say, Captain, we could lure her in close and try to board." Ivanos, standing astern at the steering-oar, called out his plan. "A dozen of us can leap across and hack up her paltry crew before they can unleash any of their ensorcelments. If we strike before the other two draw near, we might still dodge a ram."

"And avoid catching fire, as well? . . . or being set on by fanged devils in the smoke? No, Ivanos, 'tis best not to dawdle here. Oar-teams, give it all your strength," he barked to the convicts. "Pull, dogs. You toil not half hard enough!"

The rowers, still mindful of the lurid death the Admiralty had in store for them, did their best to obey. And as steadily as the pursuing ships gained on the *Remorseless*, the pirate fleet converged faster. Doubtless the captains and crews of the smaller vessels, inspired by the sight of the giant ship cruising under the skull-banner of the Brotherhood, bore some illusion that its presence would make them safer. Conan knew this to be unlikely; a large ship could be holed a good deal more easily than a small one, if its war weapons were unmanned and its fighting-decks undefended by slingers and archers. Yet even so, Conan was pleased at this show of unity, and at the impression it must make on the watching Turanians. After all, his allies might just as well have bolted for the open sea.

One ship in particular, the ram-galley *Venom*, under Hrandulf's command, raced ahead to meet the decireme. When it came about, plying oars nimbly to match speeds and stay clear of the bigger ship's ram, several figures transferred to the *Remorseless* by means of a launch.

First to come over the stern quarter was Philiope, clad in one of her cutoff gowns, with a pirate cutlass sheathed at her waist. She threw herself into Conan's embrace and pressed a long, passionate kiss on his mouth. Then she leaned back to survey him. "Oh, Amra!" she cried in dismay, taking in his bruised, battered figure and the few smirched rags that had been all but flayed from him on his plunge into the harbor. "Thank the gods you are free, in all events." She rested her head carefully against his chest. "Be it for all time or for but a few brief moments of life, 'tis good to be with you."

In her wake came several captains, including the sea chief, Hrandulf. "This is a fine ship you have seized, Amra!" The Aetolian gazed about him, impressed. "Large for a pirate craft . . . but then, if you wish to, you can ransom it back to the Turanians as you would any captured princeling or religious relic."

"Methinks I can find a use for it," Conan assured him, keeping one arm across Philiope's shoulder. "What we need now is more hands. Skilled rowers, if possible." He nodded to indicate the near-empty upper oarbank. "Can you give me the extra crew from yonder felucca, and of all those smaller ships that can travel under sail? Their main business, as I see it, will be to stay clear of battle."

"A good idea," Hrandulf said. "As time permits, I will send a galley 'round to collect them." He glanced at the fuming fireship astern. "The enemy bays close on your hells, and a fearsome pack it is! What is that evil thing? It seems like a floating funeral pyre, with that great bronze coffin awash in smoke and flame."

"Worse than rank treachery," Philiope declared, "is

necromancy. They plan to unleash the foulest sorceries on us all.''

"The bargaining fell through, then?" Conan asked her. "I feared that my capture might put the fleet in danger."

"The Turanians were never in earnest, Santhindrissa now says. They would not offer a reasonable price for our gems, yet they kept demanding to see them, likely just to learn where they were kept. Our spies heard rumors ashore that Yildiz planned to destroy us, regardless. He was only waiting for this festive day, so he could do it before an audience."

"That would be very like him." Conan cast an eye ashore, where brightly dressed crowds thronged to watch the sea-chase. "If his sorcerers cannot accomplish it, he will use the regular navy and shore batteries, I should think." He turned to Hrandulf. "Signal the fleet to go about and stay ahead of us at its best speed. We must stretch out this chase as far as we can, out toward the harbor mouth. Then, when we turn and fight, it will be with our best ships only—*Tormentress*, *Victrix*, your *Venom*, and this one. Together we can cover the fleet's escape."

Swiftly over the ensuing minutes, the pirates enacted Conan's plan. The felucca sailed with Hrandulf to gather spare crew. Signals were flown from the mast, and the whole close-knit fleet came about to run before the *Remorseless* in the mild current and the offshore breeze. Shortly afterward, fresh rowers swarmed aboard, giving the ship better speed against its pursuers. Last to arrive were a score of Santhindrissa's pirate women; they set themselves to working six oars astern, to the delight of the convict rowers. Conan guessed that the example they set, standing and toiling half-naked at the long oars, would do more to pace and inspire his crew than a dozen thumping, tweeting hortators.

The big ship's enhanced speed, as it labored ahead with a full oar-crew under broad, double sails raised by the new arrivals, stretched out the chase. Yet the *Remorseless* and the rest of the fleet were still within the broad arena of Aghrapur's harbor when it became necessary to turn and face the inevitable. By that time, the pirates' three sinister pursuers had drawn into a nearly even phalanx, their speeds almost matched, with the fiery coffin-ship central and foremost. It raced scarcely a cable-length behind the slow, bulky flagship—which, by prearrangement, was flanked by the *Tormentress*, the *Victrix*, the *Venom*, and the stolen penteconter, whose acting captain, a sea-chief, had opted to fight.

At the hoisted signal, those rearmost five ships commenced a turn to port. This bore them away from the smaller vessels, whose crews still raced for the sea under all possible oar and sail. For a brief time, the defenders' vulnerable flanks were exposed to the enemy; then their turn continued into a smooth about-face to meet their pursuers.

The *Remorseless*, ever the slowest and clumsiest, made a broader half-circle and so joined the line a little behind and off station. Although facing their pursuers, the jaded crews were not allowed the luxury of rest. Sails were swiftly lowered as impediments to maneuver, while rowers were harangued to maintain brisk speed for the sake of ramming or evading a ram.

"Steady," Conan grated to his crew from his place at the port sweep. "Keep at it smartly, your work lies ahead of you! Do not think to slack off now, you miserable curs . . ." he glanced uncertainly at the female rowers, wanting to be fair ". . . and bitches," he finished gallantly.

From his place at the portside steering-oar, he watched the squadrons converge, three ships against five, although one of the latter was an oversized galliot, barely large enough to drive a ram. The *Remorseless*'s rearmost and centermost position might be an advantage, so it seemed to Conan, if it enabled him to see the fight taking shape and to act decisively—as by letting one of the enemy ships turn aside to ram one of his fellows, then cutting it down with his own ram.

But the turn to port had made the battle lines ill-matched. Conan's ship now headed in between the two outermost enemies, the fire-galley and the mysterious, roofed-over oarship. His *Remorseless*, with Santhindrissa close on his right, and beyond her the penteconter, were all three well positioned to attack the roofed vessel. But that would leave the *Venom* cruising ahead and to port, facing the fireship alone, and Knulf's former flagship the *Victrix* against the enemy two-decker. A dangerous situation; Conan was not surprised when the *Tormentress*, pulling effortlessly ahead even though she had shared out her crew, cut smoothly across his bow to reinforce the center of the line.

The she-captain, after all, had the fleetest and best-drilled ship. She was best prepared to change position, strike unexpectedly, and snatch the greatest profit and glory from the fight. Now she steered, without doubt, for the fireship. Conan watched the oars dip smoothly, the dogged strokes of the male rowers on the lower deck meshing with the partial rank of oars on the upper one. The ram cut the blue-green water brilliantly, sending up curls of diamond spray in the bright sun. Santhindrissa herself could be seen on the afterdeck, slender and clean-lined. She steered one-handed, standing under the curving, overhanging stem of the keel, her free arm brandishing bright steel as she exhorted her crew to courage and effort. Faintly from across the water came the lilt of a flute setting the oar tempo. Agilely, like some graceful winged fish native to both sea and air, her ship raced across blue water.

Ahead, though, lay a murky enigma. The smoke of the fire-galley, borne forward on the freshening land breeze, clung and hovered over the craft like a sinister smudge of night blotting out morning. Within the gloom, at intervals, flashes of red fire could be seen, though Conan could not often distinguish the line of the craft's bows as it snorted and surged through dark-shadowed water, nor catch the sinister gleam of the metal coffin that was its heart. Toward that looming pall, and then straight into it, fearlessly plunged the *Tormentress*.

Conan watched and waited as both ships vanished from sight. He strained his ears over the puffing and rasping of the coffin-ship for the splintering noise of a ram—for shrill screams, clanking of weapons, the howling of demons or any other hint of an outcome. He watched grimly, feeling certain that the she-pirates' ship had been sucked into some dark pit of elder magic from which it could never be conjured back.

Then, as he watched, he saw a curved prow emerge from the far side of the murk. It was the *Tormentress* racing unscathed, with speed unabated and shreds of smoke swirling free as it broke into sunlight. Astern of the bireme, the smoke continued puffing and advancing.

Unbidden, a laugh rose in Conan's throat. The churning smoke, after all, had been too thick; Santhindrissa had lost her quarry in it, passing astern of the galley, no doubt, without suffering or dealing any damage in the process. Now she was loose in the bosom of the enemy, free to brave the smoke again or to take on the farther sorcerous ship, the bireme. She seemed to choose the latter course.

At once a faint, rending crash sounded away to starboard. As swiftly as it came, Conan's joy was banished. While he followed the *Tormentress*, the penteconter that raced ahead on his right flank had closed too swiftly on the enemy. The mysterious shed-covered ship had rammed home, its bow penetrating just aft of the smaller ship's in what must have been a contest of speed and agility. By rights, the well-found, nimbler warship might have had an advantage racing bow-on; but the galley had won, if only through some unguessed sorcery. Now it backed oars briskly and drew its ram out of the broken hull, letting its victim settle helpless in the water.

From where he stood on the surging deck, Conan saw and heard grinding timbers, hard-driven oars spraying water, and men thrashing and shouting aboard the stricken ship. He watched for signs of a boarding fight or of missile fire, but saw none; the plank-covered deck of the taller ship remained bare and unbroken, with none of the victim's crew contriving to climb aboard. The penteconter would not sink, Conan guessed, but float there awash. Its men were of the sea-tribes; they would easily survive in the mild harbor if not slaughtered with pikes and arrows. Any who had not been crushed by the ram would remain to be picked up—either as prisoners or by their pirate brethren, if time and luck permitted.

Watching the ramship pull free and start forward, Conan was struck once again by something he had noticed earlier. The motion of the roofed vessel's oars, though deft and efficient, was unusual. Movements passed in ripples down the oar-banks as if, instead of the beat of a single hortator, each rower was following the stroke of the man directly in front of him. It did not impede the ship, and the oars never clashed or fouled; on the contrary, the prolonged stroking likely made the oar-surge of the ship smoother and more efficient. But it was difficult to imagine what form of discipline beneath the roofed-over hull would create such a flawless, continuous effort.

In view of his own ship's slowness, Conan judged it better to take on his nearest enemy, the fireship, rather than to lumber away to starboard to face the victorious galley and rescue the islanders. Likely the roofed vessel would find him soon anyway under its own power. Steadily now, inexorably, he closed with the hellfire-ship, keeping his bow aligned with the puffing vortex of the smoke cloud. There lay the menace that most needed watching, the imminent one.

Even so, there was time for fresh disaster away to port. Conan watched the enemy bireme elude both the *Tormentress* and the *Venom*, running by means of a remarkable acceleration past the latter ship. Santhindrissa's shrewd and seawomanlike attempt to trap and scuttle the new enemy, by attacking in consort and at right angles with Hrandulf, failed. To avoid ramming her ally, she found it necessary to sheer off sharply and lose way; meanwhile, the *Venom* was forced into a slow turn, also well out of action. That left the bireme facing the galley *Victrix* alone. The smaller ship's commander Jalaf Shah, having witnessed his enemy's unnatural speed and dexterity, could not hope to turn and flee. No choice was left but to steer straight onward and fence for a ram.

As the two converged in their ill-matched joust, Conan examined the bireme carefully. Whatever sorcery it commanded had thus far been demonstrated only in exemplary speed and precision. The rowers on the upper oar-deck looked pale-faced or gray-complected, with amazing intentness and vigor in their stroke. Behind them on the poop, between similarly impassive steersmen, a white-robed figure stood shaking a raised fist. As the oars flashed through the brine, there was something about their tips . . . shading his eyes, Conan came to understand that they were metal-bladed, with flukes edged in bright steel that was probably meant to cut through enemy cordage or flesh. An oddly cruel invention of the Turanians, that; yet it did not necessarily imply sorcery.

The ships, two racing silhouettes against the clutter of Aghrapur's harbor and buildings, joined their duel at last. The *Victrix* undoubtedly would have suffered worst in a ow-on collision. Jalaf Shah, in an effort to clip the bireme's oars, must have steered slightly to port, while his own starboard oars were drawn swiftly inboard, a deft and well-executed maneuver.

Yet the larger ship, in response to a violent gesture from its white-robed commander, leaped again with sudden, unnatural speed. Its ram caught the galley aforeships, before Jalaf Shah's turn could be completed; it drove in deep, throwing up splintered oars and the bodies of rowers in a progressive, grinding chaos. The heavy keel smashed on through the small ship's bulwark, crushing and splitting mortised timbers, while the heavier hull shouldered aside the smaller ship's stem, causing a twisting and rending all down the galliot's length.

But that was just the beginning of the horror—for the bireme, engorged deep in the galliot's shattered timbers, did not back oars and withdraw. Instead, it continued its forward impetus—oars churning, driving on and riding over the wreckage it had created. Beneath the massive wallowing hull, men shrieked in agony and fear—for the ram thrust and tore, the great keel crushed and splintered, and the steel-bladed oars hacked timbers and human limbs alike, driving and churning mindlessly, stirring up bloody seafoam as they forced the great hull over and through the smaller one.

What strength it must have taken at those oars, to row through wood and flesh as if through water, was hard for Conan to understand. The gray-faced oarsmen had no human hearts, it was plain; they did not flinch, nor exult either, nor even glance aside while obeying the fisted gestures of their white-robed captain. Here was sorcery indeed, and of the most atrocious kind.

The bireme passed the length of the sinking galley, forced it under, and drove its ram out the farther side. Of the survivors who crawled free, most were hacked and slashed to pieces by oars as they tried to swim away. Conan shivered at the inhuman sight. He felt almost relieved to turn his mind back to the more imminent peril that threatened his own life.

Rather, perils . . . for the mysterious roofed galley had drawn almost even with the hellfire-ship, and now bore in on him with menacing speed. The two attackers lay at near angles, converging fast. Conan had but small hope of reaching the nearer of the two, the flameship, in time to dispose of it before the second enemy would be upon him.

He had no desire, in any event, to enter into the accursed pall of smoke. Against a single foeman, perhaps, he might have risked it—as Santhindrissa had done—with at least an even chance of finding and ramming the enemy before one's own ship was scuttled. But to grope blindly through noon darkness with two ships on his track . . . particularly if one of the two, as rumor had it, belonged to the all-seeing wizard Crotalus, the one Conan had once played cat-and-mouse with in the stifling fogs of the Eastern Vilayet. No, he would rather court death by healthy daylight. Accordingly, he leaned on his sweep, bidding Ivanos to do the same. The bireme's course shifted to starboard, toward the seaward edge of the smoke and the fast-converging ship.

He then sent Ivanos forward to carry a hasty message to the captains of every oar on his vessel—for, if he was going to fence with two sorcerers, he had best be ready with tricks of his own. He watched the roofed galley draw near the drifting smoke, then sheer off slightly. The ship stayed in plain view along the black pall's very edge, perhaps to preserve the option of veering out of sight at a moment's notice.

Conan glimpsed the devil-ship further to port, at the cloud's seething vortex—and the angry glare of red, unconsuming fire, the black-smudged demon face of a crew-

nan, the rectangular glint of the huge metal coffin at the
ship's heart. The churning oars, he noted for the first time,
seemed to be worked by an overhead beam that thrust in and
out of two metal boxes in a tireless, copulatory motion.

Gradually the huffing, hissing fury of the fireship became a tumult; it caused Conan's rowers to glance around
over their shoulders in fear. Crotalus's roofed galley came
on in silence, though the Cimmerian thought he could dis-
cern the swish of its prolonged, sinuous oarstroke as it
raced nearer.

Ivanos returned to his place at the starboard sweep, sig-
nifying with a wave that the orders had been delivered.
Conan called for more speed, and heard Yorkin's kettledrum obediently accelerate to the new pace. The first
shreds of smoke drifted in over the bows, and within moments the ship glided through sun-slanting grayness.

"Starboard rowers, ship oars! Now, at once! Haul 'em
in smartly, dogs, or you'll be picking your teeth with 'em!
Port oars, keep stroking! Helm, hard a-starboard!"

Conan bellowed his commands and threw his weight
against the steering-sweep, trusting Ivanos to do the same.
Amid the thump and trundle of oarshafts, he felt the ship
yaw and turn underfoot. The port oars continued to bite,
causing the keel to pivot faster. Then, from starboard, the
hull of the roofed galley drove against them in a crashing,
grinding collision.

The cataclysm did not cease, but thundered on and on.
Crotalus's vessel, instead of ramming the hull amidships
as the bireme's previous course dictated, struck the turning
warship a glancing blow, scraping along its overhanging
side with nothing to check its momentum. As it went, the
Remorseless's keel raked down the length of the enemy's
starboard oar-bank, snapping and splintering the heavy
wooden helves in a sustained, calamitous din. The bi-

reme's oars, having been drawn inboard a moment before, were undamaged—except for one tardy shaft that split and twisted in its thole, bruising rowers on both decks. The Turanian ship's severed oar blades whirled and flew above the bireme's bow. Some few clattered inboard, yet did no serious damage.

As the rending clamor abruptly ceased, with the enemy hull continuing to scrape past, Conan's crew looked around at each other and their intact ship. Those who were not busy straining at the port oars raised a fierce, triumphant cheer.

Alaph the alchemist, blinded and half-choked by the effusions of his fire-demons, cursed the trailing wind that sent his own stench flying after him. He cursed himself as well for—after half a lifetime as fire-tender and bakery hand—not devising some sort of chimney for his coffin-boiler. He might have changed course to escape the smoke, except for the goal that hung so tantalizingly near him: the stolen, pirate-infested bireme, whose fresh rowers and improved speed had nevertheless failed to outpace his hissing steam-demons.

Now the enemy fleet had come about to face him. The first rams had driven home, and one of the marauding ships had already ghosted past, blundering perilously near in the smoke. It would be mere moments before the grand duel, which he so feared and so desired, was joined . . . if only he could keep the big ship in sight.

Crotalus had closed with him from the north, Alaph had seen, and Zalbuvulus from the south. Each of his rivals had already vanquished smaller ships, so far as he could tell. The best way for the alchemist to distinguish himself would be to defeat the giant vessel, and possibly others as well. But now Crotalus threatened to move in on his prize. And for all he knew, Zalbuvulus's ship might lurk some-

here behind him in the smoke. He simply would have to
o his utmost, both to exceed their victories and to avoid any
eachery they might have in mind, such as ramming and
nking his heavy-laden ship under cover of his own reek.

There again, through a momentary gap in the smoke,
oomed the *Remorseless*, with white-water spraying under
s roughly handled oars. The bireme now steered to
Alaph's left, doubtless to meet the flanking threat from
Crotalus. The alchemist eased up on his port oars and
alled for his steersmen to adjust to course, taking aim at
he theoretical point where the ships would meet at their
ombined speeds. It was not necessary, he reminded him-
elf, to strike with any great force. Even a near miss or a
oarding action might enable him to use the steam ram.
He merely had to nose in alongside.

Smoke obscured his vision yet again, blown ahead by
itful morning breezes. But he could plainly hear the
ounds of the big ship over the puffing of his own launch:
he thump of the kettledrum, the captain's shouted profan-
ties, the scrape and rattle of oars. The giant lay close
ahead now; the sea felt choppy from its churning progress.

Then, almost on top him, sounded the slow, rending
crash of a collision. It was a hellish din, sharp and sustained, as of a giant ax hewing down a whole forest of
trees at a single stroke. Alaph clutched at his bronze pipe-
cocks in fear, blinking ahead across the waist of his ship
through smarting, watering eyes. Yet he did not slow or
sheer off, for fear of losing his one chance. The grinding
and scraping of hulls seemed to be almost behind him in
the murk. Then came an exultant roar from the pirates.
Alaph knew they must have driven in ahead and spitted
Crotalus's ship on their mighty ram.

Here, then, was his best chance to strike, while the enemy
stopped dead in the water. Just ahead, through drifting cur-

tains of smoke, materialized the curving wall of a hull ribbe
by oars, wheeling and turning in the water as he watched
He drove straight on, ignoring frightened shouts from hi
crew. As the ship lay dead ahead, he twisted open the meta
cocks that would send devil-force to the ram, adding its powe
to the speed of his charging ship.

Water and seething vapor exploded before the bow, with
bits of broken planking whirling on high. Alaph felt a
numbing jolt underfoot, with a thunderous crack as of a
tree smitten by Tarim's bolt. Still the coffin-ship drove
onward from its momentum, even as Alaph wrenched
down the control bars and stopped his oars from dipping.
The galley's arching prow, as he watched helpless, ground
straight on into an abyss of buckling, shifting planks before it finally shuddered to a halt.

His devil-driven ram, he realized, must have cracked
the keel of the enemy ship and broken its back. Now the
hull sagged and parted unevenly before him in the gathering smoke, settling dangerously around his bows as water surged through the shattered planks. His own vessel
looked undamaged, from the hasty glance he gave it as he
worked to adjust his controls for reverse movement. He
must back off the broken ship and get free, before the two
craft fouled together, and fierce pirates swarmed aboard
from the stricken hulk.

Then from the vessel before him, a new and hideous
tumult arose. More planks split and shattered overhead,
sending a veritable rain of fragments into the air. Ahead
in the smoke, against gray-filtered daylight, there loomed
a titanic and devilish shape. Horned, many-armed, writhing and twisting, it arched down across the whole length
of the coffin-ship to catch at Alaph with its scrabbling,
taloned mouth.

* * *

Conan, though exultant at his successful oar-rake of the enemy ship, fiercely silenced the crew's cheering. He let the port oars continue stroking, meanwhile waiting for the crippled foe to drag clear. The chuffing of the fire-galley still echoed close at hand in the smothering murk, and he blinked intently to spy it. He was amazed to note that as the lame ship scraped past his stern rail, the broken stubs of its oars still flexed and circled, rowing steadily in their odd, fluid rhythm even though their shattered ends did not touch the water.

The next moment, madder chaos erupted. Rank, fuming water splashed up over the stern, a new cacophony of groaning, wrenching timber commenced, and impacted seawater jolted under the keel. The crippled roof-ship halted dead in its progress, causing the two adjacent hulls once again to crash and scrape together.

It took a brief, confused moment for Conan to grasp the fact that his own vessel had not been holed. Instead, peering over the stern rail, he saw the flaring devil-ship driving its beak yet deeper into the hull of the same galley he had just disabled. As he watched, the flaming hell-boat ground to a halt, its crew fallen to their knees from the impact, its oars stroking level and mindlessly clear of the water.

In a flash, he understood what had happened. By passing between the two ships in the blinding smoke, turning unexpectedly and veering aside, he had not only avoided both intended rams, he had unwittingly put one of his enemies in the path of the other. Now the roofed ship, having turned blindly in place through its far-seeing wizard's unknown sorcery, was surely and utterly destroyed. He had only the smaller, more fearsome enemy to deal with. A shame it was that the flameship lay astern; there

might not be enough time to circle back and ram it befor
it could extricate itself from the wreck and get underway

He gathered breath, ready to order his starboard crev
to unship their oars and fend off from the sinister wreck
But as he turned to them, he was greeted by panicked crie
and a still greater straining and rending of wood. Along
side their benches, less than an oar's-length away, the tim
ber roof of the mysterious galley bulged and splintere
upward. Pegged woodworking gaped and flew to piece:
with the stress, and from beneath emerged the monster i
had concealed: the writhing, twisting, many-armed insec
that rowed the ship in the absence of any human crew.
With it, in its thrashing rage, came a stench that was all
too familiar to Conan—the same sour reek of the giant
centipede-thing his crew had slain on the isle of bones in
far-off Hyrkania.

As if in a dream, while he froze in uncanny revulsion,
the answer came to him. It was for the sake of the centipedes that Crotalus had traveled to that distant shore, for
them alone. They were the nimble, scrabbling creatures
that could, through his wizardly skill, be shaped and nurtured into gigantic monsters capable of rowing an Imperial
oarship. Their clawed feet, writhing in sinuous rhythms,
could ply the rows of oars more strongly and smoothly
than could any mortal crew. And they could obviously be
endowed with some form of mind, or at least with an
overbearing sorcerous will, adequate to meet the tests of
a warship at sea.

Such was the wizard's scheme, and the gems were his
means. For those jewels, the amberlike crystals with dim
shapes moving inside, were in fact living seeds, the eggs
of the many-clawed monsters. Clustered together in the
sacred tree, they had been worshipped and protected by
the Hyrkanians and the Guardians alike. What better

guardian, after all, than a parent for its own offspring? But the monstrous spawn, sold westward by the dead Knulf, had been made more monstrous by necromancy. This writhing abomination before him, caught in the foundering ship's belly, was the fruit of the single gem Crotalus had managed to obtain. More of them might serve to propel an entire fleet.

As the behemoth towered and twisted in its pain and rage, rocking and battering both ships with its frenzied weight, Conan saw that it had the same segmented body, the same armored plates and hooked talons as its smaller relatives. Whether it shared the evil will and predatory habits of the Guardians, or the more subtle wit of Crotalus, he had no wish to find out. He had seen no sign of the black-skinned sorcerer on the ship, so presumably the Zembabwan's will was somehow manifested in the bug. If so, the insect was all the more dangerous.

After the initial realization, thought and action were as one; Conan bellowed at his oarsmen to shove off from the wreck, and he leaped with Ivanos to the port sweep to achieve the same end by levering the steering blade against the wallowing, sinking hull. The enemy vessel's back was broken, he now could see, and the monster was likewise cut in half, or at least crimped in two by the invading ram. The other end—the head, presumably—had also broken free of its confines in violent frenzied pain. It now writhed atop the smoking fire-galley, making the small ship plunge and wallow with its massive weight. Of the ship's sooty crew, one bald, thick-chested swimmer could be seen splashing fearfully in the water; no other survivors were visible.

At the sound of renewed smashing and sudden, rending screams, Conan turned from his efforts at the sweep. The tail of the vast centipede, breaking through the bulwark of its own ship, had splintered his midships rail and half-crushed one of his pirates. The other brigands, doing their best to ply the heavy oars overhead, struggled to fend away the looming trunk, whose many long legs and scything hooks caught viciously at them. Conan rushed forward, seized hold of the broken oarshaft, and raised its splintered tip to prod and stab at the flailing monstrosity. The sharp point found a weak place between the segments, and the added pain was enough to make the thing twist clear of the bireme and lodge against the planks of its own hull.

But now the danger intensified, with blasts of heat and explosions from astern. Going to the rail, waving aside gouts of nauseating smoke, Conan saw greedy flames spring up out of the wreckage below. Kegs of flammable oil in the coffin-ship had been ruptured by the centipede's weight, spreading fire down its length, fore and aft of the giant bronze coffin-pyre where it had been contained. The jagged wreckage that overhung the bows was also afire, spreading and engulfing the roofed vessel in flame. The smaller ship's oars no longer flexed above the water, the animated beam having been battered down by the centipede's thrashings.

The giant armored insect was now, most obviously, feeling the heat. As Conan watched, its claws twitched and scrabbled at the wood and metal fittings within reach, which were beginning to shimmer with flame. Without warning it arched up, its hideous head looming close above the rail where Conan stood. The sharp, many-fingered mandibles clicked and chattered at him; in a hideous voice comprised of equal parts hissing and twittering, it screamed.

Conan raised his broken oar-helve and stabbed. The monster's weight could cave in his ship's stern, to be sure; worse, those jaws might easily suck or scrabble up a man whole. And if the Cimmerian was not mistaken, the twitching crescent claws at either side of its face-segment were full of withering venom. The flailing horror leaned in close, its claws scraping at the rail, and Conan drove his jagged spear straight into the joint between two segments of the armored neck. Arching back from the stern, the thing chittered shrilly again.

But now the crew, shoving and straining with its oars, finally succeeded in putting distance between the *Remorseless* and the fouled wreckage. The flailing centipede receded into the smoke, its broken, thrashing body wreaking random devastation amid the searing flames. Conan's rowers resumed a regular stroke, pulling smoothly away from the fire without the need of shouted orders. Smoke poured forth behind them, shutting off even the lurid flames and the beast's cyclopean writhings. For some moments they rowed through formless, drifting grayness.

Then from astern came an earsplitting detonation. Smoke and heated air swept over them, and the sea nearby was pattered with smoking fragments of wood, metal, and what looked like charred centipede. A brisk wave spread from the blast, as well; it overtook the pirates, splashing water over their stern rail as they passed out of the sorcerous gloom into sunlight.

EPILOGUE

"It was a perfect double ram, I tell you," Santhindrissa boasted to those present on the *Remorseless*'s quarterdeck. "One of Yildiz's admirals could not have done it better . . . my ship from the port side, your *Venom* from the starboard—" she raised her cup to the sea-chieftain Hrandulf, who nodded and drank from his own "—and that filthy sorcerer was scuppered, scuttled, finished! Even if his zombie crew had wanted to fight, our two ships would have been more than a match for them!"

"Yes, most surely," the sea-chief replied, looking solemn. "But it was strange, was it not, the way those gray-faced men just kept rowing and rowing, even as their hull filled up with water. Never did I see an oarship go down like that, so swiftly, unless it carried heavy cargo." He raised his tankard, grim-faced. "A warship should not sink, but remain awash to fight."

Philiope, from her place at Conan's side, spoke up.

'That ship belonged to the Corinthian sorcerer Zalbuvu-us, so they said in port. His crew were dead men, cruelly slain by him in his mad wish for total obedience. Perhaps they intended to go to the bottom, and drag him with them—''

''But the white-robed magician did not die!'' Santhin-drissa cried disgustedly. ''He swam clear of the hulk, and we could not trouble to turn and run him down, with the Imperial Navy on our tail.''

''It was the rowing underwater that did it.'' Hrandulf spoke up a little drunkenly, shaking his head in morbid gloom. ''The dead crew rowed their ship straight down to Dagon's weedy realm.''

''Sorcery is ever an ill business,'' Conan avowed with a shrug that was nigh to a superstitious shudder. ''That Corinthian should never have lived, not after what he did to our galliot.'' He swigged from his own cup. ''But at least we gathered up the penteconter's crew.''

''That other wizard is yet alive, too—Crotalus, was it?'' Santhindrissa challenged him haughtily. ''The one that you say ruled the giant bug?''

''Aye, most likely.'' Conan ignored the skeptical tone of her remark. ''I may just throw his vile egg-gems into the middle of the Vilayet, rather than let him rear up more giant centipedes to trouble us.'' He waved his hand out over the broad blue sea, where the pirate fleet sailed together before a stiff westerly breeze. ''That thing was as hideous a creature as I ever want to kill.''

''I should have warned you,'' Philiope said, embracing Conan's broad, bronze shoulders. ''I heard, but I did not believe. While you were a prisoner, our pirates picked up a swimmer who had escaped from Crotalus's shed in the marshes. He was a Zaporoskan, and could make himself understood to but a few of our rowers. He claimed that the sorcerer was growing a giant creature in a vat, and feeding his laborers to it one by one! It seemed too mad to be true.''

"Ah, well,'' Conan said, comforting the girl by stroking the back of her neck. " 'Tis all past us now. We have our pirate brothers back, and this fine warship, along with a passable fleet and a host of new, rough hands who may yet learn to enjoy piracy. Yildiz has been put in his place, and his infernal spell-casters are off our necks, for the time at least.''

From his seat on the steering-bench, Conan turned to the others and raised his cup in salute. "For the future, I see greater things a-beckoning: wealth and glory for our Red Brotherhood, more confusion for our enemies . . . and for Amra, the fabled pirate, mayhap the birth of a sea-kingdom!''

Ashore, meanwhile, the naval battle in Aghrapur harbor was the talk of the empire. There was ample criticism, to be sure. In the main part, it consisted of complaints that the outcome did not reflect well on Turanian leadership and naval power. But at the very least, the invaders had been kept from raiding and burning the capital, as some had feared might happen. And the naval show had been spectacular, truly diverting.

In court circles it was even rumored that the pirates' escape represented a triumph for the reigning Emperor Yildiz, that he had secretly aided them—as a means both of putting his ambitious son Yezdigerd in his place and of preventing him from seizing the reins of seapower through the expedient of the naval contest. In the aftermath of it all, no prize was awarded, and the wags subjected the young prince to a good deal more sly ridicule than they did his father.

In point of fact, the only real danger of public ferment nd dissatisfaction was over the loss of the captive pirate Amra and his henchmen, and the belief that the citizens vould be deprived of their promised public trials and ex-cutions. This complaint was remedied in some degree by he provision of various convicts out of the lesser munic-pal dungeons—and, in main part, by a drumhead court nartial held to indict and punish two naval conspirators who were seized that very day.

One of them was a blatant fraud who had made an open mockery of the naval contest by, among other absurdities, constructing a ship with wheels. The guilty one, the once-respected astrologer Tambur Pasha, was also guilty of shirking battle shamelessly, to wit hanging back near the shore while his fellow contestants faced defeat at the hands of the pirates. His sentence, fittingly enough, was death.

The other conspirator, according to evidence produced by high officers of the Imperial Court, was guilty of naval sabotage and the murder of the engineer Mustafar, all with the motive of gaining the prize money himself. This Zal-buvulus, a rank philosopher of foreign birth, was another of the unsuccessful contestants, and had to be fished out of the harbor after the battle. He was brought immediately to trial with his fellow criminal and condemned fairly. The executions were carried out promptly in the traditional manner, using eight teams of sturdy volunteers. By all accounts, it was a long and lively afternoon.